RIVER RATS

By Dorothy Weil

PublishAmerica
Baltimore

© 2003 by Dorothy Weil.

All rights reserved. No part of this book may be reproduced, stored in a retrieval system, or transmitted in any form or by any means without the prior written permission of the publishers, except by a reviewer who may quote brief passages in a review to be printed in a newspaper, magazine, or journal.

First printing

ISBN: 1-4137-0121-3
PUBLISHED BY PUBLISHAMERICA, LLLP
www.publishamerica.com
Baltimore

Printed in the United States of America

*To my dear friend Steve Birmingham,
the most generous of writers.*

Acknowledgments

Thanks to my husband Sid for the endless readings and suggestions.

Thanks to all the river people who made
my river journeys fun and who served as inspiration.

Thanks to the Virginia Center for the Creative Arts
for giving me two weeks of total peace and quiet in a beautiful
country setting where I revised this book.

And thanks to dear friend Ceil Cleveland, a great editor, grammar
guru and writer for her help and support through many years.

PART I

August 1987

The remains of several old steamboats were discovered on the banks of the Mississippi River as the biggest drought of the century shrank the waters....

Chapter 1

July 1984

It's like a Grant Wood painting, Jerry Burnside thought. The Ohio River sparkling in the sun.

He loved this stretch on the Kentucky side, between Ludlow and the little string of towns like Hebron and Rabbit Hash. Across the river were the hills of Cincinnati and the steeples of her red brick churches.

The familiar smell of oil and water that meant the river came wafting his way, along with the comforting sound of a saw whining across the water. Jerry looked down from the landing at Burnside Harbor, Inc. It was a small operation: two barges lashed to a work boat, with a trailer-office perched on top, and his harbor tug, the *Harvey C.*, tied to a float.

It ain't much, Jerry thought, but it's all mine. Mine and the bank's. Jerry slammed the door of his pickup and walked down the broken concrete launch-area. His dispatcher stood near the wood and metal gangplank, watering a sickly geranium planted in an oil can. His entire river-raddled body was intent on his task.

"Howdy Smitty," Jerry said.

"Mornin'."

"Great day."

Smitty sniffed the air. "Makes you feel like killin' snakes, don't it?"

Jerry batted at his ear as though knocking water out of it; Smitty generally made him wonder if he was hearing right.

"'Nother shootin' – up by Point Pleasant," Smitty said. "Number four, I think. It's gettin' to be a habit."

This news stopped Jerry cold. In their glass enclosures riverboat pilots were like ducks in a shooting-gallery.

"Anybody we know?"

"Nope. Man on the *Millie B.*, weren't hit, just missed 'im."

It was always something on the river. Last week some woman in a small town pushed a baby carriage with two kids in it off a dock, and a girl was found on the bank with a crossbow bolt in her chest. Now this.

Later, Jerry would wonder at the tangled events that would pull him into the center of this mayhem: a barge maneuver, an alcoholic, a death, undying love, and an old steamboat, just to name a few. His parents had taught him that he could control his life, be anything he wanted to be. Sure, he thought, provided the old ladies with scissors and string didn't decide otherwise.

He crossed the gangplank, making the floor plates rattle and shake, and ran up the metal grating steps to the office. The radio was cackling away as he read the list of the day's jobs that Smitty had written on a clipboard for himself and the *Harvey C.* They would be mildly busy, might even make the monthly bills. There was a load of groceries to be delivered to a towboat, and a barge to be taken off the bank upriver and pushed to a fleeting area on the Ohio side. No big deal.

He went into the back room of the office, on the table was a wooden model of the steamboat *River Queen*. He'd been working on it for at least a year. It was about four feet long, a perfect replica of the old packet: three decks with the pilothouse and two black smokestacks on top, every stanchion in place, the trim around the decks laboriously cut out with an exacto knife. In her day she was the most beautiful boat on the inland waterways; fancy as a wedding cake and loved by all who rode her or even saw her passing, announcing her presence with her deep chocolatey whistle.

The last time Jerry had seen the *River Queen* was on the Memphis waterfront thirty years ago. Bright orange and yellow flames shot out of all three decks and ran quickly from one end of the boat to the other. Her decks collapsed in a blaze, the smokestacks fell into the flames, the sides buckled. Two plumes of smoke poured from her, one white, one black. The firemen had a dozen hoses shooting great arcs of water on the smoking ruins – like some great Roman fountain. The smokestacks lay intact in the rubble, and the stanchion that held the lifeboat stood limp and bent. The remains of her name, *"River Qu–"* could be seen on the hull, a raft covered with steaming, smoking wood and broken rails, as the boat sank into the water.

A fully-loaded towboat passing the harbor made Jerry's office and floats dance and jogged Jerry back into the present; these modern diesel boats with their huge strings of barges the length of three football fields, or tows, would make the *Queen*, which had seemed so enormous and majestic when Jerry was a boy, look like a miniature. Jerry had piloted towboats when he first got home from Nam and before he took on this low-class harbor – which he regularly asked himself why he kept running.

He often felt out of place among the good ole boys who made up the river's work force. He wasn't educated, but he loved books and laughingly bragged of being an autodidact (a term that made him sound like an indulger in what was called, when he was a lad in the fifties, self-abuse).

The river had taken his father, his mother, some of his hearing, and had driven off the woman he would always love.

But it held him like a spell; all those lives under water that he couldn't save, questions about what happened to the *River Queen* eating away at him like the relentless bite of water on wood.

Chapter 2

"Motor Vessel *Western* calling Burnside Harbor."

Jerry answered the sing-song West Virginia voice coming through the radio's muttering, "Jerry Burnside here. What can we do for you, Cap?"

"We're up here a few miles east of you. Be stickin' our nose around the bend any minute now and we want you to take a barge out of our tow. We're turnin' with the *Plattner*."

"Our pleasure. What have you got?"

"A dab or so of petroleum." The river code demanded that the pilot sound like he was floating along on a raft purely for fun.

"Full load?"

"Seems that way."

Bit more than a dab, Jerry thought; they were talking fifteen barges, each carrying nine times the load of a freight car. Twenty-four thousand tons of trouble.

"No problem."

Jerry knew the drill well. He would have to take the barge from one tow and attach it to the other. You didn't want to let it get away from you, because a loose barge in the current would go careening down the river smashing whatever was in its way. Jerry called the *Plattner*, the boat the *Western* would be exchanging cargo with. The *Plattner's* pilot claimed to be pushing "a few buckets o' coal" – in short, it was fully loaded like the *Western*.

Jerry saw Smitty through the window, coming along the work floats toward the office. He jotted down the number of the barge they would be dealing with and walked down toward him on his way to the *Harvey*. The floats were a mess of oil drums, cable, paint cans, and coils of line.

"Hey, Cap," Smitty called. He dodged around the junk on the work barge.

"Yeah Smitty?"

"You know how to keep goats outa your yard? Get you some macaroni."

"I ain't got no yard. Later."

Jerry explained the upcoming task to Smitty and they parted company.

"That *Plattner's* a Midwest America boat," Smitty said. "They could be next."

"What makes you think that?"

"Seems like the shooter favors that company some."

The *Harvey C.*, a small version of the line-haul towboats, was looking spiffy with a new coat of clean white paint. Jerry loved her. With a few more payments – well, about a five years' worth – she would be all his.

Jerry's mood stayed up as he climbed the steep steps to the pilothouse, a glass perch on the upper deck that resembled an extra-large phone booth.

Daryl, Jerry's deckhand and co-pilot, was sleeping on the lazy bench opposite the controls. Jerry gave a sharp rap on the newspaper covering his face, and Daryl jumped up, his clodhoppers hitting the floor with a bang.

"God you scared me – thought you was that guy takin' pot shots at folks."

"We got us a big job."

Daryl sat back down, holding his hand over his heart and breathing deeply. When he was excited or mad the deep scar over his right eye filled with blood like the mercury in a thermometer.

"Wish I could get hold a that weirdo."

The shooter would be right up Daryl's alley, and maybe the end of a good deckhand, Jerry thought. Daryl could be fine company and a competent work partner, but he needed an occasional knife-fight or the sound of a bullet shattering a barroom mirror, to keep him on a steady course.

Jerry filled Daryl in on the work to be done, and stepped out onto the deck to await the appearance of the two behemoths he would be servicing. Soon the head of the *Western*'s tow came sliding downriver under the last of the seven bridges at Cincinnati. Then came the rest of the long, drawn-out flotilla: twelve more barges, three abreast, and finally the boat itself until the entire thing was spread out, hoving slowly downriver.

"If that ain't the prettiest sight," Jerry said. He gave the engineer and cook, standing on the lower deck, the two-handed river wave.

The *Plattner*, coming upriver from the west, was the size of the *Western*, but she was painted an odd shade of blue.

Jerry went back inside the *Harvey*'s pilothouse and switched on his radio.

"Come on up to our pilothouse when we're finished here," the *Plattner*'s pilot said, and Jerry said sure. He was too preoccupied to think much more about the invitation. (One of those little things you barely notice – like a tick bite – that changes your whole life.)

Jerry revved up the *Harvey*'s engines and pulled out into the middle of the river where the two tows were idling. The *Harvey* shuddered like an overworked horse. Though she was a good little boat, she was not the safest; like all harbor tugs, she was top-heavy, almost as tall as she was long and prone to tipping over or wobbling perilously in rough water. Jerry steered her toward the *Plattner* and faced her up to the rusty metal barge to be removed from the tow. It was on the head, lashed between two others. One of the deckhands trying to get lines on the *Harvey* stood on a tightly-wound steel thread while another began to loosen it with a winch.

"Careful!" Daryl called. "That cable snaps it'll send you flyin' through the air like Superman, only there'll be two of you!"

Jerry noticed the boy wasn't wearing a life preserver, safety shoes, or gloves.

Wonder who's runnin' this mess, he thought.

He told Daryl to watch out for the ugly current sloshing and pulling around the rake of the *Plattner's* head barges.

"Some bad water here," he said.

"Sure – that turkey they're callin' a boat is bright blue. Bad luck."

"That's steamboat lore," Jerry said. "This here's the diesel age." He struggled to keep the harbor tug from getting caught sideways in front of the big tow – a bad position – a push forward by the towboat could tip the *Harvey* right over, and he could feel her going. Jerry gripped the steering levers tightly, caught between the current and the barges, which gnashed and groaned like some sci-fi monster.

"Back her down some, Cap," Jerry said quietly into the radio.

Jerry got the *Harvey* out of the big boat's way, and took her upriver for another run at the barge they were trying to retrieve. This time they rode smoothly into a good position perpendicular to the head of the tow.

Jerry went out on the bridge, his knees a little weak. When everything was secure, he turned the sticks over to Daryl, and hopped on the *Plattner* to find out what the pilot's request to see him was all about – probably gossip about the shooting on the *Millie*.

He walked down the long stretch of fifteen hot metal barges with the mate, Tom, who had joined the two greenhorn deckies. He seemed like a nice guy, soft-spoken. Jerry noticed he was missing the two middle fingers on his right hand, leaving it eternally signalling a put-on. Probably in the river, Jerry thought; the river was full of fingers – and toes and arms and legs; everybody who worked on her had lost one or another body part – even hearts. The two men moved carefully, avoiding cables and "duck ponds," open spaces between barges.

"Where'd you get those boys you got deckin'?" Jerry asked.

"Oh, they come on board at the last minute. Had a couple o' deckhands quit. Lots of problems on this boat anymore, since the shootin's."

Jerry and Tom passed the equipment room on the bow of the boat, and the galley, which wasn't the cleanest Jerry had ever seen – in fact, it was a mess – with no sign, at 11:30, of lunch. He left the mate on the lower deck and swung up on the outer stairs toward the upper deck. Something wrong on this boat all right, real wrong.

In the dark inner stairway to the pilothouse, he could hear two voices: that of the pilot and another. As he came into the light room, all glass like the *Harvey*'s pilothouse, but bigger and full of up-to-date equipment, he saw the pilot, a long, lank man in jeans and cowboy shirt. On the lazy bench sat a woman dressed in suede slacks and a silk blouse. She must have a couple of hundred dollars worth of clothes on, Jerry thought. Then he recognized her; Kay, the girl he had loved since the day he first saw her – when she was three years old.

The *River Queen* had been at the peak of her glory, docked at Cincinnati. Jerry's father, Captain Homer Burnside, was at the wheel in the pilothouse atop the third deck. The roustabouts, black men in ragged trousers and torn shoes, hauled kegs of molasses and sacks of grain on their backs to the boat's overloaded lower deck. In deep sing-song voices they called to each other.

"Goin' to Marietta!"

"Goin' to Mary-whatta?"

"Said to Marietta!"

Kay's father, the new mate, was yelling at the top of his voice for them to get a move on. George the cook, usually good company for the officer's kids who lived on the boat, was chopping salads and putting pies in the oven and cleaning fish for the passengers' dinner that would be served in the gilt and crystal dining room. The entertainers were rehearsing "Showboat" tunes for the evening's performance in the salon. Mac the purser was running here and there and everywhere to keep it all straight: the destination of each barrel of pork, the name of the lucky person to whom the one automobile on board would be delivered.

Jerry, at five a seasoned veteran of all this hullabaloo, spotted a little girl who looked like she was about to cry. He pulled her out of the way of a molasses barrel rolling her way across the deck.

"It's OK," he said. "You'll get to like it here. It's fun."

The girl looked unconvinced.

"What's your name?"

No answer. The girl just kept looking glummer and more backward.

"What's the matter? Cat got your tongue?" It was the kind of thing Jerry's mother always said to make him laugh. The little girl smiled.

"Calliope's about to play. C'mon." Jerry took Kay to the top deck where a man in a striped shirt and straw hat sat at the keyboard making steam come out of the pipes along with a shrill bronchial tune: "Down by the Ohi<u>o</u>, I got the sweetest little oh-my-<u>oh</u>." At the sound of the piercing notes, the little girl cocked her head and listened. Her eyes lighted up, like the dark water when the string of bulbs along the top deck went on at night, and she smiled a smile that could always break Jerry's heart.

"Kay Kenny," Jerry said. "God, what's it been?"

"Ten years?"

"What are you doin' on the river?"

Kay looked at him with a smile he knew well.

Delight at seeing her and the pain of having lost her made Jerry's breath come hard.

"You almost ran me down," Jerry said. It wouldn't be the first time.

"Sorry. Cliff lost sight of you."

She was more beautiful than ever. And Jerry knew he had never stopped loving her for even a minute. A woman he could no more reclaim than he could the boat that held the magic and terror of his childhood.

Chapter 3

She had always been pretty, with delicate French-doll features, soft brown hair, and big dark-brown eyes. When she was a girl Jerry could put his hands around her waist. She was still trim but had gained a little all over; had lost the unearthly beauty of her twenties, but was in full forties bloom. Her hair was lighter (tinted?), cut stylishly, while before it had grown long and free. Her colors were gold: hair, jewelry, the sheen of her blouse. God, she's gorgeous, Jerry thought.

"Lookin' good," he said.

"You, too."

Jerry held down his excitement; a reunion like this on the river had to be as cool and underplayed as a couple of big tows meeting up. He said a quick thanks to the river and its hard outdoor work for keeping his stomach flat, his muscles hard, and his skin tanned. He was glad, too, he had worn the blue shirt several women had said brought out the best in his blue eyes.

"Weren't in any trouble, were you, pard?" Kay's pilot asked. Jerry knew the man from his towboat days – Cliff Cooper. He was about Jerry's age, from the Green River area of Kentucky. Looked a little like Humphrey Bogart.

"Nothin' we couldn't handle."

Through the window, Jerry saw Daryl back the *Harvey* away from the tow that Cliff was taking out of idle.

"Coffee, Jerry?" Kay asked.

Jerry nodded, and Kay poured herself and Jerry mugs of coffee from the pot that – true to towboat tradition – was hot and handy.

What on earth was she doing here, Jerry wondered. Some time after the *Queen* went down, she swore she'd never be back on the river.

"Cliff?" Her voice was still the kind Jerry liked, unusual in the women he knew: steady, communicative, no trace of hysteria or flightiness or even that wild anxiety to please that made women unattractive and easy to take advantage of.

Cliff turned down the coffee. "Keep me awake."

"See you at 5:30."

"Oh yeah – onliest job in the world where you gotta go to work two times a day."

Cliff yawned and stretched, and turned the steering levers over to Kay.

"I didn't know you could pilot a boat," Jerry said, going to stand beside her and looking down the length of the tow. It seemed endless, always intimidating. The many hours he'd spent staring at a load like this came back to him. There was the long, groaning stretch of metal barges, narrowing impossibly at the horizon. "What are you doing out here, anyway?"

Kay waited until she and Jerry heard Cliff reach the bottom of the steps and the door slam before she spoke. "Guess you heard about the *Millie*. I sent J.B. up there to give Captain Roscoe a day or two off. We're short-handed, so I'm filling in."

"Roscoe Barns?"

"Yeah."

"But what are you doing around here?"

"I've been running the barge line since Martin died. The headquarters moved to Cincinnati, so here I am."

"I'm sorry. I mean about your husband. I didn't know."

Jerry studied Kay's face to see how sorry she was. She didn't seem real broken up. Still, up close to her, he noticed a slight tightening around her mouth that could be grief or bitterness or pain or any number of things.

"Forty-eight. He was forty-eight when he died. Year ago now."

"I don't like the idea of you being out here with this crazy shooter running around," Jerry said.

"Who asked you?" Kay's eyes gave off the sparks he remembered from Joe Slack's daughter.

She laughed. His protectiveness and her resistance were old patterns they both cherished.

They passed the red-brick gothic "True-Way" Pentecostal church on River Road and its larger sister, St. Rita's, rising among the old houses below Price Hill.

"When I first moved to Council Bluffs, and saw the Missouri, I thought it might be a creek," Kay said.

She pointed to the high-rise apartment buildings on the hills, the blinding white conglomerations of oil tanks and industrial plants along the banks.

"This doesn't look like it did when we were kids."

"It does to me," Jerry said. "At least in places."

There were still stretches of feathery willows, muddy banks where a lone fisherman stood patiently in the sun. The Anderson Ferry was still going back and forth across the river all day long, hauling eight cars at a time.

Jerry pointed these things out to Kay, but even he had trouble grasping the fact that these were the same waters where he and Kay and Charlie Summers, the engineer's son, had played when they were kids, swimming off the side of the *River Queen*, canoeing, exploring the riverbanks – staying best pals until adolescence and their hormones started going crazy.

"The sounds are the same," Kay said.

They could hear a train chugging across the water, coal dropping into an empty barge, the flapping of the *Plattner's* flag. At Cincinnati, they looked up at Mt. Adams topped by Immaculata Church, a fairytale castle out of a children's book.

"I'd forgotten that skyline," Kay said.

Jerry watched Kay closely as she steered. He was used to being between those sticks himself. He looked ahead and under the bridges closer to downtown Cincinnati, hundreds of cruisers, water scooters, and runabouts were buzzing up and down, roaring from one side of the river to the other, making the water as choppy as a bathtub full of kids. It was a pilot's nightmare, made worse by the string of fancy riverboat restaurants and marinas on the Kentucky side.

"Barge crashed into one of those places last week," Jerry said.

Kay laughed at Jerry's warning.

"Talk about margaritas all over your tie."

Jerry winced as a half-mile of metal plowed toward the Brent Spence Bridge.

Kay concentrated hard, pulling the levers this way and that, making the boat hiss and groan. She cleared the first bridge by a hair, and Jerry pulled a cigarette from his pocket and lit it. "Don't you want me to take over?"

"Course not."

On the second bridge, Kay just missed a water skier – whose ilk never seemed to understand that a flotilla the size of a river tow cannot stop on a dime. Kay didn't flinch.

She seemed to have something on her mind, but was having trouble spitting it out.

She got them through the next few bridges, and then cleared the golden arch of the "Big Mac," the last of the seven. Jerry relaxed and took a long swig of his coffee. Kay poured herself a fresh cup. She had a clear path ahead now and could take it easier.

"Two of the shootings were at my boats. Almost hit Roscoe on the *Millie B.* last night."

"So I heard."

"I'm beginning to think somebody wants to put Midwest America out of commission."

"Sure. Everybody does. That's the river business. But they don't usually use bullets."

Jerry looked at the halo of gold around Kay. Out here she was just another target in somebody's cross hairs.

"All three have been right around the Big Sandy, and one was at the Kanahwa River, but not any one exact spot. Like before, whoever's doing it came within an inch of Roscoe's head. The bullet went straight on through the glass, so we don't even have a bullet to give the police."

"The riverbanks are full of crazies. My pilot, Daryl, thinks a little violence adds to life's flavor."

Jerry looked out the window. He was much farther up the river than he planned to be when he sent Daryl back to the harbor.

"This shooter is not likely to be a gentleman and would just as soon aim at a lady as not."

Jerry could see he was only making Kay more determined to stay on her boat.

"I gotta get going," he said.

But he didn't move. He could not let Kay disappear, especially into such dangerous waters, when they had just come together again after so many years.

Kay hesitated, too.

"What's your harbor like?"

"Three hots and a flop."

Jerry picked up the radio to call Daryl for a ride home.

"So why did you leave towboating for harbor work?" Kay asked.

Jerry thought a minute. "It was the same old thing – exciting to master and learn, but once learned, repetitious."

Kay seemed to turn this over to see what was under it.

"I have time for the things I like to do–"

"Such as?"

"Been makin' a model of the old *River Queen*. And I've been thinking about looking up the one or two survivors. Get their stories."

Jerry spoke casually, not letting on that his quest for the facts about the long ago explosion on the *River Queen* had become one of the most urgent goals of his life.

The *Harvey* was pulling up alongside Kay's boat now.

"It's been great seeing you, Kay."

"Yeah."

"If you need a good harbor man again, gimme a call."

Jerry tried not to start hoping for anything more.

"Oh, you haven't seen the last of me. I'm on the *Plattner* on the same basis as the crew, for thirty days."

"Kay, stay off the boats. At least until this shooting business is settled."

"I've got one boat tied off and a near mutiny on the *Plattner*. I need to find out what's going on."

"Hell–"

Kay spoke into the intercom, instructing the mate to get lines on the *Harvey*. Jerry started toward the steps.

"Wait," she said. Here it came at last. What she wanted. "How would you like to take on the *Millie B.*?"

"Me?"

"Sure."

Jerry couldn't believe that after ten years and all that had gone on, she'd just reappear and ask him to drop everything for her. But that was Kay.

"I'm through with that line-haul stuff."

"I need people I can trust."

"I'd like to help but – it's been too long for me."

"The pay's good."

"I've never been into making money. You know that."

"I need a man who knows the river, and the people especially. You've noticed the condition of the turkey I'm on. Cliff is OK, but the deckhands are right off Mount Mutant. And the cook is driving me crazy."

Jerry squinted at the afternoon sun on the water. Kay had not come back to the Ohio for him. He knew he should let go.

"You're not scared?" Kay said.

"Not of your merry marksman."

Jerry meant what he said. Kay could have his skull. Although getting shot in the head was not anything he'd wish for, he would honestly rather it be him than Kay. But with this offer of hers, he saw the big gash she might put in his life, something like she almost did to those bridge piers earlier in the day.

"It'd be like old times."

"Yeah, right."

Just what he didn't need, a repeat of the past. Nineteen sixty-two, the last time she'd broken his heart; he was lost, his parents dead and his whole world gone in one big blast of fire, and suddenly she was gone too, married to Martin Kenny and off for Council Bluffs.

"You always looked out for me when we were kids – remember?"

Oh yeah, he remembered. He took her hand swimming when he saw the current was getting her, helped her bait a fish hook because she was too squeamish to do it herself. But she fought back if he tried to get the upper hand or act the hero or treat her like anything but a total equal.

"Just wear an orange hat," Jerry said. "Your shooter is probably some near-sighted hunter."

"Looks like Daryl's ready to go. Nice seeing you, Jerry."

She had her father's blazing eyes again.

"Wait."

"What for?"

"I...." Jerry looked out the window at the barges. The afternoon sun was flat, hard, on the glittering steel. It was the one time of day he didn't like, when there were no shadows, no beauty. He felt himself being pulled away from his safe harbor, like a fleet dislodged by the pull of a towboat.

"How about old Charlie?" (Jerry wasn't serious. He knew Charlie was busy coining money with his dredging business).

"Maybe he could help out on this. He's got a good operation down the river near Paducah and runs a towboat or two. Maybe you and he could join forces."

"We already have. I thought you'd want to join in."

Jerry felt the breeze lift his colors; Kay in trouble was a temptation. Letting Charlie near her was a call to arms. Still he hesitated.

"Double dare ya," Kay said.

She gave him the calliope smile.

"Let me think about it."

"You'll help?"

"I said I'd think about it."

Kay's eyes looked triumphant.

"Meanwhile, here's a piece of advice. If you're going to run a boat, stop dressing like the boss's wife. And get out of the pilothouse and learn how to deck."

Jerry could see her holding back a retort. Typical Kay. She was the proudest girl he'd ever known. Just asking for his help had probably cost her plenty.

Chapter 4

"What'd happen to the harbor?"
"Smitty and Daryl can manage it. They've done it before," Jerry said.
Sheryl started up her sewing machine.
"I gotta get this skirt hemmed. Customer's got a big date tonight."
Jerry got up from his seat on the floor. There were pins all over the rug. He stared at the backward lettering in the window: Sheryl's Alterations.
"I'm not worried about Smitty and Daryl...."
"You've worked awfully hard to get that harbor going," Sheryl said.
Jerry laid his hand over the material Sheryl was working on.
"What are you trying to say?"
Sheryl stopped the machine.
"She's a mantrap."
Jerry clenched his jaw. Didn't say anything. There was no use arguing with a jealous woman.
"Jerry, you're nuts. She's just using you. You're gonna get burned again. Real bad."
"I'm a big boy, Sheryl."
"I remember you when you were really tore up over her gettin' married."
"You were a big help, too."
"You swore off."
"I know, I know."
"You're already gone, aren't you?"
Jerry shrugged.
"So will I see you again?"
"Sure."
"When?"
"Thirty days like always."
Sheryl pulled her material around with a jerk and rearranged it, needle ready to plunge.
"I'm not marryin' the woman. But she does need help. She can't run a barge line...."
"And you're the only guy on the river that can steer that shot-up boat...."
Sheryl was a heck of a girl, Jerry thought. With plenty of smarts.
"You're right. Me goin' out on a towboat is a dumb idea, and a god-damned invitation to replaying some of the oldest and worst pain I ever

knew."

"You got one of those – what d'ya call 'em? Obsessions."

"Could be. Maybe I need a cure. One for the road?"

"It's two o'clock in the afternoon."

"One of my favorite times."

Sheryl slid the dress material out of the machine and walked over to the door. She turned the "OPEN" sign to "CLOSED."

"I guess I'll be here when she takes off again. And she will," Sheryl said. "I just hope you don't lose your shirt along with your heart."

Chapter 5

> I asked my love to take a walk,
> To take a walk, just a little walk,
> Down beside where the waters flow,
> Down by the banks of the Ohio.

Music coming from the old French town of Gallipolis wafted across the water. A young man's voice and a guitar. Kay was standing on the second deck of the *Plattner*. Jerry noticed that she had given up her expensive slacks and blouse for jeans and a tee shirt, and looked like the river girl he loved. She was leaning against the rail and staring over at the bank.

"Remember that song?" she asked.

"Sure."

"Then only say that you'll be mine," Kay sang.

"And in no other arms entwine." The song was one of Jerry's favorites, and it sounded especially beautiful coming across the water.

Jerry was partial to Gallipolis, too, a real old town built around a riverfront park. But suddenly he was visited by a memory that he hoped Kay wasn't also recalling: he, Charlie and Kay had once gone to the movies there on a summer night long ago, and on the way back to the *River Queen*, the boys had made jerks out of themselves by getting into some male competition over who was the strongest, and they had left a furious Kay to walk back to the boat alone. He even remembered the name of the picture they'd seen: <u>Destry Rides Again</u>. Why did he have to have such a retentive memory?

Jerry tried to head off further nostalgic thoughts, and asked Kay how she and the crew were getting along.

"I could use a whip and a chair."

"They ain't the British Navy, that's for sure," Jerry said.

"It isn't me, is it? They may not respect me, but that wouldn't account for the stash of drugs in their room. One of them just about broke his neck the other night trying to follow the radar around the dial. The cook's no winner either. I think she hates me. The only two good people are Cliff and my mate, Tom."

"Yeah, Tom seems like a good man. If he hadn't come out to help those two greenhorn deckhands corral the barges the other day, we'd still be there."

"He's down on the head of the tow with Cliff. Let's go see how long it's gonna take to lock through."

Jerry and Kay walked down to the barges. Jerry could see the *Millie B.*, which he'd left tied off to some trees on the West Virginia shore. Like the *Plattner*, she was waiting in line to get through the Gallipolis locks. Because of the chambers' short length, the tows had to be broken into halves, and the going was slow.

The huge iron doors holding back tons of water were closed as a boat from a rival company cleared the locks. The water inside the rectangle was way down below the level of the surface, and water was being pumped into the tub while the tow filled all but a few feet of the space. The dam stretched across the river like a great high bridge.

Jerry figured the *Millie* could live without him until it was her turn to get through. J.B., the pilot, was back at work, and Jerry had recruited two old towboat pals, Dude and Whitey, to replace the mate and deckhand who had jumped ship after the shooting. Dude was a "Hunky" from Pittsburgh whose trademark was the several pounds of turquoise he wore on his fingers, around his neck, and on his belt. He was the vainest man Jerry ever knew, always combing and recombing his thick wavy hair and glancing at himself in the pilothouse windows, but he was a reliable crew member. Whitey was the oldest deckhand on the river, well-known for running around in a diaper-like bikini on his skinny, ropey-muscled frame, looking like the baby New Year and Father Time all in one. He was strong and one of the best workers in the business. Jerry was rather proud of how quickly he'd gotten the *Millie* running well and back in action.

A small fire glowed in an oil drum on the head of the tow. Cliff and Tom were squatting next to it, talking as if they were cozied up to a grate fire – though they were just burning garbage.

"We're gonna be here all night," Cliff said. "This is the damnedest dam on the river."

Jerry and Kay squatted down beside them, and the four sat quietly for awhile. Cliff and Tom were a sort of Mutt and Jeff, Cliff towering over the solid Tom, whose square shape seemed to bear out his reliability. They seemed to have accepted Kay with a minimum of suspicion.

"Got any idea why this crew's so out of control?" Jerry asked them.

"Could be Roscoe–"

Roscoe had been re-assigned to the *Plattner,* while Jerry was replacing him as Captain on the *Millie.* Roscoe was still somewhat spooked by having a bullet nearly crease his skull, and besides, Jerry thought, no way was Kay going to put Jerry on the same boat she was on.

"Captain out of sorts can throw everybody off," Cliff said.

"These shootin's," Tom said. "They got everybody kinda edgy."

"Maybe whoever's doin' it has crawled back under his rock," Jerry said. "Been a week since the last shooting. I still think Midwest America getting hit is a coincidence; that'd take a motive and a shooter far beyond anything this old river ever saw, and it's seen plenty."

"These farmers along the bank'll take a shot at anything that looks like a threat to their way of livin'," Cliff said.

"Could be it's another curse put on by Chief Cornstalk," Tom said.

Jerry made a noise at this remark like a miniature blast of steam.

"What's he talking about?" Kay asked.

"There was this Indian Chief over by Point Pleasant," Tom said. "White settlers drove him and his people out, killed him. But before he died, he put a curse on the town."

"This is no lie," Cliff said.

Ever since then, there has been a lot of bad things happen around here. That big bridge just up and collapsed awhile back. Then the jail exploded. People do say it's Chief Cornstalk's revenge."

"And then the shot at the *Millie B*."

"Thanks for the scientific analysis," Jerry scoffed.

"Well, you can laugh, but I never seen anything like that bridge. I was right here at the locks at the time, and it was during heavy traffic; the thing just went limp like and fell into the river and all them cars right after it. They could never come up with any explanation neither."

"They say the river right here where we're sittin' was red with blood when the Chief and his people fought the settlers," Cliff added. "Hate like that don't die."

"So they say," said Tom. "I can't think of no reason for anybody to be shootin' like here lately."

"Well, I guess your story is as good as any for now," Jerry laughed.

"All I know is," Tom said, "just when I think I've seen everything, this old river comes up with something new."

"You got that right," Cliff said.

He stood up and stirred the trash in the oil drum, reducing the light to a small glow, and gazed down toward the locks to see if any progress was taking place.

"I'm goin' on up to the pilothouse."

"I'll go with you," Tom said.

The two men left, shadows disappearing behind the hills of coal.

Jerry and Kay stayed where they were, in gathering darkness. They could hear the tree toads and katydids on the shore, the distant noises at the lock, an occasional car moving toward Point Pleasant on the West Virginia shore.

"How're you coming with your deckin'?" Jerry asked.

"Those ratchets are damn heavy. I have to drag mine out on the barges."

The last bit of spark in the oil can went out, and Kay and Jerry had only the last few glints of daylight and the lights from a distant boat to pierce the dark. It was the time of evening when the river's magic took over.

"I can almost see the old *Queen* coming down the river," Jerry said. "Lights blazin', music goin' in the salon."

With the water and the West Virginia hills soft and black as velvet and the plaintive sound of the boy and his guitar floating across the water, Jerry felt the past and present flowing together.

He took Kay's hand. He felt reunited with a part of himself.

Kay's hand slid out of his like a beautiful silvery fish.

"I wish I could love the river the way you do," Kay said.

Jerry pulled out a cigarette, to give his hands something to do.

He had thought of nothing else but Kay, and trying to revive their old feelings, since seeing her on the *Plattner*. Of course it was too soon to do anything about his hopes of getting together again. He was about to say something feeble about how surprised he was to run into her that day, when a noise behind them made them both jump: heavy footsteps on the metal deck of the barge. Jerry's fists automatically clenched and he stood up to ward off whatever was coming, when a cheery voice called, "Howdy, howdy, howdy!"

"Charlie!" Kay jumped up and ran to him, throwing her arms around him. "Are we glad to see you!"

Are we? Jerry wasn't so sure.

The two men circled each other like fighting cocks. Charlie, Jerry was sorry to see, didn't look a day older than he had when they last met. His shirt showed biceps more impressive than Jerry remembered.

"You two," Kay said, "are your going to arm wrestle?"

Slightly embarrassed, the men shook hands vigorously and thumped each other on the back.

"Hi, old friend," Charlie greeted Jerry, "how you be?"

"Damn, Charlie, it's good to see you."

"You're a sight for sore eyes!" Charlie's tone was as hearty and cheery as Jerry's – and, Jerry thought – no doubt equally phony.

Kay and the two rivals left the tow to join the others in the pilothouse. The boy in Gallipolis was still singing, repeating the song Jerry loved. But now it sounded less lovely and more sinister.

> I held a knife against her breast
> As into my arms she pressed,
> Down beside where the waters flow,
> Down by the banks of the Ohio.

Chapter 6

The pilothouse was lit only by the spinning radar and the faint moonlight. White shirts and cigarettes were the only clue as to who was sitting where. Kay's voice had taken on a lilt since Charlie came aboard, while Jerry's own mood was totally shot. He felt an old familiar tension right in the groin.

Under different circumstances, he would be truly sort of glad to see his one-time best friend and rival. It had been a long time. Charlie's dredging operation was near Paducah, miles downriver, and Jerry's work seldom took him that far away from home. But the man had interrupted a perfectly fine moment with Kay that might never come back.

"So you decided to pay us a visit?" Kay said to Charlie.

"On my way to Pittsburgh on business. Thought I'd check you out. See how things are goin'."

"I've been on the *Millie* a week – nothing," Jerry said.

"All OK here," Kay said. "Though this crew is driving me to drink."

"You ain't the only one," Cliff interrupted. "Like Tom said, Roscoe looks like he might be hittin' the bottle again."

Kay filled Charlie in on the *Plattner's* problems.

"Get a new crew."

"Might have to, though I don't know where I'm gonna get replacements. Midwest America morale's going to pot."

"I'll find you some people," Charlie said. "Wish I could be out on a boat regular, too, like old Jerry here, but I can't leave my business more than a few days at a time."

Oh gosh, Jerry thought, it was gonna be quite a war, one outside from the sniper, one inside from his old best friend.

What were his chances? Charlie was better looking than he, a head taller and quite a bit richer. And Kay might need a winner after Martin Kenny, whom river gossip had pegged as a drunk.

Cliff and Tom exchanged a few comments about the upcoming lockage, then Cliff poured himself a cup of coffee and leaned against the console.

"So are you still makin' a lot of money dredging?" he asked Charlie.

"Doin' real good."

Everyone knew Charlie's business was one of the largest and most successful on the river. Charlie ran a few towboats and did harbor work like Jerry, but the heart of his operation was dredging, pulling up sunken barges, derelict boats, whatever was worth salvaging from the bottom of the river.

Charlie, who was sitting next to Jerry, punched his old friend on the arm. "Oh God, it's good to see you all," he said, "it's been too long."

"When we lived on the *Queen*, I thought it would be forever," Jerry said.

"We did have fun."

"I'm making a model of the old girl."

"Hey no kidding."

"I'm meaning to look up the people, too. Remember Mac the purser? I hear he's still alive."

"I thought he bought it years ago."

"I 'member him," Tom said.

"He loved steamboating better than any man I ever knew," Jerry said. "He could recite the arrival time of every boat on the river. Knew the railroad schedules by heart."

"Old Mac liked little boys," Charlie said. "Tried to feel up a little passenger kid and me in the restroom once."

"I suspicioned that," Tom said. "Something about him."

Jerry, too, had a vague feeling about Mac. Funny how words said years later brought something half-hidden to the surface.

"Fine boat, the R*iver Queen*. Bill Patterson was captain on her before your father, Jerry."

Jerry recounted stories about George the cook and Mac.

Charlie didn't say much. Maybe *River Queen* memories were too painful; Charlie's father had escaped the explosion and blaze that killed Jerry's father and mother, but had been hit by a falling stanchion, and was lamed in one leg. Then Charlie's mother was sickly and his father carried around a torch for Kay's mother that everyone knew about.

Kay was quiet too. Jerry had never believed the stories about her father, but he knew she felt bad about what happened to him.

"So here you are back where you started," Tom said.

"I guess we can't stay away from this river." Jerry looked to Charlie and Kay for agreement.

"It's a living," Charlie said.

Jerry recalled some more of the old times. "Those days the river had poetry."

"Poetry?" Charlie said. "The big fish eat the little fish. Always been that way, always will be."

"Amen to that," Cliff said.

Kay didn't disagree, and Jerry let the subject drop. But the tales of old times seemed to set Cliff and Tom off, and they began trying to outstory each other with tales of giant fish swimming below the locks. When Tom's grew to 500 pounds, Cliff held up the mate's two fingered hand to show what he thought of the tale.

After the two men ran out of steam everybody quieted down, and Cliff radioed to see how traffic was doing at Gallipolis. His voice was a murmur, a familiar low river sound with the crackling of the radio in the background.

"Be another half hour," he said. He yawned and poured himself a cup of coffee. "My stomach must look like a rusted-out barge."

Tom lit another cigarette.

No matter how much they had talked about it and thought about it, no one was prepared when the window glass of the pilothouse crackled and a spiderweb spread from an ugly hole in the window all over the pane. Cliff's pilot chair went out from under him and tipped over onto the floor with a crash, taking Cliff along.

"Jesus _God_!" Jerry yelled. He dived toward Kay, but Charlie had already grabbed Kay and was carrying her onto the lazy bench with him as the bullet hit the opposite window and fell to the floor, slowed in its flight by Cliff's neck or head or whatever it had hit. A ribbon of blood went flying across the room like something squirted out of a tube.

Chapter 7

"Stay down," Charlie said. Jerry crawled toward Cliff, who was stunned and staring wildly at the ceiling.

"You OK? You hear me, buddy?"

Cliff looked terrified. Bright red blood was pouring out of his ear.

"You OK? We're gonna get you to a doctor soon as possible." Jerry pulled out his handkerchief and held it against Cliff's head.

"Here, hold tight." Jerry put Cliff's hand against the handkerchief and the wound. He reared up on his knees and peered out the window.

"Down!" Charlie hissed.

"I'm gonna go after him," Jerry said. "You call an ambulance for Cliff and take him to the emergency room at Portsmouth."

Cliff's eyes were wild and the handkerchief was turning bright red.

"And call the cops," Jerry said. He reached one arm up for the marine phone and passed it to Charlie. "I'm gonna make sure this guy's footprints don't get muddied up, and see if I can find him or if he left anything behind."

"Don't be a nut," Charlie said.

Kay crawled over to Cliff and held his head in her lap. "Oh God, I never realized how awful this was. Jerry, don't go out there."

"I think he's through shooting. He's never killed anybody yet." Jerry went to the steps on his hands and knees and then plunged down the steps four at a time. He could hear Charlie calling the marine operator and Kay asking Cliff if he was OK.

As Jerry ran down the other two flights of steps and along the spar to the bank, he felt exhilarated, as well as scared. He distinctly heard, he was sure, a note of admiration in Kay's voice when she told him not to go after the terrorist. Plunging into the trees, Jerry collected his thoughts, and geared himself up to think about what he was doing. This man had a gun, but he would not want to use it and draw attention to himself. Jerry, with his acute pilot's senses, would hear or see any unusual movement anywhere in the area. If the man were still nearby Jerry might catch a glimpse of him if not actually catch him. Jerry was well-trained to travel in the dark and to hear his way along a riverbank. The gunman may or may not be the same. He had about a five minute start.

Jerry quietly scoured the wooded area along the bank, going from tree to tree. He did find fresh footprints in the position the gunman would have taken to get a good shot at the pilothouse. From here the boat was a cut-out against the river, the pilothouse clearly outlined. Jerry placed his own nine-and-a-halfs alongside the footprints; they looked to be made by someone at least a size fourteen.

Jerry wended his way slowly to the locks. From the bank, he looked it over; the dam formed a high bridge across the river, with compartments that could open and let the river roll through when water was needed in the stretch below. The operations and lockmaster's office were in a prison-like building between the lock next to the shore and the dam. Everything looked normal. If he stood here long enough he would see the towboat in the chamber rise to the height of the lock wall like something on an elevator. The operation brought carloads of people here who seemed endlessly fascinated by the procedure. But seldom did you have observers at night. And walking away from the observers' platform was a solitary figure who might have had a box-seat on the shooting. The man had an unusually large head.

"Hey, pard," Jerry yelled. The man jumped as though shot, and froze. Now Jerry could see he was carrying a rifle he was trying to hide with his body. Oh God, Jerry thought. It's him. Somebody had told this joker to act casual, that he'd have time to stroll away from the scene of the shooting before the cops came, that no one on the *Plattner* would be brave enough or damn fool enough to come racing after him. But he didn't have the nerve for it.

The man started running toward the dam, and Jerry sprinted after him. Jerry was farther away from the locks, but the man didn't seem to know his way around, and stumbled in the half-light.

"Stop!" Jerry called. The man kept running, but luckily didn't turn to shoot again. He ran right over the top of the lock wall, a perilous, foot-wide bridge over the lock chamber's slick perpendicular sides. Jerry followed, looking down the hundred feet into the chamber where only a few inches of water sloshed between the walls and the tons of barges and towboat wanting to grind against them – being kept from doing so only by the two deckhands trying to keep their cargo off the wall. He tried not to think about what it would be like to fall in there and be mashed between the wall and the barges. Don't picture falling, he thought, just run. The shooter was sprinting along the area parallel to the chamber now, but he would soon be faced with river or running back to the bank over the other end of the lock chamber. He pitched his gun into the water, and hesitated. The man <u>was</u> like a rat. Scared. Cornered. Jerry was gaining on him when the shooter made a quick decision, and turned toward the bank. But he had lost his nerve, Jerry could tell.

"Don't!" Jerry called, but the man started over the narrow wall above the lock, moving like a tight-rope walker who's just watched the Flying Walendas. Jerry stopped his own race forward, and started inching over the wall on all fours. He saw the man he was chasing hesitate then lose his balance, and then he disappeared into the giant tub. Jerry heard a slight scraping sound and then the voices of the deckhands in the lock chamber below.

"What the hell?"

Their voices echoed, as though were coming from a well. Jerry lay face down on the walkway, afraid to look. The cement was warm. He tried to concentrate on that, tried not to think about falling into the great vat below. He could not stand up.

Chapter 8

With his ankle throbbing and his head still spinning with vertigo, Jerry peered down into the lock chamber. He saw two deckhands, looking very small from this height, working with a grappling hook in the water.

What the hell happened up there?"

"Shooter. He fell. Can you see him?" Jerry called.

"Naw," yelled one deckhand.

"Guy shot the pilot on the *Plattner*, Cliff Cooper. I was tryin' to catch him."

"Know him?"

"No."

"I heard there was some shootin's," said the second deckhand. "So he got Cliff. Is he dead?"

"Hope not. He's at the hospital."

"That's good."

Jerry forced himself to his knees, took a deep breath, and stood up.

"Boy, we sure got surprised," called the first man. "All of a sudden, plunk. This guy comes outa the blue, hits the end of the barge, goes into the water. We ran down to this end of the tow fast as possible, but he's a goner sure."

"Yeah."

The description wasn't helping Jerry's balance any. He teetered across the wall on rubbery legs. Once safe, he limped toward the lockmaster's office. Several lock workers in orange vests scurried around with walkie-talkies. In the office, Jerry got on the radio and called the *Plattner* to tell them what had happened. Charlie had taken Cliff to a local doctor, but he said Roscoe, who should be taking over for Cliff, was drunk as a skunk.

"I'll stay here," Jerry told Kay. "The Coast Guard'll want to talk to me. They'll be here soon. Save that bullet, Kay. It's the only piece of evidence we've got. I doubt there'll be enough of that guy left to identify. The barges'll be taking care of that."

In due time the Coast Guard arrived, two men in a small runabout.

"Not much we can do," a young lieutenant told Jerry. "We're not cops. Doubt there's a survivor."

Jerry agreed.

Nevertheless the two men climbed down the ladder into the lock chamber and questioned the deckhands as to what they had seen. Several policemen arrived and questioned Jerry. They had other men on the *Plattner*.

The lockmaster's voice came over the loudspeaker, "This lock is closed down until further notice. All traffic stand by for further instructions."

Jerry walked slowly back to the *Plattner*. A policeman was in the woods with a flashlight, and Jerry helped him locate the footprints he had seen. The first light of dawn was beginning to show upriver and white mist was rising off the water.

There was another policeman in the pilothouse with Kay. She was handing him the bullet, which she had wrapped in a Kleenex.

"Twenty-two," the policeman said.

"The guy pitched the rifle into the river," Jerry said.

"You're the guy that chased him?"

"Yes."

"Did you get a good look at him?"

"I saw him from a distance near the lock platform but he was backlit by the moon. He was biggish, had a large head. I was too busy trying not to fall into the lock to be concentrating much on his appearance."

When the police had gone, Jerry sat for a moment on the lazy bench.

"God," Kay said.

"Yeah."

Jerry breathed deeply, squared his shoulders.

"So what about the peerless captain of this vessel?" Jerry asked. "You said he's a little inebriated?"

"To put it mildly. He's in his bunk, paralyzed."

"Let's go roust him out."

"The situation wasn't bad enough."

"Let's go take a look. Lock's closed down. We're not goin' anyplace anyway, but neither is anybody else. We got time to get this turkey back into circulation. Lemme just call the *Millie B* and make sure Dude's got things under control."

After a brief chat with Dude, Jerry waved to Kay to come downstairs with him, and he limped toward the stairwell.

"You hurt?"

Kay's tone was so full of concern and sympathy, Jerry exaggerated his difficulty walking.

"Just a flesh wound."

At the door marked <u>captain</u>, Jerry and Kay stopped and knocked. No answer. Jerry pushed the door open and beheld the dispiriting sight of the boat's senior officer lying on his bunk like a barge bumper.

"Roscoe?" Jerry was answered by a regular tone poem of snores.

"Maybe we could let him sleep it off," Jerry said, "though the man looks like he's seriously pissed. Wonder how long it'll take to get that lock open?" The reason for its being shut down hurt to think about. No one deserved to be crushed between cement walls and steel barges.

Jerry checked his watch. The darkness had lifted off the river and morning sun was lighting the surface with a few glints of silver.

"Let's go find your cook and get her to take Roscoe some hot coffee. She oughta be about ready to start breakfast." Jerry and Kay walked down to the lower deck and along the outside walkway to the galley.

There was no sign of breakfast, no cook, not even a light turned on. There were a few dregs of evil-looking coffee bubbling in the pot and a package of "store-bought" breakfast rolls on the sideboard.

"That woman," Kay said. "She is such a loser. Yesterday she had the 'punies'."

"Can she cook if she wants to?"

"Maybe. Her problem is she thinks spaghetti is a vegetable."

"Let's go see if she's on her way." Jerry and Kay went down the hall to the room marked cook. It was open and they peered in at a tangle of bedclothes, stockings, unwashed laundry, makeup and stacks of romance novels.

"Wonder where she is. Look in the bathroom, Kay." Kay went into the cook's room and tapped on the bathroom door. No answer. The two walked on to the bow of the boat, where they found Tom looking over the tow.

"Where's Nettie?" Jerry asked him.

"Beats me. Ain't seen hide nor hair of her nor Dave since the cops was here."

"Hmm. Were they together?"

"Last time I seen 'em."

"Thanks."

Jerry and Kay went to the engine room and looked around: bright-painted machinery, the boat's enormous twin engines below deck, blue rudders in a separate compartment – gauges, valves, wheels, alarm bells, the engineer's booth where the Chief spent most of his time. No sign of life anywhere.

"Well I'll be damned," Jerry said. "How've you been gettin' along with this Dave?"

"Oh – he's extremely quiet. I seldom get a word out of him."

"Let's check his room."

Jerry and Kay returned to the hall leading to the officers' rooms, and knocked on the engineer's door. No answer.

"Dave – what's up? Where's Nettie?" Kay called. Still no answer.

Jerry banged on the door.

"Dave, open this door the hell up!"

The door opened a crack and a frightened man's face appeared.

"What the heck's goin' on?" Jerry pushed against the door.

"We're goin' up the hill," Dave said. "Soon as we can get Nettie packed."

Jerry pushed the door all the way open. Nettie was sitting on Dave's bed in a kind of trance, while the engineer, a three-hundred pounder, sitting next to her, hauled himself to his feet. When he moved, his fat rolled like a waterbed. Nettie was also overly plump, with steel-wool hair just like Little Nancy's in the comics. She looked like a prime candidate for exorcism.

"What's the prob here?" Jerry said.

"What do you see, Nettie?" Dave asked.

"The same face as before." Nettie was trembling all over.

Tom appeared at the threshold of the room.

"Cap, I mean Miz K," Tom said, "those two crazy deckhands claim they're seein' ghosts."

"They got nothin' on these two," Jerry said. "Now Dave, take it slow, pard. What's got hold of Nettie?"

"The man that was hung on this boat one time a long time ago. Nettie saw him up in the pantry. She came down and told me. She thought he was someone got on the boat somehow from up on the bank, but then he just disappeared. She come down to me and described exactly the man was hung on this boat way back in 1950 – a black man wearin' a blue cotton jacket and had one them little funny beards."

"Jerry, that's the same thing those boys are seein'," Tom said.

"Right after that, the engines just conked out," Dave said. "Went cold stone dead."

"Oh. Oh," Nettie wailed. "This boat's got evil on it."

Jerry could see the hairs on Tom's neck stand up. His own neck felt a little chilly – not because he believed in Dave and Nettie's 'hants,' but because this was a problem he'd never faced before. He'd dealt with electric fires, near collisions, loose barges, pugnacious deckhands, thieving wharf agents, floods and drought, and shut-out fogs, but never the spirit world.

"There's a curse on this town," Dave said.

"Something awful's gonna happen," Nettie said.

"It already has. Cliff was shot and the man that did it got crushed to death in the lock – you know that. I think it's been upsetting for us all and maybe got our imaginations workin' overtime."

Jerry reached out a hand to Nettie but she pulled away as though he were Satan himself.

"We need to get this woman to a hospital. Or maybe a little glass of brandy'd help. I know where there's a bottle." Jerry tried a little humor, but Nettie and Dave grew more hysterical.

"Maybe we better let these two be for awhile. Dave, shall I call you a taxi? If you and Nettie want to go up the hill, why, we certainly can't stop you."

Jerry, Kay and Tom backed out of Dave's room and closed the door.

"What do we do now?" Kay asked.

"This is a new one on me," Jerry said. "But damn! Dave has always been a top notch engineer and a good man far as I know. Not a lunatic like he's acting now."

"Not one thing has gone right on this boat since I got on it. Maybe it *is* me," Kay said. "They're testing me to see how far they can go."

"They look really spelled," Tom said. "I've seen folks like that before. An' well, you can disbelieve in Chief Cornstalk if you want, but there does happen a lot of strange things around here."

"Tom, let's go see what's goin' on with those engines," Jerry said dryly. He hoped his tone would snap Tom back into a navigable channel.

"I'll see what's going on with the deckies," Kay said.

Jerry and Tom went to the pilothouse. Jerry turned the key in the ignition. Not even a rumble came from the bowels of the boat.

"No warning about this?" Jerry said. "Everything all right till last night?"

"Far as I know."

Jerry took the key out of the ignition and fiddled with the steering, then inserted the key again.

"I'm still thinkin' about Nettie and Dave," Jerry said. "Usually when people start seein' ghosts there's a reason. It's like any other kind of acting up. I learned that watching my kids. Why, one time one of 'em managed to raise the biggest welts you ever saw all over his body and they never went down till I found out he'd gotten himself expelled from school for smoking in the bathroom and was afraid to tell me."

"Nettie don't get along with Kay," Tom said. "Says Kay thinks she's better 'n her and is always tryin' to tell her how to cook."

"Somebody ought to from what I've seen of that galley. Nevertheless, that old sayin' about two women in one kitchen is probably still true." Jerry turned the ignition key a second time. There was still no response from the engine. It was dead as the kid at the locks.

Chapter 9

"Here comes Charlie and Cliff," Tom said. He pointed to the pilothouse window through which the two men could be seen coming out of the wooded area on the bank.

Jerry went out on deck. He was overjoyed to see Cliff walking.

"How you doin', Cliff?" he called.

Kay's pilot made the thumbs up sign and yelled, "Fine! Fine!" He had a bandage on his right ear and a tape around his chin holding it in place.

The whole group, Cliff and Charlie, Tom, Kay, and Jerry, met in the galley a few minutes later.

"You look like Van Gogh," Jerry said to Cliff. He slapped him on the back.

"Thought you always said I look like Bogie."

"I mean with the bandage."

"Oh yeah – that guy cut his ear off."

The four men stood awkwardly around, looking to Kay, the only woman in the group, to fix breakfast in the absence of Nettie. Kay started toward the stove and then stopped in mid-step and drew back. She sat at the head of the table, making it clear that she was not about to put on an apron. Jerry smiled as he took in the situation.

Finally Tom said, "I guess I can rustle up a little breakfast." He broke eggs into a frying pan and placed the coffee in the machine while Jerry filled Charlie and Cliff in on the night's events.

"The man fell into the lock chamber?" Charlie asked. "Did you get a look at him?"

"Not much."

Tom served bacon, fried eggs swimming in the grease, leftover biscuits and hot coffee to the group seated around the oil-cloth covered table.

"Boy, my ear is still ringin' from that bullet," Cliff said. "I don't relish that ever happenin' again."

"Maybe we won't have to worry anymore," Kay said. "If this shooting spree was just one man's fun and games."

"The shootin's are all so similar," Tom said. "I think maybe you got your man." He raised his lonely pinky as he took a sip of coffee.

"Could be," Jerry said. "But something tells me this guy was just a flunky. He was so dumb."

"I say your unions," Charlie said. "They been tryin' to get into my business for years. In which case they won't give up just because their man got killed."

"What about this craziness with Nettie and Dave?" Kay asked.

"Don't know. Have a few hunches. I'll talk to them again after breakfast," Jerry said.

Everybody dug into the food. Tom passed another platter of eggs and bacon, and poured fresh coffee.

"Wow, we forgot all about old Roscoe," Jerry said. "We were on our way to get him some coffee to sober up on when we ran into the children of the damned."

"What <u>about</u> Roscoe?" Charlie said.

"Pissed. Comatose."

"Christ." Charlie plunged a piece of toast into the gooey center of his egg.

"Oh yeah, and the engines don't work," Jerry said. "We'll have to call the office."

"Oh hell, I'll fix 'em," Charlie said.

"Can you?" Kay's eyes were full of hero worship. "I bet you didn't think you'd get into all this when you said you'd help me."

Charlie puffed out his chest – like an ugly bull frog, Jerry thought.

"Nothin' to it anymore. All the modern engineer needs is a slide rule and an oily rag."

Kay obviously, Jerry noted with annoyance, thought this cliché an original and colorful epigram made up by Charlie on the spot.

"When my father was engineer on the *Queen*, you really had to work: stand there all day in a boiling hot engine room and listen to the captain bawl orders through that old tube. Then turn the rudders by hand. Took some thought and a lot of muscle."

Charlie sort of flexed his pecs to underscore his point, while Jerry absorbed the fact that the captain "bawling" orders was <u>his</u> father, and he didn't like the unflattering description. Even though Captain Burnside had been a bit of a martinet, he didn't take kindly to anyone else saying so.

"So where do we go from here?" Jerry asked.

"Well first we gotta get this boat moving," Charlie said.

"And get the captain started on the twelve steps. He's either got to go to AA or back to milkin' cows out on the farm."

"He's good people when he ain't hittin' the bottle," Tom said.

"Give him another chance," Charlie said to Kay. "But get rid of those two punks you got deckin'. I'll send you two new hands." Charlie wiped his mouth and laid his napkin on the table. "I'll go fix those engines now."

"Let's see," mused Jerry, "we've got one 22 bullet and one footprint cops say was from size 14 work shoes."

"Great," said Charlie. "We know that the shooter, who even if they find his body is now about as recognizable as hamburger, was a guy with big feet wearin' clodhoppers and carryin' a 22 rifle. That really narrows it down, here in West Virginia."

"So we're nowhere at all."

Everybody at the table looked depressed. They finished their coffee and each carried his dishes to the sink according to galley rules. Jerry stepped out on deck. The locks were open now. He could see movement downriver. Presumably the body of the man, or what was left of it, had been found.

Jerry left the others trying to get the *Plattner* underway, while he went to the lock. The orderlies from the morgue were there and the Coast Guard and the police wanting a statement from Jerry. A few reporters were hanging around and a TV crew trying to get pictures. Jerry asked to look at the body, hoping somehow that it would tell him something, but Charlie's prediction was all too accurate. The man's face was battered beyond resemblance to anything human. One arm was dangling. The shoes and feet were gone. The man's clothes and skin were both hanging in shreds.

Jerry pushed away the Betacam the TV cameraman was sticking between him and the corpse.

"Let the guy have a little dignity," Jerry said.

A young reporter who had just arrived on the scene, asked, "How many people killed?"

"One," said the cameraman.

The reporter's face fell.

"Only one?"

As Jerry left the area, a crew member said to a young deckhand, "That could be you, Jim, you don't stop takin' weed down in the lock."

"Ee-you," the deckie said, "he looked like road kill."

Here was one kid who might learn the river could be deadly and dangerous, Jerry thought, just a little moreso when a sniper was running loose.

Chapter 10

On his return to the *Plattner*, Jerry found Kay in the engine room admiring Charlie's mechanical genius as he tinkered with an engine. Squatting together before the huge cylinders, the pair were too close for Jerry's comfort. Besides jealousy – he hoped the damned engines were busted beyond repair – he felt a distinct sense of *déjà vu*. Perhaps it was Kay's fetching ass, with her jeans pulled tight over it.... No, it was something about the two of them together. Jerry stared hard; they were still unaware of him, Kay handing Charlie various tools.

Now he had it: the tableau took him back to the *River Queen* and Kay and her father. Charlie had a distinct resemblance to Joe Slack; they were both dark, well-built, and had an air of command. And Kay followed the *River Queen* mate as he worked. Jerry must have seen them hundreds of times: the busy father, the adoring daughter hoping for a little attention.

"How's it goin'?" Jerry asked.

Charlie frowned, preoccupied. "Not bad. We'll have 'er up and runnin' soon." He pulled a dip-stick out of the oil container and stared at it. He took some oil on his finger and tasted it.

"I'll go see Roscoe," Jerry said. "Maybe Tom'll have him sobered up by now."

Jerry reluctantly left Kay and Charlie in the lower region of the boat and climbed up to the captain's room. He found Roscoe sitting on his bunk with his head in his hands. He was about Jerry's age, near fifty. His face was puffy and a distinct pout made him look babyish. His belly bulged out from between his loose shirt and pants from the twenty years he had spent eating on boats. An empty coffee cup and an ashtray full of cigarette butts testified to his attempts to get sober. The alcohol fumes rolled off his body like smoke off dry ice.

"Wow, you sure tied one on," Jerry said. "What brought that on?"

Roscoe groaned.

"I dunno," he confessed. "Jerry, I'm about burned out with this river."

"Maybe you don't cotton to almost gettin' your brain scrambled and made into an omelet...."

"That didn't improve my mood. But I was already down. This ain't no way to live. Thirty days at a stretch out here gives your wife too much time on her hands and you too much time to think about it."

"True, true. We all been that route."
"I just got divorced."
"Uh-huh."
"It has really tore me up." Roscoe smacked his fist into his hand. "The bitch!"
"Was she foolin' around?"
"All she cared about was gettin' dorked."
"How 'bout you?"
"A little. And now I'm workin' my ass off to pay rent for her and the guy she's livin' with."

Roscoe looked out toward the river. His eyes were bloodshot and his hands trembling as he reached for a cigarette.

"You know the old story; she got the goldmine and I got the shaft."
"Ain't that the way?"

Jerry joined Roscoe for a quiet smoke.

The two men sat pondering the ways of women and the world until their cigarettes were gone. Then Jerry got up from his seat at the foot of Roscoe's bunk.

"Well, Roscoe, what are we gonna do about this? Drinkin' yourself silly won't change nothin' – except your liver. Ever see a guy with cirrhosis?"

"My daddy died of it."

"Can you think about lookin' into AA?"

Roscoe turned away, plucked at the blind.

"What time is it?" he asked.

Jerry looked at his watch.

"Time to get goin'. The lock's open. You heard about last night?"

"Tom told me – who was the poor son of a bitch?"

"Don't know. Too late to find out. His mama wouldn't know him now."

Roscoe got off the bed and searched in the dop-kit on his dresser for shaving gear.

The floor under Jerry and Roscoe's feet began to move and a gigantic rumble shook the boat.

Shit, Jerry thought, that damned Charlie's got the boat going. He'll be strutting around all bloated up like one of those big harbor worms, and Kay'll be all aflutter.

"Engine's fixed," he said. "Think about AA, Roscoe. There's really no choice. You're in charge of a lot of lives out here."

"I never drank when the boat was goin'." Roscoe shoved his shirttails inside his rumpled pants and rebuckled his dangling belt. "When I do get off this damn river, I'm takin' an oar with me into the country, and I'm goin' so far away from the river no one will know what it is for."

"Everybody says that. I've used the line myself."

Jerry left Roscoe to put himself back together and headed toward the galley. No boat could travel far without good food and plenty of it. And not only was food needed from the cook, but sympathy and certain motherly ministrations as well.

The galley was still deserted, so Jerry returned to Dave's room. Nettie's eyes were still blank as canned grapes. Dave seemed to be returning, with the growing sunshine, to reality.

"Roscoe's up and about," Jerry said to them. "He'll be needing some lunch, Nettie, and so will the rest of the crew. Are you gonna do your job?"

"She's scared as a rabbit," Dave said.

Jerry pondered his choices.

"Do you two really want to go up the hill then? What will you use for money? I doubt Kay's gonna be in any mood to give you references."

"We'll get by."

"Yeah – you can sell your story to the *National Enquirer*. How a dead Indian Chief put a curse on you and a bullet came from Hell. That's about it, Dave."

"You don't believe we saw that spirit."

"Put it this way. I've never seen a spirit that didn't have some real reason for showing him or herself. Like some gripe – maybe a legitimate one that a person can't spit out."

Nettie retreated farther into her silence. Dave looked as though he might be thinking. The effort was evident in his clenched jaw and the way his heavy eyebrows drew together.

"Engine's are goin'," Jerry said. "Charlie fixed 'em."

"Charlie Summers?"

"Yeah."

"I don't want him messin' with my engine room."

"Well, then get down there and take over."

"You OK, Nettie?" Dave asked. He moved to Nettie's side and patted her steel-wool hair.

"Tell him about what we heard," Nettie said. Her sepulchral voice was replaced by a more normal one.

"Well," Dave said. As with many of the folks on the river, Dave's thoughts and feelings came from down deep and did not easily find their way into words.

"Seems like she's goin' to fire everybody that was on here before she took over."

"She'll have to if folks are layin' off their jobs," Jerry said.

"She's gonna sell to some big company."

"Where'd you hear that?"

The two looked spooked again. Jerry held up his hand.

"Don't answer that," he said. "I know you got your sources."

"Seems like there's spies around," Dave said.

"Spies?"

"Company spies."

"Like who?"

Nettie shook her head.

"Can't say any more," Dave said.

Jerry decided to quit while he was ahead. The boat should get moving and it was probably not wise to try to replace the whole crew. Barring another shooting – in a vicinity already suspected of being under an ancient curse, in the dead of the night a belief the most prosaic person might flirt with – Dave and Nettie would probably be OK. Kay needed to talk to them about their legitimate gripes. But Jerry judged them to be basically sound, just scared, like everybody else.

Nettie added, "Can't no good come of a boat that's painted blue."

"That's steamboat lore," Jerry began. Then gave up. Fuel for river boats might have changed, but the same old myths still fired up folks' brains.

Jerry left Dave and Nettie and went to the galley. There was Charlie sitting at the table, and Kay standing beside him, serving him a sandwich.

Chapter 11

"So where do you go from here?" Jerry asked Charlie. He was trying to wait him out, as he'd done as a kid, so he would have a few more minutes with Kay.

"Goin' on to Pittsburgh. Driver's out there now waiting for me." Charlie took a big bite of the sandwich Kay had fixed for him.

Kay poured herself a cup of coffee and sat down. She didn't ask Jerry if he was hungry.

"Jerry, did you know Charlie's father died this year? Not too long after Daddy."

"No, I didn't hear. Sorry, Charlie."

"Heart attack."

Charlie and Mr. Summers had worked together in their dredging business ever since the *River Queen* burned.

"What about your Mom?"

"She's still alive. Pretty much an invalid. She lives with me."

Jerry poured himself some coffee and sat down. Charlie took another big bite of his sandwich.

"You'll have to stay tied off till those two new deckhands get here," Charlie said to Kay. He looked at his watch. "Shouldn't be too long. They're comin' up from Paducah. Been workin' for me."

"Thanks for getting them, Charlie. And for getting rid of those two awful jokers I had on board."

"No problem." Charlie looked so smug Jerry wanted to slug him.

"I'll be callin' you from Pittsburgh. See how things are workin' out." Charlie gulped down what was left of his coffee and pushed back his chair. "Mighty tasty." He stood up, smirked at Jerry, shoved him playfully on the shoulder, and gave Kay a quick kiss on the cheek. "Be seein' you all soon."

Kay walked Charlie to the galley deck and stood waving as he went over to the bank.

With a hearty cry of Hi-ho Silver, Jerry thought.

When Kay returned to the galley, Jerry said, "You and Charlie looking mighty domestic when I came in."

Kay's whole body stiffened.

"What do you mean?"

"Oh he looked real comfy and Lord of the Manor sittin' here while you waited on him."

"The man worked like a dog all morning fixing that engine." Kay took her cup and Charlie's plate to the sink. "But domestic? That'll be the day. I am <u>finished</u> with all that!"

"Why so vehement? You're young, and still beautiful, you know that."

"No more marriage."

"May I ask why?"

"You may not. Though I'll probably tell you anyway one of these days." Kay was laughing now.

"I feel kind of bad toward Charlie," she said. "Daddy treated him mean – never did like him. He disliked the whole family as I remember it."

"Your Dad didn't think I was too cool either."

"True. He didn't want me to have anything to do with river people. Thought they were all low class, except for Captain Gray. And Mother looked down on Charlie because he didn't finish high school."

"I was a drop-out and a delinquent, too."

"I know. She didn't like you either. The only thing she and Daddy ever agreed on was that you and Charlie were no good and that I was too fine for the likes of you."

"Probably true."

At this juncture in Jerry's extra moments with Kay, Nettie came into the kitchen. She looked as if she still had one foot in the twilight zone.

"Oh, are you doing something here?" Nettie asked.

"Just fixed Mr. Summers a sandwich. He had to go," Kay said. "Are you feeling better? Over the 'punies' or the 'hants' or whatever?"

Nettie looked stricken; Jerry would have to remind Kay to go easy, and he took a softer tone.

"The men need lunch. We'll get out of here, and you get busy now. I hear you can whip up some of the best biscuits on the river."

"I been makin' biscuits since I was seven years old."

"Cap'll be needin' some good strong coffee, lots of it."

Nettie pulled the coffee out of the cabinet and laid a can of Spaghetti-O's on the counter.

"I think we ought to have some vegetables today," Kay said. "We've been going pretty heavy on the starches and red meats."

Nettie stopped working and looked to Jerry as though she were about to pull her apron off and fling it at Kay. Better separate the two, Jerry thought.

They would be natural enemies under the best of circumstances. Kay was tall and slim, beautiful, rich (or so Nettie would think), well-read, and she spoke good English, while Nettie was next to illiterate, a country girl, short, fat, and poor. Put the one in charge of the other, and look out. To avoid further friction, Jerry asked Kay to accompany him to the pilothouse so he could call J.B. and see where the *Millie* stood in terms of locking through.

They passed Roscoe in the hall on his way to the galley. His skin was rosy, pink, and smooth. Aftershave and the licoricey smell of Sen-Sen masked the alcohol odor.

When the captain was out of earshot, Kay said, "Charlie told me he talked to Roscoe and he promised to go to AA. We said he could stay on. Charlie took all Roscoe's bottles and poured them overboard, so he'll be OK for the rest of this run."

<u>Charlie</u> talked to him? Jerry thought. What about his own lengthy man-to-man with the captain?

"Charlie really knows these river people," Kay said. "And how to handle them. They respect him so."

Jerry wanted credit for <u>his</u> work with Roscoe; after all he had primed him for any efforts Charlie might have made. And as for knowing river people, hadn't Kay noticed Jerry's tact with Nettie? He could tell her of his efforts to get Dave back onto Planet Earth, too, but it would all sound so defensive, so childishly competitive, so self-serving. Jerry hoped he had learned something since the days when his and Charlie's idea of wooing Kay had been to compete at arm-wrestling and to brag about who was the toughest.

One of the last times they were all together, just before she married Martin, in fact, Jerry remembered trying to outdrink and outstory Charlie. Charlie had bragged about working iced-over barges and saving a pleasure boat full of children from drowning, while Jerry recalled his legendary fight with Beany Fuller, a Neanderthal deckhand who had made a pass at Kay. He had fought until his knuckles were shredded and his face like a deformed apple, and finally kicked Beany through a wooden guard rail.

It's a new world, Jerry reminded himself. And your rival is a man Kay feels close to because they both just lost their fathers, a man who has spent his life caring for his invalid wife and mother, a man who "really knows river people," has fixed an engine, and recruited fresh help for an ailing boat.

Damn! If only he'd been able to catch the guy that shot Cliff. Surely that would be worth at least the new deckhands or the invalid mother.

When Jerry and Kay reached the pilothouse and Jerry had assured himself that all was well on the *Millie B*, he told Kay the full story of his encounter with Nettie and Dave; she had heard only Tom's report of their seeing ghosts, and obviously dismissed it as one more silly aberration on the part of the crew.

"I couldn't get a whole lot out of Dave," Jerry said. "But I know he and Nettie are afraid the barge line is going to be sold and that they'll be fired. Then he said something about spies on board the boats."

"Spies?"

"Are there? Can you think of what they might mean?"

"I do have a colleague who rides now and then," Kay said. "He brings in a report on general efficiency. Rates the various boats for safety, morale, communications, and so on."

"To these folks he's a company spy."

"He's been very useful. We have to keep the boats up to face the competition."

"The river's been a last place for people to be independent."

"Fine," Kay said. "But they have to realize I have a business to run. We have to show a profit."

"Are you thinking of selling in the near future?"

"I might. If I get the boats to where anyone would want to buy. If I get a good offer."

"Would the present crews be secure?"

"Some. It depends–"

"On how the spy rates them."

"On the personnel reports. And for that matter, if they're worried about security, I might add that the so-called spy has been trying to convince these people to put a certain amount of their pay into a plan that would give them a good future on retirement or job loss."

"River people value their independence more than money. They don't want other folks making up their minds for them how to spend their pay."

"They'd rather be stupid."

"Maybe."

"I understand where Nettie and Dave are coming from," Jerry said. "I think while all this shooting is going on, you should cool the boat rides by your man. You've gotta think about morale."

"The *Millie*'s startin' into the lock." It was J.B. on the radio.

"Be with you in a trice," Jerry said.

He took the same liberty Charlie had, and kissed Kay on the cheek.

"Gotta go. Remember what I said about the people you're dealing with."

"Thanks for the advice."

As he headed for the steps, he said, "Kay, as far as Nettie goes, it would help to forget about heart-healthy menus for the time being. She has her own way of cooking and by and large the men would rather risk a coronary than give up meat and gravy."

"I cannot have the crews jeopardizing their health. I'm sending Nettie to a nutrition course as soon as she gets off the boat."

Jerry caught sparks off Kay's expression. All this trouble and mess was getting to her.

"You've got Joe Slack's eyes," Jerry said, "and lady you're as stiff-necked as your old man, too."

"And you're just like yours. Captain Jerry Burnside. Everyone else is a fool – especially women, stevedores, and mules."

It seemed Jerry's plan to win Kay back was not getting off to a very good start.

Chapter 12

Damn that Jerry!

Charlie watched the West Virginia hills fly by on his right. What could he offer Kay that Jerry couldn't? The two of them always had something special that he couldn't quite figure. Like books. They would listen all day to Jerry's mother reading. Now here they were alone together on that boat. Well, that wouldn't last long.

Charlie glanced back downriver to see if any movement had taken place in traffic. Jerry always brought out these painful feelings. That's why he never sought Jerry out even though they weren't all that far away from each other. Now he was right back to the old unhappy days on the *River Queen*. He could almost smell the hot steam in his father's engine room where the men shoveled coal into the open fireboxes to build up pressure in the boilers. They would be stripped to the waist, muscles glistening with sweat, straining over the heavy shovels full of coal. The red fires lighted their faces red. The boilers growled like animals.

"Watch that needle," his old man would say, pointing to the pressure gauges. "If it goes into the red, come and get me. We're goin' sky high."

And then the boat did explode and after that everything was different. No more Three Musketeers stuff for him and Jerry and Kay. He knew Jerry and Kay dated for awhile, and he, Charlie, asked her to marry him, but she went off to college and married that guy from Iowa.

Well, it wouldn't do to think about that. All water under the bridge. He couldn't get the pictures out of his mind, though, of him and Jerry as kids. It was always a contest. He almost fell onto the big paddle wheel once and could have been killed, challenging Jerry to run through the opening where the pitmans turned the big wheel, creaking and splashing, tossing its hundreds of buckets of water into the air. But he went farther than Jerry that time. He took his canoe closer to the wheel, too, when they rode the wake. Jerry won in wrestling, but Charlie beat him in boxing, and Jerry was chicken on heights. Charlie chuckled remembering his own quick climb to the top of the roller coaster at Coney Island. It was winter when the park was shut down. While Jerry only made it half way up the steep track, he climbed all the way to the top. King of the Mountain.

He needed a Queen. And he would get her. They were both free now. Surely it was time for him to have some luck. All those years taking care of a woman in a wheelchair.... And he never cheated on her, at least not with anyone she would know about and be hurt by. His few affairs were conducted far from home territory, so as not to pollute the ground around her.

And then there was his mother and his son down home.... He had to take care of them.

"Speed up," he told his driver.

Chapter 13

Damn Charlie, Jerry thought. Here they were back in the same old lockhold just like on the *River Queen*. All the emotions of those days had sprung from hiding like a Jack-in-the-Box. Surprise! You still love Kay, and Charlie is still around. And the game is harder: find the sniper.

The renewal of old rivalries intensified Jerry's obsession with the *River Queen*. His recurring dream was back in which the victims of the explosion whispered insistently in his ear that he must finish the model and find Mac Lodder, the only survivor besides himself, Kay, and Charlie.

Flames appeared in this dreams and he relived the day the *Queen* burned: his whole life, his mother and father, the people of his world – gone – in seconds.

Even his time in Viet Nam had not been as bad. His world had already exploded. The Army, which he'd joined several years before the war started, had given him the structure he'd been searching for in the years after the *Queen* blew and he'd gone to pieces. Jerry had stopped his heavy drinking after Nam, and lost his taste for bar fights and whores.

Of course, the service was one more wedge between him and Kay. While he had been acting the fool during his limbo years, she had been dutifully finishing high school and starting college. Then when he straightened out and was about to be shipped to Nam, and they met and he thought she'd be impressed by his uniform and his good resolutions, she had merely given him a lecture about how stupid the war was. The next time he heard, Kay had married Martin Kenny, moved to Council Bluffs and had a baby.

How did his parents actually die? In Jerry's mind he saw them as the stick figures in old etchings – flying through the air among splintered planks and balls of fire and other bodies.

All before he could prove himself to his father or tell his mother how much he loved her. Would his father be proud of him if he could see him today? Probably not, Jerry decided. He wouldn't understand the harbor work or the model-building or his love of poetry. The past was all water under the bridge, Captain Burnside would say. He respected only two men that Jerry knew of: Captain Dan Gray, owner of the Gray Packet Line, and Captain Jim Hale, the pilot who had taught him the river.

"He didn't go in for worrying about how you felt," Captain Burnside would say – especially when Jerry's mother interfered with his attempts to "make a man" of Jerry, a program consisting of endless errands, chores, and public bawlings-out. "If we did something wrong, Captain Hale let us know right quick, and good and loud."

"You could give Jerry a little credit now and then," his mother would say.

"I give credit where credit is due."

And then he went and died, Jerry thought, and Jerry had tried that "water under the bridge" outlook, but it didn't work. He had to build that model, including every detail of the *Queen*, and know what happened to her.

Jerry glanced at his navigation charts with their blue ribbon of river laid out on long pages. He was close to Marietta and suddenly had an idea of how he might find Mac.

Chapter 14

Damn Jerry and Charlie! Kay didn't want to be thinking about them. But as she looked out at the river from the pilot's chair in the *Plattner*, she wondered where they were and what was happening to them.

She had not come back to Cincinnati to be tangled up in their competition. The headquarters of the barge line moved here and that was that. If she were to run it, she had to be here.

Of course she had to admit she had been curious about what had become of her old boyfriends. And she wanted to prove to people that Joe Slack's daughter was capable and honest – and show off her position as owner of a big operation, even if it was in the red. Everything in business was in the red, she'd discovered.

She was sure, with Richard's help, she could pull Midwest America out of its slump. If only this insane shooting would stop. Since Cliff was shot, she was convinced more than ever that it was aimed at her. There had been some trouble with some very tough people when Martin and his father were running the business. She had heard talk, and knew they had hired private police to patrol the wharf in Council Bluffs. But that was some years ago, and at the time she had been busy with the children and household, and had known little of what went on aboard the boats.

She had made a mistake coming here. But what was the alternative? Let others run the business? It was her only way of getting her children through college. On her desk were tuition bills for Rob and clothing bills for Sally. They would get good educations. No one would ever call them river rats.

Like they had her. That Kay was dead. Her past on the *River Queen* was gone, buried in the mud with what was left of the boat. Or it had been. Now seeing Charlie and Jerry again, her own old feelings were stirred up, like mud on the bottom of the river; ruffle the nice clean surface, and it's all brown and cloudy.

Why wouldn't Jerry let the past go? That model she'd seen at his harbor showed how perfect his memory was of every detail of their former life. And now he was hunting down Mac Lodder, and dragging her into the past....

Out here on the river she was a child again, forced back by Jerry and his talk and her need of him and Charlie, into painful memories. Once again she sat on the stairs just above the *River Queen* salon; she saw her mother and father at the door. Usually Joe did not go near the salon while his wife was performing. He'd patrol the lower deck, checking on the horses or cattle tethered in their stalls. Maybe he felt the way Kay did, that this 'Linda Lyn' who sang sultry ballads was not the same person as her mother.

This night Linda was about to go on-stage in a transparent chiffon harem outfit with a few bangles covering her breasts. She had a figure considered sexy then: plenty of cleavage, a small waist, generous hips and long legs. Rita Hayworth and Jane Russell were popular, and Linda fit right in. Her face was made up to look exotic: lots of black liner around her eyes and thick mascara on her long lashes – red cheeks and a pouty, bright red mouth.

"You're not going out there like that!" Kay's father shouted. His face was red with rage, and Kay was scared; he could blow up suddenly like the boat's boilers down in Chief Summers' engine room.

Joe Slack was at least a foot taller than Linda and built like a bull, but she stood her ground. Kay was afraid he might someday actually hit her.

"Going out there like what?" her mother said.

Kay slunk into the shadows behind the lifeboats.

"You look like some – floozy."

"I'm supposed to. This is a Barbary Pirate number. I'm in a harem."

"I don't care what you're in, put some clothes on. What if your daughter saw you like that?"

"What if she did?"

Her father clenched his fists. He could easily kill her mother with a good strong blow.

"Just do as I say," he said.

"Don't tell me what to do," Linda replied. "I'm not one of your damned roustabouts."

"And watch your language."

"I'm late," her mother hissed. She backed away from her husband and went around to another door to the salon, leaving him blocking the one where she had planned to make her entrance. Her father didn't follow. Kay had never seen another person on the boat say no to Joe Slack and get away with it. The stevedores and roustabouts were afraid of him; George, the cook, stayed out of his way at all times, and Mac deferred to him in matters of loading and unloading. Even Captain Burnside was respectful of her father. If challenged, he would quit on the spot as he had many times, dragging her and her mother to some new place.

After her mother went into the salon, Kay stayed hidden. She felt so ashamed. Of her mother showing off her body, of her father's anger.

Joe stood for a moment staring after his wife, then stomped away, headed for the lower deck.

Kay slid onto the stairwell and watched as he made his rounds of the cargo. He kicked a barrel, pulled a layer of canvas tighter over some bales of straw, looked into the pen of a particularly dangerous bull that the roustabouts had had a hard time getting on board. Kay could smell the cattle and horses' sweat and manure, hear them shifting in their wooden stalls.

"Ned," her father yelled, and a black man slowly and sleepily appeared from his bed among the barrels. He was one of the roustabouts who was always nice to Kay and the boys; he had a big grin, and liked to kid them about being sweethearts.

"Get that bull secured. He'll be in the river again. He's already broken a leg," her father said.

Ned did not move.

"Get on it."

Ned still didn't move.

"Do as I say." Joe moved toward the man, threatening him with his fist.

"I already got tromped by that shit kicker," Ned said. He held up a swollen foot. He was a big man, taller than her father and with muscles bulging out of his white undershirt.

"You're drunk!" her father said. "Give me that bottle. You know Captain Gray doesn't allow liquor on board."

"Up you."

Her father cracked Ned across the face and pushed him toward the bull's pen. Ned leaned against the wood for a second, staring at her father. He jumped forward then suddenly and came at Joe with a razor.

"Get off my god-damn back! I'll kill you."

Ned slashed her father across the cheek with the razor, and Kay bit her lip to keep from screaming. She could see blood seeping from the wound and dripping down her father's neck. He wiped at it with his hand, then grabbed the razor, and twisted it out of Ned's hand. Then he beat him until Ned was on his knees. Kay ran up the steps and headed for the pilothouse, as far away as she could get from the lower deck and the rage of the two men. As she ran, she could hear the sickening sound of fists hitting flesh.

Kay stayed under the pilothouse steps for a long time, until she heard the sounds of people leaving the salon. Then she ran down to find her mother. Mr. Summers was coming out the exit. He was grinning and talking about "Luscious Linda." Charlie and Jerry, who had sneaked into the show, were right behind him. Kay hid behind a partition, then followed her mother to their small cabin. Linda was excited, sweat streaking her makeup. She had a glass of wine on her vanity table. She couldn't stop talking.

When Joe came up to the cabin, Linda told Kay to go down to the galley and get herself a piece of cake from George. Kay reluctantly obeyed, afraid of further violence. When she came back, the cabin door was locked.

In the afternoons, when she wasn't being Linda Lyn, Kay's mother was not like the salon performer. Her face was clear of makeup. Her breath was sweet. She would ask Kay what Mrs. Burnside was reading to her and Jerry.

"You get an education," she would say. "Don't be like me."

After the *Queen* blew up, Kay's mother and father were quiet and bitter. No more arguments. No more locked doors. No more glamorous steamboat life. Joe took a marina job. Linda sold makeup in a department store. She turned all her attention to Kay, obsessive as Miss Haversham.

"Stay away from river men," she advised. "They're nothing but trouble."

Chapter 15

Marietta, full of century-old houses and Victorian shop buildings, was one of Jerry's favorite places. He walked up the cobblestones to Main Street, at the confluence of the Muskingum and the Ohio, thinking of the many times he'd blown his top on beer and martinis in the Lafayette Hotel's cozy bar overlooking the water (it was strange how river people swear up and down on their days off that they'll get as far from the river as they can, and then at the first opportunity seek out riverfront bars and restaurants). He hiked a few more blocks to where the shops ended and the nice houses began.

There was no problem finding the place he was looking for; the yard was surrounded by a fence made of steamboat hog-chains and a trellis leading to the garden was made of two steamboat wheels – the old wooden type that were steered by hand. A large gray steamer bell was the centerpiece of the front yard, and the house was painted a fresh, neat steamboat white. Everything was ship-shape, battened down, trim, ready to sail.

Jerry pressed the front doorbell; it rang two longs and a short – like a steamboat announcing arrival. He hoped he hadn't chosen the wrong day to drop in.

He soon heard slow but firm footsteps, and the door was opened by a man in his nineties. He was slight and white-haired and wore rimless glasses that cut into his nose. Just behind him appeared his mirror image. The Fitzgerald twins, as they were still known on the river, looked so much alike, even their wives, Queen Lizzie and Jewel, both long dead, hadn't always been able to tell them apart.

Both men looked doubtful about who Jerry might be, until he identified himself.

"Oh yes," said Captain Jesse. Jerry knew which twin he was only because he was wearing a cardigan with a "J" on the breast pocket. His brother, Captain Harold, wore an "H."

"You're Captain Homer Burnside's boy," Captain Jesse said. "Sure thing."

"We've got the glaucoma," Captain Harold added. "We don't see so good anymore."

"Gosh I'm sorry." Jerry felt really bad. The twins had been pilots for forty-five years, and were the memory of the steamboat era. Whatever was lost to time and flood and fire was in their hearts and minds. They were like gods, revered, respected, almost worshipped by the river people.

"Come in and sit yourself down," Captain Harold said. "We're just waiting for my daughter to come and take us to supper."

"I hope I'm not intruding."

"Captain Burnside's boy is always welcome," Captain Jesse said. "What can we do for you today?"

"I've been putting together a model of the *River Queen*."

"Beautiful boat." The Fitzgeralds led Jerry into the parlor. "Built down at Howard Shipyards in 19 and 20."

"Originally called the *Republic*," said Captain Harold. "Had an unusual pilothouse. Trim designed specially by Captain Dan Gray himself. Have a seat."

Jerry looked around the parlor. Like the exterior, the interior of the house was strictly steamboat style: green satin draperies like those in the ladies' parlor on the *River Queen*, red plush carpeting with a pilot-wheel motif, oil paintings of the Fitzgerald boats the *Peggy Ann* and the *Americana*, a brass telegraph standing by the fireplace, and a grouping of several Victorian chairs and a loveseat from an 1870's sternwheeler. Jerry sat on the loveseat.

"It was tragic what happened to that boat," Captain Jesse said. "She was a fine packet. Ran the Cincinnati-St. Paul trade till 1956 or thereabout, then she operated as an excursion steamer."

"Her bell was made right there at Cincinnati," added Captain Harold, "at the Verdin Brass and Metal Company."

"I'm trying to look up some of the survivors."

Jerry suddenly felt shy. In spite of their passion for recovering every splinter of every steamboat, the Fitzgeralds must think it strange that he was here, almost thirty years after the boat's demise, suddenly interested in it. Why had he waited so long? Of course he had had to make a living. He'd served in the Army, he'd raised a family – he'd been busy. But why had he not asked questions or sought answers right after his parents' death? He had run away. He'd wasted four years bumming around, getting into fights, drinking beer, chasing girls, generally messing up his life.

"I thought I'd like to see if I could find Mac Lodder, remember him?"

"Mac Lodder," Captain Jesse was saying, "the *River Queen's* purser. Served on the Gray Line boats for thirty-five years. Started out clerking on the *General Grant*. Came from up in Pennsylvania."

"He might be able to tell me what happened that day," Jerry said. "I never got it straight."

"Weren't you there, boy?"

"Yes," Jerry said. "Of course, I remember the day, the uh – the fire and all. But I just walked away after." He did not want to tell the twins that he could barely remember where he went that afternoon. He thought maybe to the Salvation Army. He remembered trying to sleep on a hard cot that smelled like Lysol.

"Well it wasn't too unusual for a boat like that to die violently," Captain Jesse said. "You've heard of the *Sultana*? Killed a thousand Civil War soldiers returning home."

"The *Washington*," Captain Harold added. "1820, all lives on board lost."

"The *River Queen* killed fifteen," Captain Jesse said.

"Wind was high. She was building steam awful fast. Explosion caused her to burn."

Captain Jesse and Captain Harold's voices sounded like a scratchy old phonograph as they recalled the extent of the damage, and talked on about the type of fuel the *Queen* burned, and how many buckets of water the wheel worked.

"She was widened to fifty-two feet just prior to getting out of the packet business and into the excursion trade," Captain Jesse was saying.

"That was right after she struck the lock at Markland Dam."

Pain tore through Jerry's head, and unshed tears gathered, as the twins continued their litany of steamboat facts.

"Do you know where Mac lives now?" Jerry asked. "Is he still alive?"

"Oh, he's alive," Captain Jesse said, "but I don't know if you'll get much out of old Mac."

"Pretty much the hermit," Captain Harold added. "Lives off to himself – someplace in Indiana." He named a town likely to be Mac's retreat.

"He and Wendall Summers jumped from the upper decks and saved themselves the day the *Queen* burned," Captain Jesse said. "Chief Summers got a bad leg from it, but poor old Mac was never quite right in the head after that."

"Stayed in the hospital a long while after the fire, then a sanitarium."

"They say he's still a good six bubbles out o' plumb."

"Is there anyone else who would remember?"

"Not any more. Mac's the only survivor but you children."

The Fitzgeralds' front doorbell rang.

"That'll be Hilda," Captain Jesse said.

"Coming to take us to supper."

"Oh right." Jerry got up from the loveseat and shook hands with the two old men.

Captain Harold's daughter appeared at the parlor door, holding car keys in one hand and her purse in the other. She and Jerry were introduced and exchanged a few pleasantries, and she herded the aged twins to the door.

"Wait," Jerry said, "who caused the fire?"

The twins stopped and stared at each other.

"Some say Joe Slack the mate," Captain Jesse said.

"I do believe he was the one," added Harold.

His daughter jiggled her keys.

"It's quarter past five."

"We go to the mall for dinner as a rule," Captain Jesse said.

"For the Senior Special. Pretty good deal. You get a main dish, a salad, a potato, a roll and a drink for $3.50 if you get there by 5:30 p.m."

"Joe Slack couldn't have done it," Jerry said. "Why would he?"

There was no reply. By now the old captains were being helped out the door.

Jerry suddenly realized that his quest to find answers might be misguided. Of course, like everyone, he'd heard the rumors about Kay's father, but never from a source as reliable as the Fitzgeralds. Suppose, like other fantastic river stories, Joe Slack as the guilty party had a grain of truth in it? He might be hurting rather than helping Kay with his digging around.

It was well-known around the *Queen* that Joe was furiously jealous of his wife and Wendall Summers, Charlie's Dad. Because of the rumors. No one really knew, of course, whether Wendall and Linda were actually having an affair, but everyone gossiped about the fact that the engineer never missed a show he could afford the time to attend. Even the children knew what was going on: they heard things, saw things. And Joe Slack was a violent man.

Chapter 16

Someone somewhere knew why one tow was exchanged for another, Jerry supposed. But he certainly didn't and neither did any of the boat crews. All they knew was that they would be shoving thousands of tons of coal toward Pittsburgh, only to be told by the office to turn with a tow carrying coal to Cincinnati. According to some such decision, after visiting the Fitzgerald twins at Marietta, Jerry found himself going toward home with a different set of barges.

The day had changed character since he left Marietta. A wind had blown up and was making little whitecaps on the water. A marina on the West Virginia shore was taking the wind and the wake from a passing tow, and its long strings of floats danced like a Chinese paper dragon.

The sky was dark now, and little lights began to appear along the bank: from an open fire where some tramp or a pair of lovers was camping, from the lamps of small houses and shops. They looked cozy and homey, increasing the loneliness and isolation of the pilothouse above the long, dark, silent length of barges.

"Comin' up on Blennerhasset Island."

Jerry jumped when Dude spoke from behind him. Dude had come up the steps quietly.

Jerry turned on the searchlight and surveyed the shore. The thick beam of light swam with so many moths, it looked like a blast of snow. Its farthest reach lit up the woods as it moved from point to point, as though searching out the secrets of the dark. Strange, strange, to be gliding down the river, poking here and there into the vast lonely shores. And poking around in the past.

Jerry turned off the searchlight, and the river and hills were dark again. A crescent moon was the only light. The long dark flotilla hoved toward the south. With his night eyes re-established, Jerry could see Blennerhasset Island to the starboard, a long strip of land just off the West Virginia shore. He thought about old Aaron Burr over there in the Blennerhasset mansion, plotting treason. There was a big hollow tree – Jerry's ruminations were interrupted by a sharp, loud whizzing sound next to his ear. His heart pumped about a gallon of blood to his head. Amazed, he saw a bullet break through the far window and disappear into the night. For a minute he was stunned. He thought crazily about what a steel missile traveling at the speed of a bullet could do to a skull, when another shot roared past his cheek, so close he swore he could feel it. Jerry dropped to the floor, his forehead pressing into the tile. He reached an arm up to the console and grabbed for the intercom and called his engineer.

"I'm stoppin' down. Did you hear the shot?"

"Had the radio on," the Chief said.

"OK, you get J.B. up here on the double."

Jerry switched to the galley where the crew on duty would be watching TV or sitting around the table.

"Whitey, meet me and Dude in the equipment room right away." Jerry set the controls for the boat to stay put, and raced to the first deck, deciding what to do as he ran. There was no time to wait for the cops to arrive, and he had to get the shooter while he was still on the island.

When Jerry and Dude reached the first deck, Jerry grabbed a life jacket and a hardhat from the piles of safety gear. Whitey arrived seconds later.

"Did you hear the shot?" Jerry asked. Whitey had not. Jerry explained what had happened.

"I'm goin' over to Blennerhasset," he said. "If you two are game, you can help me. Need help rowing and more than one pair of eyes and legs. It's a big island. If we can spot him and get a description, that'll be good. We can take some lines and maybe even hog-tie him if we can sneak up on him."

Jerry looked at his chosen team; Whitey was dressed in his usual bikini, having added only a puffy vest against the night air.

"I'm in," he said. "Get the son of a bitch. You got a gun?"

"Nope." Firearms were not allowed on river boats, and Jerry thought, with good reason.

"I'll get my Nigger-Knocker," Whitey said. "Be back in a second."

A quick resolution to chat with Whitey about his racism crossed Jerry's mind, but this was no time to worry about a social conscience for a sixty-three year old deckhand.

"Dude? You're in, aren't you?"

"I'd do anything to get offa this boat." Dude dropped his turquoise necklace inside his shirt and reluctantly donned the hard-hat Jerry held out. "Hat hair" was his greatest fear. He fastened a bulky orange life jacket around his big chest.

"We're takin' a chance. He's armed and we're not." As Jerry spoke, he and Dude put an inflatable boat in the water. Whitey returned carrying three homemade bolos – baseball-sized lead balls covered with woven line on a lasso, folk art Whitey created on long winter nights in the galley. He also brought a good-sized butcher knife. The men threw more line into the boat and Dude grabbed a grappling hook. Jerry spoke into the intercom.

"J.B., are you there? Douse all the lights on the boat and keep the engines off."

Jerry and the two crewmen slid into the rubber boat and paddled as softly as they could toward the island. The moon gave very little light, so it was quite possible they could surprise the man.

"Head for the leeward side," Jerry said. "That's where he would leave his boat. We'll be able to tell if he's still around. If there's one there, we'll cut it loose."

"How do we know there's only one guy?" Whitey asked.

"I guess we don't. We're gonna have to be real careful."

Whitey nodded toward the bolos.

"We got these handy N–"

"Right," Jerry definitely would have to talk with Whitey later. How could the man be so good-hearted and such a fine shipmate and be so prejudiced against his fellow man?

"Now look, don't take any chances. We'll stay together. Dude, you were in Nam weren't you?"

"Yeah."

"We'll do what we did in the jungle."

By now, they were in the water between the island and the West Virginia shore.

"Keep your eyes peeled for a skiff or something," Jerry said.

The men searched the island inlets for signs of a boat as they dipped their oars quietly into the water and pulled their boat along.

They paddled on, each one dreading the whiz of a bullet. Jerry patted his hardhat. He hoped it would work if anyone started shooting. He kept a close eye on the woods all along the shore. He saw nothing suggesting a human form and heard nothing except the sound of crickets and tree toads.

They covered the whole island. There was no boat.

"Let's tie off right near that sycamore," Jerry said. "Take a look around the island. Can't understand how he got away so fast. Didn't hear an outboard, did you?"

Jerry knew the island well from the old days when the *River Queen* made it a tourist stop. He led the men to the hundred-year-old hollow tree where the visitors took pictures of themselves, and the excursion boats docked. There was nothing among the tall weeds and the willows, except dead grass, like the hair of corpses.

The men crept through the woods behind the Blennerhasset mansion, a sprawling three-winged Colonial. The place stood white and huge and empty on a green lawn, a house of plots and secrets. They heard the horses that pulled tourist carriages along the lanes, nickering in their stalls.

"Wait," Dude said. "What's that?"

Something crept across the lawn. It stopped and sat in a patch of moonlight.

"What the heck?" Jerry said.

"A painter," Whitey said. He used the locals' word for panther.

"Wow." Jerry had heard reports and rumors of panthers along the river ever since he was a kid. He'd stopped believing in them.

"God Almighty."

Whitey waved his bolo at the animal, but Jerry stopped him.

"You might kill him."

The panther sat regal and tall, coal black, yellow-eyed. It seemed magic, unreal, giving the moment an air of enchantment.

"What d'we do?" Whitey said. The animal was too close for them to try to creep past it; it could easily spring.

"We best just stay down wind of him," Jerry said.

They waited quietly for several minutes – minutes that gave the men they were chasing time to get away.

Finally, as if released from a spell, the animal sprang to its feet and ran off into the woods.

"Whoever did the shooting is long gone by now," Jerry said. He walked over to the spot where the panther had sat, only half-conscious of checking to see if the grass was tamped down – it had been so like a vision.

The men walked back to their boat, guided by the white branches of the sycamore, "the pilot's friend," and rowed back to the *Millie*.

J.B. turned from the steering levers laconically as they reached the pilothouse.

"What'd you all run into over there?" he asked.

"Painter," Dude said.

"You're kiddin'."

"We did," Jerry said.

Whitey shook leaf dirt and mud off his legs and arms. "Think it was the shooter. Turned himself into a painter to throw us off. Some folks can turn theirselves into animals like that."

"That's just a folk tale," Dude said. He tried to see himself in the slight reflection the controls made on the pilothouse window, and he whipped out a comb. "But they do say a devil can do it."

"We know one thing for damn sure, there's several guys involved in these shootings," Jerry said. "There's the kid I tangled with, and this shooter couldn't have gotten away so fast without help – someone waiting with a motor running to take him off the island – so it's two more guys, or one and a panther."

Whitey flexed his ropey old muscles. "I ever catch any of these guys I'm gonna turn 'em into catfish bait."

He would do it, too, Jerry thought. Whitey was one of the toughest guys on the river in spite of his age and small size.

Dude was still trying to smooth down his hair. "Damn," he said, "I got hardhat hair."

Whitey was scratching his arms and legs raw.

"Well I got chiggers."

The next morning, Jerry and Whitey and Dude went back to the island to take another look in the light of day. There was no sign of the beautiful black panther, and nothing on the island to lead to the shooters. But there was a boat on the West Virginia shore that seemed to be abandoned; a skiff containing a set of the nets used by mussel fishermen and hundreds of vicious hooks linked together in what resembled chain mail.

Chapter 17

"You're fired," Kay said. "I'm sending out a relief pilot."
"I signed on for thirty days."
"Right, not for eternity."
Jerry rejoiced at the concern in Kay's voice. Could she love him?
"He just straightened my part a little."
Jerry couldn't admit to being scared. He tried not to think about his head split open by a bullet, though he kept picturing his brain like a scrambled egg, the carefully collected thoughts and memories, the facts and feelings stored in its intricately folded tissues blown out like a blob of bloody snot.
"You knew this could happen when you invited me to run the *Millie*."
"I didn't quite believe it would happen again – and again."
Kay's voice had taken on a desperate note since the attacks on Cliff and Jerry.
"I need to talk to you in person," Kay said. "Not on the radio."
"That's a different story." Jerry agreed to take the company van back to Cincinnati as soon as it delivered the relief pilot. He could use some time off to check in at the harbor to see for himself how things were going at Burnside, Inc.

The van followed the river along highway 50 the whole way from Portsmouth to Cincinnati. There were so many roots of frustration on these banks. The shut-down steel mills of Portsmouth, their windows broken, conveyor belts stilled, spoke of failure and abandonment. Further along, Jerry saw a band of picketers protesting a new power plant. All along the banks, it was the forces of change against those who were trying to save the river's trees and towns and ancient burial grounds.
He passed Manchester, then Ripley, the old underground railroad stop. The past was everywhere, in his whole world as well as his life. Nothing was ever all the way gone or buried or sunk into the years; time was only a thin layer of sand.
As the van reached the outskirts of Cincinnati, it passed the race track and Coney Island, now almost totally abandoned, but still lush and green. Jerry could see the picnic groves on the river, the artificial lake where he and Kay had rowed many times, the tower of the obsolete roller coaster sticking up

through the trees, where he and Charlie had tried to see who could climb highest.

The approach to the city continued pretty, not like the entrance from the north with its stretches of car dealers, malls, fast-food places and other eyesores. Soon he could see the red brick spires of St. Rose's church, on a bend in the river, its big steeple clock for over a hundred years letting riverboats know the time. It was only when he turned off Columbia Parkway onto the expressway and then onto a main northward street that Jerry began to feel the familiar dis-ease of being on the banks. He could never quite believe, coming from his still basically beautiful world of water and weather that his fellow man could live among chicken shacks and tacky signs and endless billboards. He was back in the land of car exhaust and Muzac, and of being put on hold.

Kay's building was characterless and plastic; canned music hit Jerry from the time he entered until the Midwest America receptionist took his name. The elevator was alive with the sound of non-music. Jerry looked at his watch; an hour of being in this trashy world and he already felt tacky and diminished.

"Mrs. Kenny will be right out," the receptionist said. "Can I get you something?"

"Earplugs."

The woman looked at Jerry quizzically.

"Kidding."

Jerry longed for the sound of a hammer ringing far across the water. The noisy engines of towboats, a constant rumble and rattle, would be better than the roaring of the stream of traffic flowing past the building.

"Coffee?"

"Coffee would be nice."

He sat down and thumbed a magazine, a terrible thought suddenly hitting him. Maybe Kay had needed to see him for something personal. Anything else could surely have been communicated on the radio or marine phone. She had something to tell him about herself and Charlie and was letting him down easy. While he was out running around Blennerhasset Island, taking the chance of getting his head divided into equal parts, Charlie was further impressing Kay with his engineering skills and his way with the river folk.

"Jerry, I'm so glad to see you!" It was Kay, coming toward him, throwing her arms around him. He could smell her delicious perfume; it was sweet, like something you could eat – not that vaguely alcoholy disinfectant that so many women took for a seductive smell. He could stand here all day, bodies touching, his nose almost nuzzling Kay's neck. But now, Kay was backing away.

"Would you like coffee? Soda?"

"Your girl – woman – reception-type lady already asked. She's bringing coffee."

"Come with me, then. She'll bring it along. I'll show you the layout here."

Still wondering what Kay wanted enough to drag him off the boat, Jerry followed her into an inner room.

Chapter 18

Just inside the room Jerry and Kay entered was a desk and an electronic board running the length of the wall. Small squares blinked on an electronic replica of the river, each standing for a towboat or a barge. You could look at it and tell from minute to minute what boat was pushing what barge and where it was located. As the boat moved up or downriver, its square moved to a different location. This was a new one on Jerry. Even since he had gotten out of towboating, things had changed. This new computer-age set-up was disturbing. While he was thinking about the cosmos and the strange concatenations of human events, and was feeling transcendent and in tune with nature, a little blip on a lighted board represented his importance to the world.

Kay studied the board with businesslike concentration.

"The *Plattner*'s at mile 371," she said. "I got off her soon as I heard about you. Now tell me more about what happened last night...."

But before Jerry could start his tale, a well-tailored yuppie-type demanded Kay's attention. A blow dryer was obviously all the wind and weather the guy had ever experienced. Jerry wondered if he'd ever been on the water or outside an air-conditioned office. He detested guys with manicures.

"Kay," this denizen of boardrooms said, "I have something to discuss with you. Could we?"

"Oh Richard, this is Jerry Burnside. I've been telling you about him. You can talk in front of him."

Richard glanced at Jerry. Jerry took a second look at Richard. He guessed he was good-looking. Like a shirt ad.

"Captain Burnside." Richard nodded in Jerry's direction. "Kay?"

"Go ahead, Richard."

"Well, it seems Cliff Cooper has been seen with some union men."

"This is what I wanted to talk to you about, Jerry. Besides that, a union rep has turned up on one of the boats."

"So what are you saying?"

"That they might be behind the shootings."

"As we all know," Richard added, "they're quite thick with organized crime."

"Some are."

"Maybe it's time to replace Cliff."

"You don't think Cliff had anything to do with the shootings, do you? He got winged pretty bad himself, remember?" Jerry could still see the ribbon of blood spurting from Cliff's ear.

"Could be a diversion."

"You'd have to trust your sharpshooters not to hit you. Dick, you been reading too many murder mysteries," Jerry said.

"I'd hate to drop Cliff," Kay said. "He's one of the few reliable workers on the *Plattner*, and we've had such a turnover. It's like a cursed boat."

"Cliff's OK," Jerry said. "Even if he has been hanging around with the wrong people." To Jerry, Cliff was a simple good old boy with a penchant for good stories. He would never take part in rough stuff or nose into the business side of towboating, There were a lot of sea lawyers on the river, but Cliff wasn't likely to be one of them.

"Go ahead and find out anything further that you can," Kay told Richard. "But at the moment, let's keep Cliff on. We're not having much luck getting help."

"I'll do what you want, but I've got real problems with it." Richard's eye contact with Kay was something to be envied, and Jerry didn't like the proprietary tone he took in regard to company decisions.

"See you at lunch," Richard said to Kay.

He moved over to the electronic board. Kay and Jerry proceeded into her private office.

"Who is that guy?" Jerry asked.

"I knew you wouldn't like Richard," Kay said. "But he's been a big help."

"He's the company spy, right?"

"If you insist on calling him that. Actually he's a vice-president of the company. He was here with Martin's father."

Kay sat behind a big desk littered with papers and Jerry took the seat across from her.

"Charlie agrees with Richard's approach," Kay said.

"Then it must be right," Jerry snapped.

He was tired, feeling let down after the high as well as the terror of his recent close call.

"How are Nettie and Dave doing? Seein' any more spooks?"

"Nettie cooked broccoli last week."

"No. How 'bout Roscoe?"

"Roscoe's definitely promised to go to AA on his days off," Kay reported. "Meanwhile he's been sober as a judge."

"Have you met Judge Harry Plum of the Hamilton County Court of Appeals?"

"No," Kay laughed.

"Check him out sometime on a Saturday night at the Marina bar. But really that's great about Roscoe. I think he's basically an OK guy. That episode at Gallipolis is the only time I ever heard of him drinking on the job."

"That's what Charlie said. He was the one who got him to go to AA."

What other Helpful Harry thing had good old Charlie been up to? This visit to Kay was giving Jerry a headache.

"Where is old Charlie?"

"Back home."

"So are you beginning to take the offers to buy Midwest America more seriously?"

"They're looking better. I want to get back to Council Bluffs. But I can't do anything till this shooting ends. It's bringing business to a near stop. Customers don't trust me to get the boats there on time and crews are harder to get every day. Nobody wants to go into a set-up like that."

"It's a bummer, I can attest to that."

"God, I feel terrible about getting you shot at." Kay and Jerry reviewed the events at Blennerhasset Island, but there was little new he could add to what he had told her from the boat.

"The cops tried metal detectors on the *Millie*." Jerry described how they had scoured the island that morning and found little beyond a handmade bolo. "Oh, one thing we might check. The skiff the men might have come to the island in had mussel nets. We can check out the locals, look at licenses."

"So where do we go from here?" Kay asked.

Jerry shrugged.

"We know for sure now it's more than one guy."

"And no other boat company but mine seems to be the target."

Jerry and Kay sat silent for a moment, both absorbing the facts. Then Jerry said, "Kay, are you sure it's an outside job as they say in the movies? That VP of yours has upwardly mobile written all over him. He was with your father-in-law? Resents the wife of the boss's son taking over? Starts or encourages trouble among the crews? Pays someone to terrorize the boats? Little woman caves in and turns business over to bright young veep?"

Kay shook her head.

"Richard has been a help from the beginning. I just can't–"

"Has he ever worked on a boat?"

"Probably not. But he knows how to run a business."

"The river is more than a business."

"The river has always been a business."

"There was more...."

"As Charlie says, the big fish eat the little fish," Kay said. "Period."

Jerry hated that saying; it was too – true. He could see he and Kay were on different wave-lengths, and that she was going to ignore his theory about Richard. And there was something he definitely didn't like about this guy. Maybe it was jealousy at work. But maybe not.

"Remember that story Mac used to tell?" Jerry said.

"Which one?"

"About the rats."

"Rats?"

"The *River Queen* – oh back before we were born – was overrun with rats. And no matter what Mac and George and the mate did, they couldn't get rid of 'em. Got into the grain and scared the pigs and one got into the ladies' parlor and had the ladies all screaming over their tatting. And then somebody got the bright idea of getting a ferret on board – somebody told Mac and the others a ferret would get rid of the rats. Well, they got this big ferret and turned him loose on the lower deck. And everything was quiet for a while. But what happened was that instead of killing the rats, the ferret was mating with the female rats, and they produced a whole race of monster rodents."

"So – is there a point to this story?"

"It's just – your vice president has such sharp little teeth. Make sure he's not in bed with some rat that wants the barge line."

Chapter 19

While he had the advantage – Kay's sympathy for his close call and Charlie back in Paducah – Jerry called Kay and invited her to dinner. Under the spell of a river view and the sunset, he would tell her what he had learned from the Fitzgeralds, and maybe what he had wanted for so long, would happen at last.

He supposed she was still at her office. He'd been gone only a few hours, long enough to check in at his apartment and reclaim his bit of turf.

"About six," Jerry said. "I know this nice little place in Petersburg."

Kay hesitated.

"You'll have to pick me up," he added. "My car's at the harbor."

"OK," Kay said. "I'll drop you there after dinner."

Under his breath, Jerry added, "And then we'll come back here."

Jerry looked around the apartment trying to see it through Kay's eyes. The small living room had a nice bay window overlooking a garden; otherwise it was undistinguished. It was cozy though, with a wall of books and records, and some nice prints of river scenes. He kept his place neat and reasonably clean.

Jerry plumped up the couch pillows and filled the ice cube trays. Beer was all his had in the fridge. He looked at his watch, and decided to rush to the corner deli for a bottle of champagne.

He noticed a neighbor kid's tricycle sprawled on the tiny lawn, and he picked it up and put it in the side yard. The row of houses that made up his block looked pretty good, mostly 19th-century brick jobs. The neighborhood was only slightly tackied up with flimsy new stuff and signs for palm readings.

Kay arrived right on schedule. She was driving a Jaguar. Was she looking at his building with pity?

Luckily the restaurant Jerry picked was open and had room for them. He never called ahead on matters like eating, and so was noted more for being "interesting" than for possessing *savoir faire*. While he had observed that unsatisfied hunger could reduce the most romantic moments to a debacle of growling stomachs and arguments about reservations, he still didn't have a backup in mind.

He was pleased that the hostess at the River View treated him with special attention, remembered his name and that he liked a table by the window where he could enjoy the scenery. She took their orders for home-cured ribs, and popped a reserved sign on their table. Jerry and Kay went outside and across the road, and sat on the white wooden lawn chairs the restaurant had placed on a lawn overlooking the water. Jerry settled down with a beer, and handed Kay her white wine. The sun was setting, beginning to blend in with the banks, a soft pink glow coloring the daytime gray-green water. It changed every minute, from demure to dangerous. It was never boring. That's why Jerry loved it.

Jerry told Kay about stopping in Marietta.

"I know – it's all over the river that you went to see Captain Harold and Captain Jesse, and that you found out where Mac Lodder is."

"I guess I shouldn't be surprised – channel 13 is like a party line. I know who's got hemorrhoids and who's gettin' divorced."

"Jerry, I'd like to ask you a favor. Please don't pursue this *River Queen* business."

"I'm sure your father had nothing to do with it. It wouldn't make sense."

"One of your most endearing qualities has always been that you actually believe things make sense."

"I guess."

"The whole thing is making me feel – well, I've got enough on my plate."

Kay was remembering her father after the death of the *River Queen*. He took a job at a marina catering to boaters who used the river as an excuse to drink right after breakfast.

"I guess your reunion with this old river hasn't made you love her any better, has it?"

"Not really."

"It'll be different when we get this sniper. You'll see."

"I'm just on the river long enough to get the business going again. Martin drank up a lot of it."

"You belong here, Kay."

"You can't go home again, and I don't want to."

"But if–"

"Face it, Jerry, the *River Queen* days are over. In fact, they never were. That's poetry. I have to live in the real world."

"Poetry is real. And I have the feeling the sniper is connected some way to the *River Queen*."

"How?"

"I don't know. But it's like the old girl doesn't want to stay under water forever. The river has a way of taking things and then sending them back up to the surface."

"Now you sound like Nettie."

Jerry could see how upset Kay was and he changed the subject to something that would remind her of his recent close call.

"I saw one of those fabled 'painters' over on Blennerhasset Island the other night."

"Really?"

"Honest. I thought the sightings were just stories. Always something new and beautiful turning up on this old river. Look at you."

Kay stood and headed for the restaurant.

"We better go in."

Chapter 20

After dinner, Jerry and Kay drove along the river to Burnside Harbor. The first sight of it gave him a stab of regret; how could he have left his place to others? He felt the sweet sensation of coming home. He could smell the musky wild geraniums and the honeysuckle on the bank mixed with the river fumes of oil and mildew.

As he and Kay walked over the gangplank, their feet made that clatter that meant return – metal on wood. A towboat was passing and the harbor boat swayed slightly from the wake. He was back on the jiggle of the water – to terra-infirma where everything constantly shifted – and stayed the same.

Then up the metal grating steps to the office where Smitty's small night light cast tiny gleam on the black mirror of the river – lonely as an Edward Hopper painting. Smitty was in his accustomed place, tipped back in his chair, radio cackling, an old *Hustler* and a religious pamphlet side by side on his desk.

"Jerry!" Smitty said. His feet hit the floor with a thump. "Well, I'll be. And Missus." Smitty pushed the dirty magazine under a sheaf of papers. "How you doin', Jerry? That bullet scare you out of a year or two's growth?"

"Who me? Bullets never stopped my old man and they won't stop me."

Jerry looked around the office and peered out the window at the work barge and float.

"How's the *Harvey*?" he asked. "Is she keepin' busy? Her vitals in workin' order?"

"Pretty fair. We ain't been swamped but we're not out o' business neither."

"Where's Daryl?"

"Well now that's a good question," Smitty said. "I ain't seen hide nor hair o' Daryl all day. An' that's unusual for him not to show up or have his mother call. He's hardly ever late."

"Probably having a satisfying bar fight. There's nothing like the sound of breaking glass to make a coal miner's son feel alive."

Smitty chuckled.

"That Daryl, he's a pistol all right. He'd fight a porkypine if it was to talk back to him."

Jerry wandered into the back room and turned on the light. His model of the *River Queen* was there and waiting for him to come and put the finishing touches on it. Almost complete, all there, except for the story it hid.

He returned to where Smitty and Kay were quietly reviewing the Blennerhasset episode. While they talked, he glanced through the file cabinet to see what was going on at the harbor. Through the window just beyond, he saw car lights in the trees, two yellow eyes like a 'gator's in a swamp. They blinked out, and a car door slammed, and he saw somebody coming down the path to the boat.

"That sounded like Daryl's car," Smitty said. "Got a croupy sound to it."

"Looks like Daryl. And he's moving pretty fast."

They heard the clatter of the gangplank, the hollow metal plunk of feet on the steps, and Jerry's pilot was at the door to the office.

"Wait'll you hear what I got to tell you," he said. He put his hand on the door frame to steady himself after his speedy ascent. His scar glowed red like a neon tube. "I was pretty far downriver last night. Got to talkin' with some boys from Kentucky River way. This one guy's cousin is from a little town way back the hills and he said his cousin told him there's a guy been missin' from town. Left quite awhile ago and nobody's seen him or heard from him since."

"What's his name?" Jerry asked.

"The guy didn't know. His cousin told him but he forgot. Didn't think too much about it, but last night we got to talkin' about all the peculiar stuff goin' on by the river, and he had to match it. Lots of shootin's up his way he said."

"You're thinkin' it could be the guy I chased around Gallipolis lock?"

"Could be. Never heard anymore about that and I figured this guy's been missin' about since you was in Gallipolis."

"What's the name of the town?" Smitty asked.

"Gar's Hole. Little teeny place way out to Hell and gone."

"Do you have the cousin's name?"

Daryl reached in his shirt pocket. Jerry noticed his knuckles were scraped and raw.

"I wrote it down," Daryl said proudly, handing Jerry a crumpled matchbook from a bar, with a penciled name on it.

"Bobby Bolton," Jerry read. "Where's this cousin now?"

"This guy didn't know for sure. Thought maybe back in Gar's Hole."

"I oughta go up there," Jerry said. He turned to Kay. If he left, his relief pilot would have to stay on longer than she had planned.

"Oh no. Just call the police," Kay said.

"Nobody in Gar's Hole would talk to no police," Daryl said.

"You got that right," Smitty chimed in.

"He's right," Jerry said. He could tell by Kay's expression that she too understood.

"I think it might lead someplace," Jerry said, "if I could find out who the man is that's missing, and who he was associating with. We know our shooter was part of a group, not just a lone nutcase."

"Jerry, you've done enough. I'll go," Kay said.

Smitty looked like a carp caught on a fish hook. He spit out what he was trying to say.

"You don't want to do that – bein' a woman an' all."

Daryl seconded Smitty's opinion.

"There's some pretty rough customers up that way. Most of 'em are OK, but there's some that like to – well, they go for pigs even – much less a pretty woman–"

"You're needed here anyway," Jerry said. "I don't want you to turn your back on that VP of yours for any length of time."

"Jerry, really, Richard's all right."

"It ain't all that safe for a man to go up there, neither," Daryl said. "Leastways someone like you, Jerry, they ain't used to the type of. I could go."

Jerry shook his head; Daryl might be too tempted by the 'shine and fisticuffs to keep his wits about him and to return in one piece.

"I think I better go," Jerry said. "You and Smitty are doin' a good job, looks like, on the harbor. I'll be OK with this cousin's name to drop around. Besides, my daddy was originally from up that way and I might have some kin in town."

Jerry made himself sound jaunty, but even as he spoke, he remembered getting lost down an out-of-the-way lane near the Kentucky River, not too far from the old Shaker colony where tourists went. The people sitting in front of a row of rundown houses were straight out of *Deliverance*. He would not have gotten out of his car for anything. He didn't even roll the window down.

"Be careful," Kay said.

"The back country may be safer than piloting at this point," Jerry said, even though he had never forgotten his scary experience. "The guy I'm lookin' for is not doing any more shooting and his friends are presumably still out on the river. You be careful."

When Jerry and Kay left the office and walked up the hill to the parking lot, he took her hand. This time it didn't slide away.

"I still don't think you should go down there," Kay said. "You guys like to play down the risks."

Jerry pulled her to him in mock passion.

"I shall return to you."

Did he detect a response? Kay didn't pull away. He felt like a man about to be struck by lightning. His whole body shook from the current charging toward him. When it hit, he was holding her in a desperate grip. He kissed her on the mouth as though he had always had that right, and she greedily opened her lips for more. The fireflies in the dark pines sparkled like Christmas tree lights.

"I don't have to leave till tomorrow," Jerry said.

"I know."

Holding Kay tight, Jerry steered her toward his car. He had waited for this moment for thirty years. If it weren't for Daryl and Smitty nearby he would pull her down right here among the trees. He couldn't wait till they got back to his apartment. She kept her arms around his neck even as they moved.

Jerry and Kay fell locked together into the front seat of the car. He had never been so on fire. He kissed her through her blouse, and she grabbed at his hair.

"Kay! Kay!" Daryl's voice came from the darkness around them. Jerry and Kay both looked through the open car window and saw Daryl running in their direction, waving frantically.

"Wait! Kay! Your veep called. Said they need you right away."

Daryl panted from the effort of climbing the hill at a furious pace, and Kay and Jerry tried to put themselves together.

"I was afraid I couldn't catch you."

"Oh God," Jerry whispered.

"Hoses broke on the *Plattner* and some guy at the fuel depot is threatening somethin' or other. It's a mess."

Kay straightened her hair and prepared to get out of the car. Jerry pulled at her arm.

"Let Tom take care of it."

"Tom ain't there. He said he needs Kay," Daryl said.

Kay smiled regretfully at Jerry. "Gotta go."

Daryl looked over the situation and tactfully retreated.

"What shall I tell them?" he asked.

"I'm on my way."

Daryl, embarrassed, left.

Kay pulled away.
"No," Jerry said.
"Have to...."
"Damn."
"I won't be long."
"Call me later."
"I'll try."
"You will."
"I will."

Jerry walked Kay to her car and she got in. He kissed her one last time. She started the ignition.

"You be careful," Kay said. She sped away, leaving Jerry in the dark parking lot.

Back at his apartment that night, Jerry waited several hours for Kay to call, but she didn't call. He tried the harbor and her apartment but got machines in both places.

Around midnight the phone rang.

"Jerry?"

It was Sheryl.

"How are you? I haven't heard from you for so long, I thought I'd give you a ring."

Jerry tried hard to keep impatience out of his voice. But what if Kay called while he was on the phone?

"I'm fine."

"That's not what I hear. The story of you almost getting shot is all over the place."

"It was no big deal."

"No big deal. You're awfully cool."

"Look Sheryl. I just got home and I have to get up early tomorrow, could I call you later?"

"Fine."

"Good." Jerry hung up. He hated himself.

Sheryl deserved better treatment, but he had to keep the phone free in case Kay called. Where in the world could she be this late?

Chapter 21

At last, Charlie was alone with Kay. Charlie had promised her he would ride the *Plattner* a few days, and straighten out the glitches. He hadn't planned on the hoses going haywire or the snafu at the fuel depot, but they worked to his advantage. Got Kay to the boat without that damned Jerry hanging around. Now he had gotten the hose repaired, and had put the rip-off artist at the fuel depot in his place, and the midnight moon was lighting up the water, turning it silver as mercury.

He and Kay were standing near the gangplank.

Charlie felt the same old heat, being around Kay; his body burned with anger at Jerry and desire for Kay. She was so sexy. So beautiful. She was his by rights. If only he had the smooth-talking ways of a Jerry. This should be their moment. He would ask her out for a drink, they would recall old times; maybe she would remember, as he often did, the nights they went up to the top deck of the *River Queen* where the couples went to "neck."

"Thanks so much," Kay said. "How can I ever pay you back for all you've done?"

"No problem…." Charlie glanced at a couple of ducks swimming in the water near the dock, and pointed them out to Kay. "Look."

Three ducklings joined the party. Kay watched until the babies were guided over to a safe spot near the boat hull. A breeze lifted her hair. Charlie could smell her perfume.

She was different tonight. She looked flushed, distracted.

"Let's go get a drink," he said.

Kay looked at her watch.

"Better not. It's late."

"It's only twelve. The Water Witch is still open till three."

"The same old Witch? But…. I really can't."

"You have a late date?"

"Of course not. It's been a long day. Let me have a rain check."

"I won't be around for awhile. Taking the *Plattner* down to Louisville, remember?" He hoped reminding her of his service might change her mind. But why was he begging? He didn't have to beg for women.

"I'd love to. But – I really have to go."

Kay started to cross over to the dock.

Charlie seized her arm. She didn't pull away. She turned and seemed to examine his face, as though searching for something.

He wasn't conceited, but he knew the look of a woman hungry for love. Now she took his hand away from her arm. Gently, Charlie thought.

"Thanks again," Kay said. "I just can't – "

She walked over the gangplank. "You coming?"

Charlie followed her up the hill to where the cars were parked.

"You shouldn't be driving around alone at night," Charlie said. "Not with all the stuff that's going on."

"I'll be OK."

"I could drive you home."

"You have to be on duty soon. Take care, Charlie."

With that Kay was into her car.

"Is it Jerry?" Charlie said. "I can't believe you could go for him. He's so full of it."

"Jerry's a poet," Kay said.

"And a dipshit."

Kay laughed.

Charlie was glad she agreed with him.

"When I get back to Cincinnati–" he said.

Kay waved, and pulled away.

He knew damn well she wanted to see what was left of their old magic. Where in hell was she going?

Chapter 22

Kay undressed and lay down, her body restless. Through her window she could see the lights of the bridge and the river boats, the highway going south from the little apartment where Jerry was waiting for her. She pushed her pillow between her legs.

She could hear her own voice on her phone machine, then Jerry's saying, "Is everything OK? Call me as soon as you can."

All she had to do was pick up the receiver and they'd be together. When they had kissed earlier, her whole body felt young. She was free. She could do what she wanted. She wanted a man.

But it was a good thing Daryl had interrupted them. Jerry would take the whole thing seriously.

It wouldn't be fair. Not when she'd felt the way she did when Charlie grasped her arm as they stood together on the dark water.

Maybe she was like her mother. Linda had loved Joe Slack, but she couldn't stay away from Wendall Summers.

What was it? The thrill of being wanted by two men? Kay had told herself there was no way she had gotten together with Jerry and Charlie to start anything. She was in trouble with the barge line and needed people she could trust. Of course when she saw the sign "Burnside Harbor" she couldn't resist wanting to see what had become of Jerry. And the same with Charlie. She knew of his operation; it was big and known even in Council Bluffs.

She wanted a man. But she wanted to test her own powers. See what she could do with the business – and first thing off the bat she'd gotten herself involved.

She was so lonely. Why shouldn't she be wanting a man? In her last days with Martin, all feeling between them was gone. His eye was on the bottle. He drank before sex and couldn't wait for the after-lovemaking wine.

She put the phone in the living room and shut the door to keep out the sound of Jerry's voice, calling again.

She must have been crazy letting old feelings creep up on her. Letting the two men put her in the same old position of having to choose. Jerry's worship was touching and sexy, and he would never leave her. But he was such a dreamer. He would pull her under.

Charlie would be as domineering as her father. Though he seemed to respect her work on the barge line, he would take over her life like he took over everything.

She pulled the phone on its long cord into the living room, turned down the volume of the ring, closed the bedroom door and put a pillow over her ears.

Her mother was right. Stay away from river men, they're nothing but trouble.

PART II

Chapter 23

Jerry's pickup had a bad tire, so rather than take the time to drive back to Covington and have a new one put on, Jerry borrowed Daryl's Chevy to drive to Gar's Hole. Daryl had gotten directions from his bar buddy. The place was not on the map, and far from any other town, on an unmarked road, but Jerry felt sure he would be able to find it, by following the Kentucky River. He was eager to get there; this tip about a missing man, though fourth-hand, was the only promising lead that had come up in the shootings.

The day was hot and humid. Jerry drove west along a former state route arched over with trees. He watched the woods, thinking of the danger they harbored along with the questions and mysteries of the summer's events. He was about half-way to the Kentucky River, when the "croupy" condition of Daryl's car began to sound serious. More on the order of tubercular, Jerry thought. He was far from a gas station or garage; in fact, looking around with the first flutter of panic, he realized he was completely away from any sign of civilization. He would give anything to see a garage or a business area with a phone booth. The croup was sounding terminal.

Jerry tried to wind his way back to a more populated route, but by the time he reached the turn-off that led to it, the car was racked by a new and more violent coughing fit, and came to a stop at a crossroads.

"God damn." Jerry got out and looked into the black oily bowels of Daryl's car. Several jerry-rigged features, obviously Daryl's homemade remedies, explained the breakdown. Jerry tinkered a bit, but there was really nothing he could do to get the motor going again. There was no alternative to simply sitting and waiting for someone to come along and pick him up.

Jerry closed the hood of the car. The bang of metal on metal resounded through the trees growing close over the pock-marked two lanes of blacktop. He leaned against the fender and waited, listening for the sound of an approaching car; but for a good twenty minutes he heard only the birds chattering loudly, "sincere, sincere, sincere – chi-chi-chi." He kicked a tire.

More time went by. Jerry looked at his watch. The sun was directly overhead now and he was getting hotter and thirstier by the minute.

At last his ears picked up the sound of a truck approaching the intersection. He stood straight and put on his friendliest, most guileless smile. But of course, serial killers and satanic ritual murderers – both of which had been in the area recently – would probably arrange themselves to look equally harmless. For that matter, for all Jerry knew, the guy driving the truck was presently adjusting the features of a werewolf, to take in this lonely, stranded traveler.

There was no choice of Samaritans however, and Jerry continued his effort to flag down the truck as it came closer. He was relieved to see it come to a stop, and a head lean out the window.

"Car break down?" The face was that of a beefy good ole boy, probably not more than 17 or 18 years old. He wore a heavy black beard and a billed "John Deere" cap. Just the type Jerry hired as deckhands, and usually good-hearted, if not always in the top intellectual percentile.

"Yeah," Jerry said. "Completely busted down."

"Wanna go to a garage?"

"Naw." After opening it up, Jerry didn't think the car could be saved, and a day spent at a garage debating the particulars, locating parts and getting repairs would be a waste of both time and money. "I don't think she can be saved. Maybe you could just give me a lift. I'm headin' for Gar's Hole."

"No kiddin'?"

Jerry looked around at his situation, inviting the driver to do the same. Was this the place to kid? "You know Gar's Hole?" Jerry asked.

"Get in."

In spite of the boy's ambiguous answer, Jerry climbed into the pickup and settled himself in the passenger seat. The next vehicle along might be even less inviting. He felt around for a seat belt to buckle himself onto the cracked and slippery plastic seat, but found only a shred of webbing that had been hacked off.

"Jerry Burnside," he said.

The boy started the truck up and the two lurched forward as it zoomed away from the Chevy's death scene in a whirlwind of gas and crumbling blacktop. As his driver did not return the favor of introducing himself, Jerry asked his name.

"Ed Crocker."

Jerry was glad to be moving again, but remained apprehensive; though Ed looked like a familiar type, he drove like a drag racer, and Jerry noticed an almost decimated six-pack on the floor next to his foot.

"Beer?" Ed asked.

Jerry looked at his rescuer's porky red face.

"No thanks." Jerry decided one guy full of alcohol was enough per pickup, even though he was parched with thirst.

Ed looked down at the plastic beer holder and the remaining two cans of beer.

"'Bout time for a pit stop," he said.

He stepped on the accelerator. As he whizzed around the curves and unrepaired berms of the back road, he reached for a fresh beer, popped it open with his thumb and gulped it down.

"You know folks in Gar's Hole?" Jerry asked.

"No."

"Ever been there?"

"Nope."

In the hope of getting a little more information from his driver, Jerry offered his own credentials.

"I run Burnside Harbor – near Cincinnati. Lookin' up a friend in Gar's Hole."

Ed reached for the last beer and consumed it with the same efficiency he had before.

"Town's pretty poor from what I hear," Ed said. "Folks eatin' polk salad."

"That's poor."

Jerry was unable to pry more conversation from Ed, and concentrated on fighting panic.

Jerry, looking down into a wooded ravine where metal from an ancient wreck gleamed in the sun, said, "Maybe we ought to get onto the expressway."

"This is a short cut."

Another hair-raising hour went by, with Jerry alternately holding onto the outside of his door and cramming his fist into his pocket to keep from biting it off.

"We must be getting near the river," he said hopefully.

"Print near."

If Jerry had seen any other way to get back to civilization, besides riding with Ed, he would have grabbed it, but the only sign of habitation was an occasional shack that did not even have a TV antenna, a sure clue there would be no phone. He could hear the birds squawking and insects buzzing as they careened along. Occasionally Ed stirred up dust and loose rock as he came close to a drop-off; he didn't seem to read road signs too well, if the fact that he speeded up at every "dangerous curve" sign was an indication. Jerry was thoroughly jittery by the time they reached a small settlement of stores and houses.

"Pit stop!" Ed announced. "I gotta take a whiz bad. How 'bout you?"

He came to a tire-burning stop at a small gas station. Jerry, feeling as though he had jet-lag, slowly and gratefully climbed down from the pickup and stood on solid ground. It seemed to be moving slightly. But the sensation went away after he urinated and drank a coke.

"How much further to Gar's Hole?" he asked Ed.

"Not far."

Jerry was calculating the chances of his arriving there as a corpse against the delay that going into town and finding someone to drive him the rest of the way would involve. Postponing decision, he called the harbor, told Daryl where to find his car – hoping it would not be stripped of all parts by the time Daryl reached it – and asked him to have Smitty drive to Gar's Hole to pick him up. By the time he came out of the phone booth, his nerves were steadied enough to face the prospect of another short distance with Ed at the wheel. Though the male code he knew forbade one man telling another how to conduct himself in his own vehicle – especially as an uninvited guest – Jerry asked Ed if he might buy him a cup of coffee.

"No thanks, I'll just have a beer. Sure you don't want one?"

"Sure. Would you like me to spell you on the driving?"

"Naw, I ain't tired."

Jerry took his seat alongside Ed in the truck.

I just can't believe, Jerry thought, that God has it in mind for me to die on a back road somewhere near Gar's Hole, Kentucky, at the hands of a drunken hillbilly. Something more subtle, more heroic, more poetic – even ironic – this is too silly. He even hoped that Ed was less drunk than he appeared, though he himself had seen him put away three beers and had seen the empty six-pack. Regardless of his hopes regarding his Samaritan's level of sobriety, Jerry's fears were given no rest.

"Nice little town," he said to Ed as they left Milton in the distance. "Madison across the river's real nice, too."

"Yeah. My neuralsurgeon lives there."

Jerry held onto the door grip. Why did Ed need a neurosurgeon? He hoped the good doctor had gotten whatever it was under control.

"Almost had my whole head decapilated," Ed said. He pulled back his beard, showing a red scar running from ear to ear.

"What happened?"

"Racin' my old truck. Totalled it. Hee hee."

RIVER RATS

Jerry wished he had waited a little longer at the crossroads, for a serial killer to come by.

Chapter 24

Jerry had lost sight of the river. The town was far behind. Ed slowed his pickup from time to time as roughly-sketched dirt roads intersected the deeply-shaded macadam.

"Around here someplace," Ed said. He headed for a wooden sign almost covered by overhanging branches.

"What's that say?" he asked.

"Jesus comes as a Judge."

They drove on.

Ed slowed down at the next side road. "I'm sure that's it. That stump is where the sign was at."

Jerry glanced down the muddy brown byway.

"It's supposed to be on the river," Jerry said.

"It is. Just walk about a mile down that way. You'll come to it."

"Don't you want to drive down? Make sure?" Jerry didn't want to let go of his transportation, however risky, until he was sure he wasn't lost in the middle of nowhere.

"Couldn't get my truck down there – it's pretty steep."

"You're positive this is it?"

"Yeah. Sure you wanna go there?"

Jerry had little choice but to take Ed's word for his whereabouts. Thanking the boy, he got out of the pickup and began the hike toward what he hoped would be Gar's Hole. Looking back, he worried about Smitty finding this turn-off.

Ed was right about one thing, and that was a good sign; the road descended steeply and would not take a truck. It was mostly loose rock, mud, and tangled vines. In spite of the covering trees, the air was humid. Jerry wiped his face with his handkerchief and slapped at the mosquitoes and gnats that hovered around his face.

He had been vaguely aware of dogs barking, and the sound grew louder as he descended. They grew angrier as he moved on. Soon he saw a pen with at least four Dobermans jumping, barking, and hitting the wooden planks, threatening to break them down. He'd seen the bites of these animals on a little girl Daryl once brought down to the harbor. As he tiptoed past, the dogs got more excited.

"Nice doggies," Jerry whispered under his breath. He walked steadily, as unobtrusively as possible. He was relieved when he was past them. He didn't look back.

Still going down, Jerry definitely felt the presence of the river, and soon he could see it through the trees. A few feet further he stopped, hearing a voice raised as though in some sort of public speech. He peered between the branches of a wild rhododendron that had grown as tall as a man. He had not figured Gar's Hole to be a metropolis; at the same time, he had not quite imagined being so totally cut off from the outside world in such a small settlement where he was a stranger.

The town was spread out along the water: twenty or thirty houses in all states of repair, a few outlying lean-tos – apparently even Gar's Hole had its slums – a fishing dock, three or four rowboats bobbing in the current.

The town was gathered around at this moment, faces turned toward a small houseboat where a man stood addressing them with a Bible in his hand. Jerry moved forward and lurked at the edge of the crowd. The number of people appeared to be greater than the small grouping of houses would account for; he was lucky to be in town when there might be a few outsiders. Still, it was obviously a very tight place. The people who turned as he approached looked at him with blank or hostile faces. A woman pulled her child closer to her, and her man, a thin but tough-looking character with the taut aggressive look of the dogs Jerry just passed, indicated that Jerry should not make any sudden moves. Jerry had only the name Bobby Bolton – who, he just realized, might be public enemy number one – as a calling card. He considered how to get himself accepted here – not only enough to find out what he came for – but to escape in one piece.

The man on the boat was saying, "And so Jesus said to the people, you will be clothed and you will be fed. He took the five loaves and the five fishes and he told his disciples to eat of them and to take the bits and pieces among the people. And the disciples did as Jesus said. They didn't look to the government or the welfare to feed them."

Miraculously Jerry could smell fish frying, and it smelled damned good. He looked in the direction from which the odor was wafting. Two women were standing over fires in barrels, dipping fish into cornmeal and then into skillets full of hot fat.

"And so let's thank the good Lord who has provided for us this day and has put fish into the water. Thank Jesus who walked upon the water – the same water that's in that river right there – didn't have no water skis. No sir. Anybody here want to try 'er? You'll drown, my friend. Only Christ, the

Savior, the Son of God, could walk upon that river."

Jerry edged closer to the preacher. If he could get him in conversation pretty quick, the other people might accept him. As he disturbed various townspeople on his way toward the front of the group, he got a series of stares, some hostile, some puzzled, but most closed, like the town doors in a plague year.

The preacher wound up his sermon with the announcement that he had fifty pounds of fish to feed the people.

"Let's all thank the fine women who brought the grease for our fish fry and made the bread and the men who caught the fish. For while I am only a servant of Christ, I find that when I speak to folks, the food does multiply and come forth from the waters and the people are amply fed."

The preacher closed his Bible and went inside the cabin of his houseboat. Jerry spoke to the woman next to him.

"Could you tell me that preacher's name?"

The woman looked fearfully at Jerry.

"Just preacher," she said. "He holds a fish fry now and then so people will come to hear him talk. Don't live here. Lives on that boat."

Jerry approached the boat and called to the preacher through the printed cotton curtain that served as a door to the houseboat cabin.

"Hello – permission to board?"

"Come ahead."

Inside, a small space holding a few decrepit chairs, a wood chest, some books and a cot, the preacher was fanning himself with an old cardboard church fan. He was a good seventy-five or more, Jerry judged. His clerical collar was gray with many washings and he wore it with a neat denim shirt, a white belt and white shoes probably ten years old.

There was little in his appearance to inspire Jerry's trust in a total stranger. He looked over the man's books: *Pilgrim's Progress*. a Bible Concordance, Emerson's essays. Good reading.

"I enjoyed your sermon," Jerry said.

"Thank you, son." The preacher continued fanning himself, and studied Jerry's face.

"You're not from around here, are you?"

"Cincinnati."

"I was there many times. Used to have the old 'Chapel on the Water' – oh twenty-thirty years ago. I preached to the steam tows on the Ohio. All gone now."

"I remember that boat." Jerry could just see it bobbing next to the photography boat, the dish boat, and the one with the "Monster Whale" you could buy a peek at for a nickel. Jerry had wanted to go take a look, but Captain Burnside said it was just a come-on for suckers like Jerry.

"A good place to spread the good news, the old river," the preacher said, "for the towboaters and steamboat men need much help in finding their way. I'm the Reverend Daniel Zecariah."

"Jerry Burnside."

"Pleased to meet you." Jerry looked around. Behind a worn cloth hanging across the cabin, was a dish pan on an orange crate and a rough shelf holding salt, Corn Flakes, sugar and a can of Planter's Peanuts. The bedclothes on the cot were gray and frayed.

"But what can I do for you?" Mr. Zecariah asked. "I'm about to go and try the fine picnic the ladies are fixing up."

Jerry had little choice. He decided to trust the man. Now how to explain his mission? His story suddenly sounded so bizarre, even to himself.

"We both seem to be strangers in town," Jerry said.

"The messenger of Christ is a stranger to no one."

"That's kind of what I'm bankin' on. I just got into Gar's Hole and I think I'll need a little help getting acquainted."

"Depends on why you've come."

"I'm tryin' to find the name of a man that's missing from Gar's Hole."

"A lot folks disappear from around here."

"Uh huh."

"Why do you seek this man?"

"Well this fellow might have been involved in a shooting. He was killed, and his identity was never discovered; then a Bobby Bolton from Gar's Hole told a friend of a friend of mine there was a man missing from here. He was gone about the same time the man was killed."

The preacher thought over what Jerry had said.

"These folks like to protect their own. If they think the man is being looked into by the law...."

"Yeah," Jerry said. "I see what you mean." His mission seemed increasingly foolhardy – a good idea from the vantage point of safe, secure Burnside Harbor, but in the reality of Gar's Hole, tricky and more dangerous than he had thought.

"I would think they would like to know what happened to the missing person – his friends, family?"

"People missing aren't all that novel hereabouts. If you get on the wrong side of people, you could be one of them…. These are fine folks. But they are rightfully suspicious of outsiders."

"That's why I'm thinkin' if I'm with you, I can kind of ease my way in."

Mr. Zecariah studied Jerry's face. He seemed to be reading Jerry's soul. Jerry tried to will himself to look trustworthy. Ultimately Mr. Zecariah's scrutiny let up, and he appeared impressed with what he found.

"Well, stay with me then. But Mr. Burnside, I'm just a visitor here myself, like you are. You're here fishin' for information. I'm fishin' for souls. The folks are fishin' for their livelihood. We're all fishin' for something, ain't that right, son?"

"Sure thing."

"Just be sure you don't catch anything you can't land."

Chapter 25

Jerry and the preacher left the cabin and climbed over the little wooden gangplank back onto the muddy bank. The Gar's Hole folks were lined up at the fires getting hot fried fish piled onto their plates. A big platter of greens had appeared and a galvanized tub full of cider.

"Come on up, preacher," said one of the women serving the others. "You don't need to wait."

"No special favors are required for me." Daniel Zecariah stood at the end of the line, but everyone gave way, and the preacher and Jerry found themselves provided with plastic plates and tin cups of cider. One of the women piled their plates with good-smelling fried fish and dollops of cornbread fried in grease. The women stared at Jerry curiously, but did not question his right to be fed.

"This is Mr. Jerry Burnside from Cincinnati," Daniel Zecariah said to a matron in a housedress and ancient Nikes. "He's a visitor in town."

"Come to hear the reverend's talk," Jerry said.

"How did you know about it way up there?"

"He's a friend of mine. I told him." The preacher and Jerry took their food over under a tree and squatted down to eat.

Daniel Zecariah bowed his head over his food and said a short prayer of thanks and contrition. He ended, "God forgive me for that lie I just told."

"I think he will," Jerry said. "Your motive was to help your fellow man."

"God does not judge my motive but by law," Daniel replied. "The law came to us on stone tablets; thou shalt not lie. Nevertheless I would like to see a fellow river man accomplish his purpose here – supposing it is truly a Christian one – and get away without incident. I trust you have truly come to stop the violence the person you seek was involved in and not for revenge."

"I have." Jerry noticed various men and women looking his way as he and the preacher ate. Their eyes were not friendly.

"Can I get you another cup of cider?" Jerry asked Daniel. The preacher nodded and Jerry took their two cups to the woman at the tin tub.

"Mighty good," Jerry said jovially, holding forth the cups. The woman filled them, not saying a word.

"Wow, it's hot isn't it?"

The woman nodded. Jerry moved on to the women who were still frying fish, and filling plates with second helpings.

"That's catfish, isn't it?" Jerry asked. "It's sure delicious."

The man with the Doberman eyes stepped between Jerry and the woman.

"You're a friend of the preacher's?" the man asked.

"Mr. Zecariah? Sure am."

The man looked at Jerry suspiciously. He glanced at the preacher's houseboat as though asking why Jerry hadn't arrived on it and whether he would be leaving on it.

"Say," Jerry said. "I told a friend of mine I'd look up a fella from here named Bobby Bolton."

The man's eyes became more dangerous than before.

"Is Bobby around?"

"I ain't seen no Bobby Bolton."

Jerry decided this wasn't the person to level with. He would look around for someone friendlier.

"Nice town," Jerry said.

The man grabbed a little boy by the arm and thrust him away from the cider. "Set over there under the walnut tree, or I'll set ye afar'."

Jerry joined the preacher in the spotty shade provided by the mulberry tree. Some of the children were picking up the little purple berries and eating them. Jerry sampled one, recalling a delicious pie George had once made from mulberries a farm wife gave him. Kay and Jerry and Charlie had eaten the lattice crust off the top. Charlie got a whipping, Kay was not spoken to for a whole day by her father, and Jerry was bawled out in front of the entire *River Queen* crew. This berry was sour with a white center, nasty and soft as a grub worm.

Nobody joined Jerry under his tree or spoke to him as they passed. Well, my legendary charm ain't workin', Jerry thought, spitting out the berry. He got up and walked around the little settlement, checking out the rotting tires, rusty hubcaps and old tires that marred the place. The houses needed paint and repair, and the gardens were sparse, pitiful attempts to force growth out of unyielding clay. Jerry walked by the river's edge, trying to think how to ask his questions so as not to arouse hostility. The fear suddenly hit him that if Gar's Hole was indeed the home of the man he had chased at Gallipolis, the man's accomplices who shot at the *Millie B.* at Blennerhasset Island might be among the silent men by the riverside. Not knowing who was who, or where an attack might come from was worse than being in the pilothouse.

He approached a group standing around the fire and decided to drop cousin Bobby's name one more time.

"Anybody seen Bobby Bolton lately?"

The men turned to stare at Jerry. One had an eye full of blood like a fertilized egg.

"What do you want him for?"

"Just to say hi. He's a friend of a friend—"

"He ain't around. Ain't seen him for a while. Where you from?"

"Cincinnati."

"Cincinnati, eh?"

The men exchanged glances.

"That's up near Pittsburgh, hain't it?"

"Sorta." Jerry was on a dangerous wild goose chase, a bad combination. He joined a circle that had formed by the water's edge. Families and children were grouped around an older man who was playing songs with a set of spoons. He held ten or twelve in each hand and beat them on his knee, his head, his listeners' heads, the side of the cider tub – anything handy – producing brisk, rattling tunes. From time to time he would sing.

Jerry knew the songs. The *River Queen* crew used to sing them on summer nights out on the deck.

"I'm 400 million years old," the spoon man sang. This one was about Noah and Jonah, the flood waters, the whale, and the beginning of man.

"They left the Garden of Eden, to return there never more."

Jerry took over the last line, "Adam ate the apple, and I ate the core."

The man laughed and started another tune. "Where do you know that from?"

"River."

"You a river man then?"

The spoons never stopped their rhythmic clatter.

"Sure am."

"Know any stories to tell these kids?"

"A clean one, I guess you want."

"Clean as you can make it."

"Well, how 'bout the guy who claimed to be the fastest man in the world?"

The children in the circle turned to Jerry, their pinched faces alive with excitement and interest.

"I guess you all done heard this one."

"No," the kids murmured. "No, we never heard it."

Jerry told about how this man bragged so much his neighbor said he had to prove how fast he was.

The spoon man played a suspenseful riff.

"He gave his neighbor a bucket of water to pour onto the ground. He would catch it before it got there," Jerry said. "And while the water was in mid-air, the fastest man in the world ran in the house, got a fresh bucket and caught the water before it hit."

The children laughed and the spoon man nodded approvingly.

"A good story," he said. "Now I'll tell one"

He did, and he and Jerry kept the children, and gradually some of the adults who gathered around, entertained, until the sun began to dissolve and the tree shadows crept half-way across the river. Daniel Zecariah, noting Jerry's integration into the community, said goodnight to him, and waved the good-bye to his flock. He unmoored his houseboat, and went floating down the stream to his next stop.

Jerry was on his own.

Chapter 26

Nettie dreaded the Gallipolis locks. This was where that kid got killed and she saw the ghost. And now they were coming up on it and it was getting dark, too.

Nettie was at the sink, washing some dishes the men had left from their evening snacks. She laid the detergent on the sink top and pulled off her plastic gloves with a plop. She could hear the big iron gates swing open and she felt panic as the *Plattner* slid inside the chamber and the gates swung closed. She could hear the clank and thud as they gripped one another tight. The tow was being raised now. The cement walls were all around her. She wished one of the men would come in for coffee, but they were way out on the tow, keeping it off the wall, the very wall where that kid was crushed to death.

She never liked being down inside the huge chambers where everything echoed. The lights in the galley flickered. Nettie picked up a nice warm dishcloth and held it against her face. She dried a glass carefully and laid it on the counter. Usually she just let them drain, but she did not want to move from the galley, where, if anywhere, she felt safe. A low faint moan came from the direction of the barges. She was hearing things sure. She held her ears. But it wasn't in her head; with her ears covered she could hear nothing. It had to be a cable; they sang as they were pulled tight on the barges. Or it would be the wind blowing the ventilator on the open deck. She took her hands away. There was definitely the sound of a person moaning. Nettie went to the doorway. It was louder now, though still faint. It was coming from under the barges, echoing in the chamber. The voice of a young boy.

Nettie ran to the bow of the boat and looked down the long, dark length of the barges filling the chamber. The alleyway of metal and heaps of black coal were full of shadows and weird shapes, but then she saw a distinct form emerge from behind a closed barge. It was a young boy. He walked toward her slowly. It wasn't any of the deckies on board. He had a large head, that was all she could tell, and he held a rifle in his hand. Nettie ran back to the galley, and locked the door to the deck. She called the engine room on the intercom. No answer. She called the pilothouse. Charlie Summers, who had been on the boat since Cliff quit, answered.

"Charlie," she said. "Is Dave up there?"

"Sure thing, he's right here. Want me to put him on?"

"Hurry."

Dave came on the intercom and Nettie told him what she'd seen. He didn't reply at first.

"Are you sure it wasn't one of our boys?"

"Sure. It was that boy that was killed in this lock."

"I'll be down in a minute. You stay there."

Dave came puffing into the galley, and he and Nettie went out on deck and walked down the tow together. Dave shone his flashlight into every cranny. Nettie jumped at each pile of coal. They found no trace of the boy, just two bottles of whiskey – one half empty – that someone had hidden among the barges.

"Somebody been drinkin' down there, sneakin' it," Dave said. "Ghosts don't drink."

"I <u>know</u> I saw that boy," Nettie said.

"I know you did." Dave steered Nettie back to the galley.

"Ain't nothin' we can do to stop it. But if you see it again, or I do, we're gettin' off this turkey. I'll take a look from up in the pilothouse. OK?"

Nettie reluctantly agreed, and let Dave take her to her room, where she locked herself in.

Dave went back to the pilothouse, out of breath from hauling his great bulk up and down the steep steps of the boat. He found Charlie waiting for him anxiously.

"Take these sticks a minute, will you, Dave? I got to go to the head bad."

Dave took Charlie's place, while Charlie shifted from foot to foot, thinking Christ that man has the biggest ass I ever saw.

"Nettie saw that boy that was killed here. Heard him moanin' from under the barges...."

"No shit." Charlie moved toward the steps. "You can put the searchlight on. I think Nettie's seein' things though."

"I just don't know."

Dave fiddled with the console. Which button controlled the searchlight?

"Wait Charlie, show me how to work this thing."

Charlie impatiently returned to the pilot's chair, and turned the right switch. A blaze of light swept over the locks. Charlie saw red, and his head felt as if it might explode. He reached his hand to his temple. When he lowered it and looked down, as if at a mosquito he'd just swatted, there was blood on it. He felt surprised, kind of numb.

Chapter 27

"That's all for now," the spoon man said. The children begged for one more song, and he obliged with "Goodnight Irene," but then he piled his spoons in a little plastic case and went to the tub for a fresh cup of cider. Jerry remained sitting on the piece of driftwood he had occupied during the singing. He hadn't gotten very far. The people were a little less fearful. Several smiled at him as they pried their children away from the circle and toward their houses, but he hadn't found out anything helpful, and was not looking forward to the mile walk back to the road through the deepening gloom.

"What's your name again?" the spoon man asked, returning to his seat. Jerry told him and complimented the man on his music and story-telling.

"Oh, this ain't nothin'," he said. "I used to have an act I took around all over. I'm Sam Spoon. Maybe you heard o' me. I played up in Cincinnati – little club on Main Street."

"Sure," Jerry said. "Bluegrass Mattie's."

"Nobody cares no more," Sam Spoon said. "I came back here where I was raised."

Jerry nodded.

"Everything's all glitz and MTV...."

"Right you are."

Jerry was getting more fearful by the minute of his long walk back to the highway.

"I hear you was askin' about Bobby Bolton," Sam Spoon said.

"Yeah." Jerry's hopes revived. "You know him?"

"Could be. I tell you what." Sam Spoon paused and took a long drink of cider and stared out at the river. "Got a cigarette?"

Jerry took a pack from his pocket and shook the cigarettes out so Spoon could select one.

Spoon lit up and sucked in several deep lungsful of smoke.

"You tell me a story and then maybe I'll tell you one. Tell me about why a Ohio river rat ends up in a place like Gar's Hole to hear a country preacher and look up somebody he don't really know."

Jerry laughed, but Sam Spoon's expression was deadly serious. His face, jovial while singing and trading stories, now looked frightening with the puffs of smoke coming from his red lips. He reminded Jerry of an old Camel cigarette billboard where smoke poured from a hole in a flat painted surface. There were faint signs of a drinker in Sam's nose, a grossness to the jovial face. Nevertheless, Jerry decided to trust him – with at least part of the truth.

"There was this riverboat pilot tootlin' along mindin' his own business, when all of a sudden a bullet came whizzin' through the air and took his ear print near off. Another man on board the boat went runnin' after the gunman while other folks took care of the pilot. Well, durin' the chase, the gunman got killed." Jerry gulped. He hated thinking about the fate of the man he had chased; he felt responsible. He would have to mute this part of his story, not only for himself, but for how it would play with Sam Spoon, who might well be a friend or relative of the man. He studied his companion. Sam Spoon was finishing his cigarette, holding the butt between thumb and forefinger and sucking the last bit of smoke through less than a half-inch of cigarette.

"So anyway," Jerry continued, "there were some more shootings. No one was hurt, but nobody likes to think he's a sittin' duck. A grudge fought out in the open's one thing, but sniper-fire's against all rules of fair play and decency, ain't it?"

"Most times," Sam Spoon said. "Go on." He pulled a harmonica out of his back pocket and accompanied Jerry's narrative with a casual, plaintive air. Even if he learned anything from this person, Jerry thought, what could it prove? He had just about convinced himself Kay's veep, Richard, was somehow behind the shootings, and he had trouble making any connection between Sam Spoon and Kay's slick yuppie vice-president.

"Well," Jerry went on, "nobody knew anything about the gunman that got killed – not his name nor where he came from nor anything. So we – they – the people bein' shot at – wondered if he didn't have a mother or a dad or a sweetheart or somebody lookin' for a person that just up and disappeared.... Then one night a fella, nevermind his name, a real fightin' trick who likes to hang around in bars, heard tell of a lad missing from a little nearby town."

"So?"

Jerry figured he had said enough.

"A story without an ending."

Sam Spoon looked skeptical, but did not press for more.

"There's lots of those."

He played a short tune on his harmonica, his eyes closed.

"Got another fag?"

Jerry offered the pack again. Sam Spoon accepted and lit up the cigarette.

"Now I'll tell you a story," he said. "It seems like there was this man livin' in a small settlement on the river. Didn't have much. He'd been strip-mined out in more ways than one: where he came from the coal owners used up the coal and moved on, and his wife cleaned him out and she moved on too, so he was pretty much alone – lived on catfish and polk salat. Had him a little lean-to kept the rain off his head. Well, one day a boy came into the settlement. Nobody knew from where. He was real shabby and acted like a stray dog that's been hit. Kinda cringin' and likin' to fight at the same time. Nobody wanted him. Just another mouth to feed and nobody had any extra. Big boy he was: big feet, big hands, great big head."

Jerry was sure now this was the gunman he'd chased over the locks at Gallipolis. He remembered the head, like a Jack O'Lantern against the night sky.

"Well, this man that was all alone took him in. Give him food, a place to sleep, taught him to fish."

"And?"

"He was with the man for a year or two, followed him around like a dog. But then one day, some time back, he was maybe seventeen – eighteen at the time, he just went off and left and nobody has heard from him since. His daddy that became so has been real desponding, keeps off to himself mostly."

Jerry waited for the rest of the story.

"Do you – does the story tell where he went or what happened to him?"

"Nope. That's as far as it goes."

"How about the man that took the young man in? Did he go lookin' for him? Did he want to know what happened to him?"

"He might have," Sam Spoon said. "Might still. It would all depend. He wouldn't want no police mixin' in. If the boy done anything bad, he'd take care of it hisself."

"Sounds like our stories mesh," Jerry said. "Like they might almost be about the same people."

Sam Spoon was close to burning his fingers on a cigarette butt again.

"I told all I know," he said. He flicked away the cigarette, packed his plastic kit of spoons into his back pocket, and stood up. "Hey, you ever see Mattie or anybody anymore?"

"Not for years."

"I could use a gig. This here's a good place, but I'm in Show Biz, son."

"I'll look her up," Jerry said. Now where was he? Led on by Sam Spoon, but still basically in the dark. He watched the man's preparations to leave with dismay.

"I'm not any kind of fuzz," Jerry said.

"I know you ain't. If you was, I would of smelled it on you. Well, I'll say goodnight to you."

Then he added, saving Jerry's life, "You might want to talk to Harlan Huff down in that cabin right there between them two piney bushes. He tells some good ones, and with your love of stories, you might enjoy talkin' to him. Tell him I sent you."

Harlan Huff was sitting in his cabin, staring at the four walls. Just him and the four decrepit walls covered with pages from old magazines and newspapers. He wasn't smoking, watching TV, listening to the radio, talking to anybody, playing with a dog, or doing anything at all.

He was a tiny man; he looked to Jerry like a shrunken Abraham Lincoln – same unkempt dark hair, square jaw, deep-set eyes, bony frame – all condensed and squeezed into about a hundred and fifteen pounds.

"Sam Spoon told me I should come and talk to you." Jerry explained how he thought the man that had been killed on the river might be the boy missing from Gar's Hole. He didn't mention the shooting or the way he died.

"He fits the description," Jerry said. "Especially the big feet and head. And nobody ever came up with anybody missing till we heard about a boy gone from Gar's Hole."

"Who told you that?"

"Bobby Bolton, from here, told a friend of my harbor man."

"It's true my boy left here and we ain't heard," Mr. Huff said. "We thought he was murdered."

"Do you know anybody that'd want to murder your son?"

Harlan Huff thought.

"No," he said. "No I don't. Slag was a quiet boy. Got in a fight once in a while, but...."

"Slag?"

"That was his name when I got him. Didn't have no last name, he said."

Mr. Huff's eyes looked empty and sad.

"How long has Slag been gone?"

Mr. Huff went to a calendar hanging on the wall amid the newspapers and magazines. He pointed to a date some weeks before Gallipolis. Jerry figured the time. The boy had been missing since the first shot had been taken at one of Kay's boats.

"Did your boy have any friends in town?"

"Not that I know of."

"Did he have a job?"

"Him and me fished."

Jerry paused, thinking where to turn next. How could he track the movements of a boy named Slag who had no job, no friends, no last name?

"How come you to take such an interest in the boy if you ain't the police?" Mr. Huff asked.

Jerry himself was convinced by now that Slag was the dupe of somebody with far more smarts and a lot more viciousness. "He got mixed up with some bad people, took a shot at one of our towboat pilots on the Midwest America Line. But I'm sure it wasn't his idea."

"He wouldn't do something like that for no reason."

"He was running away when – he fell – and drowned. Somebody probably paid him to take the shot – told him it wouldn't hurt, not to come too close. The other pilots that got shot at weren't hit."

"He didn't have his own gun yet. And mine ain't missin'." Mr. Huff glanced toward the corner of the small room, where a 22 rifle glistened in the low light.

"I think he was used by somebody," Jerry said. "Think again. Is there anybody your boy might have gone off with?"

"He was hangin' around with some deer hunters awhile back."

"Did you know any of them, or anything about them?"

Harlan Huff shook his head. "You lookin' for 'em? That what you want with Slag?"

"Yes," Jerry said. "I'm lookin' for 'em. Or is there anybody at all in town that you think might be the persons I'm after?"

"If there was, you wouldn't have to worry about it." Mr. Huff's sad eyes hardened into steel and his square jaw was thrust out defiantly. "I'd take care of 'em myself."

Jerry stood to go. He thanked Mr. Huff and shook his hand.

"Any friend of Sam Spoon's a friend of mine."

Jerry was sure he had the right person, but he was still a long way from solid ground. He felt better in himself for having talked to the father of the dead boy. The man ought to know what had happened to his son and where he was buried – even if it was only the potter's field for unclaimed bodies the West Virginia morgue couldn't keep forever.

Chapter 28

Dark overhanging trees blotted out the ground and Jerry had to maneuver carefully to keep from getting off on a side path. He should be about halfway to the road. Maybe he had gotten lost. There was something strange about the woods. Then he realized there was no sound of dogs barking. He stopped to get his bearings, leaning against a tree. He looked down, took a deep breath. When he raised his head, preparing to move on, he saw a black form coming his way.

"Smitty?" he called.

There was no answer, but the form came closer.

"Smitty? Over here."

A flashlight made Jerry blink like a possum hunted down at night. He held his hand up to shield his eyes.

"Howdy."

The man was upon him now, pointing a shotgun at his chest. This is it, Jerry thought. Really it.

"What do you want?" Jerry said.

The man drew closer, lighting his own face; it was the man with the fertilized-egg eye.

"C'mon with me."

"My dispatcher's on his way to meet me. I gotta wait for him."

"Move." The man pointed his rifle in the direction he wanted Jerry to go, and kept it close to his ribs as they walked to the lean-to where Jerry had seen the Dobermans. It was a pile of tin sheets and logs pitched together into a small cabin with an ancient TV antenna on the roof.

The room inside was lit by a kerosene lamp. The mystery of the barking dogs was solved. Three Dobermans sat in a row as steely taut as barge cables stretched to the limit. Their eyes were beady bright. One moved very slightly as the man closed the door.

"Nup. Nup," the man said. "Stay put." He laid his gun across an old picnic table. "They won't hurt you as long as you don't scare them."

Me, scare <u>them</u>, Jerry thought. He tried not to breathe.

"Who are you?" Jerry said.

"You can call me – let's see – Reggie – that's a good name."

"Reggie."

"Suits me, don't it?" While they talked, "Reggie" pointed Jerry to a chair and tied him to it.

"Your dogs look kinda uncomfortable," Jerry said. "Don't you want to let them out?"

"They're fine. They'll do exactly what I tell them. I got them trained. You wanta see something?"

Reggie went over to the dog on the end of the row.

"Gonna see how much you love me," he said. The dog remained at military attention.

Jerry couldn't care less what happened to his captor, but he prayed this nincompoop wouldn't set the whole bunch off into a rage with whatever he had in mind.

Reggie pried open the rigid jaws of the Doberman, exhibiting his black tongue and two angry-looking rows of sharp white teeth, then he leaned his face as close into the dog's mouth as he could get it. The teeth were right against his skin. Jerry held his breath. Reggie, after a long moment, raised his face from the dog's jaws and said, "good boy."

"You see, I don't even need that gun to make you heel. Cause these dogs do exactly what I tell 'em."

"I get the point."

"You try it," Reggie said. "Put your face there like I did."

"No thanks."

"He won't hurt you. Not if I tell 'im not to."

"What exactly do you want?"

"C'mon, try it. It's fun. See how brave you are." Reggie came toward Jerry as though to untie him so he could experience the thrill of sticking his head into a cluster of teeth.

Jerry tried to pull away, but the dog began to growl. He didn't know which would be worse, to be chewed up or shot. He went rigid.

Reggie sat back down and picked up his shotgun.

"Just kiddin'."

"What have I ever done to you?" Jerry asked. "I don't even know you."

"I don't like your looks. You look like one of them boat pilots to me, think your shit don't stink."

"That's no reason to shoot a man."

"What were you doin' pokin' around down in town, asking all them questions?"

"I was looking for Bobby Bolton,"

"Yeah, what did you want him for?"

"Me and him were gonna go huntin' together."

"You don't even know Bobby Bolton."

"Sure I do."

Reggie looked toward the dogs, who seemed as though they were about to pounce, with or without orders. He fondled the shotgun.

"What do he look like?" Reggie brought his face close to Jerry's. "Do he have an eye like this?" He pointed to his bloodshot eye.

Jerry took a big chance, hoping Daryl's friend would have told him if Bobby had any unusual features.

"No."

Reggie said nothing. He looked as though he were weighing the evidence.

"Well then what do he look like? He got a beard?"

Jerry glanced at the dogs, imagining the teeth, dog breath on his skin. Every man that Jerry knew had a beard at one time or another. "He did once. I haven't seen him for awhile."

"Is he a big guy?"

"Bigger than me." Most of the backwoods men Jerry knew were taller and heavier than he.

"You could be talkin' about anybody," Reggie said.

"But I'm not. Honest."

"We'll see. We'll let Satan here decide. He knows when people are tellin' the truth or lyin'. You put your head in his mouth there like I did. If he don't bite you, you're tellin' the truth."

"Honest, my dispatcher is on the way down here. He's got a gun."

"Bullshit." Reggie started untying the ropes holding Jerry in his chair. If he tried to bolt, Jerry thought, he was sure to be shot. He wished Smitty were somewhere near and did have a gun.

His heart beat against his chest like someone trying to break down a door.

Reggie kept Jerry's hands tied and knocked him onto the floor. He prodded him in the back with his foot and pushed him toward Satan.

The animal stayed taut and controlled. Only his upper lip moved slightly, quivering as though waiting for the least sign of permission to snap.

Jerry was right next to the dog now. He could smell his musty fur, see the tiny flecks of red in his black eyes. The white deadly needles waiting to puncture his flesh.

"Are you tellin' the truth?" Reggie said.

"I am. Honest. I told you so."

"I don't think so. I think you've been lyin' right along. An' it looks like

Satan thinks so too...." Reggie pulled the dog's black mouth open. Jerry could see saliva glistening between the teeth.

"Now put your head there right between those jaws and me and Satan will give you a little lie-detector test."

Jerry felt Reggie's hand pushing his head toward the dog. He could feel its breath on his face.

Chapter 29

Damn all orange barrels. The highway was one long corridor of bright-colored witches' hats and stalled traffic. Smitty had taken the super highway to get to Gar's Hole by the time Jerry needed him, but he would have been better off on the side roads. He sure hoped he could find that little town.

When he got free of the tie-up around Covington – everybody driving south and down home for the weekend – he ran into another snafu: trucks and cars not moving at all outside of Rabbit Hash. What in the hell? Smitty switched on the radio. He could walk faster than this. He looked over at the car next to him, its windows rolled down, a family jammed into the small seats, the back ledge full of stuffed animals, blankets, and picnic gear. On the roof of the car were two or three folding lawn chairs. Hanging from the front visor was a plastic Virgin Mary, pale blue and pink. Oh yeah, now he remembered what this mess was all about. Some gal named Kelly had seen the Virgin Mary in a field near here and thousands of people were coming from all over to watch for her to come back again. They had tied up traffic for days. The kids in the back seat waved at Smitty.

Goddamn, he swore under his breath, the folks around here were always seeing something that wasn't there; if it wasn't UFO's it was the Mother of God, or it was Big Foot or a "painter" or Nettie's ghosts. Smitty crept along in the line of pilgrims until he could cut away on a side road. He hoped he would be doing the right thing. The traffic on the expressway showed no sign of letting up. But Lord only knew what he might run into on some of these out-of-the-way routes.

He eased his truck onto an exit, and headed toward the river. He found himself on a steep grade through heavy woods. The shoulders of the road were soft. The guard rails were smashed in a lot of places, and he looked down into the hollows for wrecked cars. He kept his foot on the brake, riding it. He was just glad it wasn't raining; last week a boy and his girlfriend had slid off the road and into the river and drowned, trapped in their car.

Even now it was hard to see the water. It was misting over in the fading light. You couldn't tell where the water ended and the banks began. When the river was like this, Smitty could fathom why people could be afraid of it, and how people could see almost anything in it: ghosts or dead relatives or will o' the wisps or whatever. The mist and fog could make you see all kinds of stuff.

Get a grip on, he told himself. What would Jerry say?

Smitty speeded up a little. He was already late, didn't want to keep Jerry waiting in that out-of-the-way place. He sure hoped he could find it. But the mist was getting thicker. He wasn't sure if he was lost or not. Then he guessed that's what lost was –

Chapter 30

My God, with Jerry down in that terrible hill town, and blood reddening the towel she'd wrapped around Charlie's head, Kay wanted to wail loud as the siren screaming in her ear. This had to end. It had to.

"How're you doin'?" she whispered to Charlie. He didn't answer. She looked to the ambulance attendant. He shrugged.

"Oh please be OK," she said. She really didn't care right now if the shooter got her as well. Was he still out there in the dark on the river bank?

When the police reached her, Kay had rushed to Charlie, wakened Roscoe, called an ambulance, and left the boat. She hoped the *Plattner* would go on without her. But poor Nettie was hysterical and Dave wasn't much better off. Roscoe's eyes looked distinctly bloodshot and his breath was strong. He had noticed her looking at him and said it was mouth wash. Well, she had to trust him. No choice.

Charlie groaned faintly and Kay leaned her ear close. Was he trying to tell her something? She kissed him on the forehead, getting a slight taste of dried blood.

Hurry, hurry, she thought. She lay her head lightly on Charlie's chest, listening for the sound of his heart beating. Sweet good Charlie, hang on for me.

She needed Jerry.

Chapter 31

Jerry's face was so hot he thought it would explode.

"Easy, man," Reggie said. He opened the dog's jaws and pushed Jerry's cheek next to its teeth. Its breath was foul. "Satan, is this guy a damn liar?"

Jerry told himself to stay completely still, to play dead. Once as a kid he'd been caught under a moving train on a railroad trestle; he had not breathed, not moved a single muscle.

"This one test you better pass, friend."

Jerry was afraid to even swallow.

"Now tell me why you're way down here where you don't belong."

About to faint, Jerry felt a cool breeze on his neck and heard a slight sound. The dog stiffened.

"Nup," Reggie said. The dogs stayed put.

Jerry heard a quiet voice say, "What you doin', Donny?"

It was Harlan Huff. Jerry raised his eyes only, fearing to move a single muscle. He saw Huff standing in the doorway.

"Are you gone nuts?" Huff said.

"This guy was down in town askin' a lot of questions. Says he knows Bobby...."

"He's tryin' to find my boy."

"He's lyin'. He don't know Bobby. Says he was a big guy with a beard. He's a little bitty guy and couldn't never even grow a mustache."

"That ain't no reason to torment nor to kill him. You want to bring the whole world down on us? Let him up."

Donny made a brief try for his gun, but Mr. Huff said, "No," and brought forward the rifle that he carried by his side.

"Untie him."

When Donny hesitated, Huff brought his gun nearer to Donny's chest.

Donny loosened the rope around Jerry's hands.

"Jerry! Jerry!" A pounding on the door sent the dogs out of control. They rushed at the men with the guns, biting and scratching whatever they could get hold of. Huff hit one on the muzzle with his rifle, while Donny tried to shake off the other two. Satan grabbed his hand with his teeth, and the other was jumping at his chest as Smitty rushed through the door. Jerry tried to pull off one of the dogs, but Mr. Huff shook his rifle at him.

"Go on, git!" he yelled. "I'll take care o' this. Get out of here!"

"Jesus God!" Smitty screamed. "What's going on?" The dogs were barking and slavering and going for more blood.

"Run!" Jerry said. He and Smitty dashed out the door and ran up the hill toward the car, crashing into trees and loose branches. It hurt Jerry to breathe. They could still hear the dogs and the men and the rattling of the tin lean-to. Then they heard shots, and then there was only the echo of dogs barking and gunshot ricocheting through the woods.

As Jerry and Smitty drove the dark roads taking them home, Jerry could still feel the splintery floor of the lean-to that had scraped his knees, the dog's disgusting breath on his cheek.

"You OK?" Smitty said.

"Fine."

He kept seeing Donny with his bloodshot eye, Mr. Huff at the door. Who were these strange people and how were they tied into his life? He knew he would have nightmares about Gar's Hole to the end of his life and his ability to dream.

Chapter 32

Jerry dialed Kay's number as soon as they arrived at the harbor.

"C'mon," he said to the phone. Kay's machine said to call the dispatcher for her whereabouts. Jerry rang the office number.

"Where's Mrs. Kenny?"

"May I ask who's calling?"

When Jerry identified himself, the woman on duty reported, "She's on the *Plattner* with Captain Summers, on their way back from West Virginia."

"God Damn!" Every time he was out risking his life, that damned Charlie was getting tighter with Kay. What Helpful Harry thing had he done now? Didn't the man have a business to run?

"They should be in soon," the phone voice said, "Mrs. K. asked you to meet them on the boat."

"Roger."

Jerry drank some coffee, ate a stale doughnut, and lay down on the cracked leather couch. Smitty dozed in his chair.

Jerry couldn't drop off even though he was dead tired. Last night he had waited for Kay to call until he saw light streaks in the sky. He had been worried sick that she was in trouble, while she had merely been out on the river with Charlie. She could have called to let him know she was OK.

He and Kay must finish what they had started. Why did Charlie have to be hanging around? Well, at least he would be able to one-up Charlie with his close call in Gar's Hole. It wouldn't hurt Kay's opinion of him, and as for their lovemaking, the stinking breath of the reaper so recently on his neck would make their passion more intense than even last night. So why did he feel uneasy?

When he heard the call numbers of the *Plattner* from the Cincinnati dock, he rushed to his truck and sped over to the boat.

He ran up the steps to the *Plattner* pilothouse, and burst into the room, all ready to tell his tale of near death.

Charlie, his temple bandaged, was sitting on the lazy bench with Kay. Roscoe, smelling of Sen-Sen, was hovering about. They barely noticed Jerry.

"What happened to you?" Jerry said. "Looks like somebody tried to scramble your signals good." He tried to make light of Charlie's situation. Probably cut himself shaving, Jerry thought. He was obviously OK, healthy enough to be enjoying Kay's concern.

"Charlie was shot by the sniper," Roscoe said. "Last night." He and Kay stared at Jerry with disapproval.

While Jerry hadn't shot Charlie, he felt guilty. He'd wished him dead enough times. Especially today.

"My God, how bad off are you?"

"I'm OK," Charlie said.

"He's going to check into the ER soon as the car comes," Kay said.

"Naw. Doc in Point Pleasant's got me fixed up good."

"How'd it happen?"

Charlie told how he had been in the pilothouse with Dave, and gotten hit.

"That Gallipolis lock," Jerry said. "It always was a bummer." His little jest fell flat.

Kay gave him a dirty look. But Jerry was so angry and frustrated, he couldn't let up. Besides he could tell Charlie had told his story at least ten times, and when Charlie saw Jerry getting jealous, he winked at him.

"Must of turned you religious, Charlie," Jerry said. "A bullet grazin' your skull that way."

"I did think I was about to see what's on the other side."

"Please," Kay said.

Jerry tried to simmer down.

"Any ideas who did the shooting?" he asked Charlie.

"None as usual."

"Dave and Nettie took off," Roscoe said. "She was seein' hants again. Said there was gonna be trouble. She got it right this time."

"It doesn't take a psychic to predict trouble on this river," Kay said.

"Why'd she leave?"

"Said the boat's cursed."

"Great."

Kay examined Charlie's bandage again, and re-filled his coffee cup. She seemed to have totally forgotten that Jerry had gone off to hunt for the shooter, and been in danger himself.

He sat down heavily in the pilot's seat.

"Little bushed. Just got back a few hours ago."

"Oh yeah," Charlie said. "I hear you been down in Dog Patch playin' Sherlock Holmes."

"It sure can't compare with a slight grazing of the skull. But it was wild."

Jerry told the story of his hair-raising ride with Ed, meeting "Preacher" and Mr. Huff, and almost being killed by Donny.

"That does it," Kay said. "I'm pulling this boat off the river and we're out of here. All of us."

"We're just making progress," Jerry said. "The man missing from Gar's Hole has got to be the man I chased at the Gallipolis lock when Cliff was shot. But he's not the big cheese. He's the kind of loser somebody would pick to do the dirty work."

"He have a name?" Charlie asked.

"Slag."

Charlie and Kay both looked unimpressed with Jerry's findings.

"Last name?" Charlie asked.

"He has none. Though he might go by the man's name that took him in, Huff."

"Wow, it's not much."

"This is our man."

"But there are plenty of folks missing around there I bet."

"This boy was the right age. I could tell the guy I chased was young by the way he dashed over the lock wall, and green because of the way he panicked. Then I'll never forget the size of his head."

"You're grasping at straws, Jerry," Charlie said. He smiled indulgently, and Jerry could swear that Kay was smiling, too.

"Hell, every Saturday night some hillbilly catches steel in a bar fight."

"I think this Donny might be in on the shooting, and we should find out who that boy was hangin' out with."

"How are you going to do that?"

"I got my sources. I still ain't found this Bobby Bolton that's talkin' around about Slag."

"Now who's Bobby Bolton?" Charlie asked.

Jerry told Charlie about Daryl's encounter in the bar where he heard about the missing boy.

"I'll ask around about this Slag," Charlie said. "Maybe somebody down my way has heard of him."

"It's an unusual enough name," Kay said.

"Mind you, I'm skeptical, Jerry. 'Cause while you were huntin' snipe – I mean snipers – it seems the guy you were lookin' for was up here taking a pot shot at me."

"We find Slag's friends, we'll find our Blennerhasset boys and your shooter and whoever put 'em up to it."

"Could be. Oh, by the way," Charlie said. "I checked with the wildlife department about your mussel fisherman at Blennerhasset. They got one mad old man on their hands – had his boat stolen."

Kay shook her head. "This Kentucky trip is the end."

"You were crazy to go down there without a gun," Charlie said.

"You did that?" Roscoe asked.

"Don't cotton to guns."

"Bet you were glad that man had one, though."

Jerry had to admit he had been glad to see Mr. Huff and his firearm.

"Well," Charlie said. "This boat's got work to do, curse or nor curse."

Kay made one more pass at getting Charlie to the hospital, and gave up. She and Jerry went down the steps and to the dock together.

"You should have seen Charlie when we took him off the boat," Kay said. "I've never seen so much blood."

"Scalp wounds bleed a lot."

Jerry was dying to take Kay's hand, but she seemed so upset he backed away. She was pale and tired-looking, not in any mood to take up where they left off.

"The way Charlie told it, it looks like somebody is after Dave," Jerry said.

Kay just frowned, as though she couldn't handle any more.

She got into her car.

"Take care," Jerry said. He wanted to say so much more.

They left the dock and went off in different directions.

Chapter 33

"You oughta take the day off," Smitty said. But Jerry didn't feel like resting. Why hadn't he said something to Kay on the boat? Why hadn't he grabbed her, kissed away her fears? She couldn't love Charlie. She just felt sorry for him because of his getting shot. She loved him. She just couldn't show it. Still, he burned over the vision he had of Kay in Charlie's arms, holding his injured head. If Jerry was any judge, Charlie's wound was very superficial....

Charlie was on his way downriver. Good. But what a man. Jerry had to admit his rival was cool. Maybe cooler than he would be with a damaged brain pan.

When Daryl arrived at work, Jerry told him about Gar's Hole, and then drove him to the abandoned Chevy. It had no tires left, and was clearly useless. Daryl looked as mournful as a cowboy forced to shoot his horse. As in all romance, Jerry thought, a time came when the scars on a guy's eyes fell and he saw a wreck for a wreck.

After the car had been towed to a garage to be sold for parts, Jerry returned to the harbor. He was tired and shaky. He looked over the work sheets Smitty had prepared for him, wiping away the greasy thumbprints that covered everything at the harbor. He checked supplies, cleaned out his desk, and walked down the float to look over the *Harvey*. She was bobbing happily as a puppy, rubbing against the rope bumpers that a tow stirred into syncopated movement.

"We'll put you to work soon," Jerry said. He patted a bulkhead. But nothing could put his mind at ease He must have it out with Kay. Damn it, he had risked his life for her three times. He deserved to know where he stood. Was it him or Charlie?

Jerry lit a cigarette and stared at the Cincinnati skyline across the river. Kay lived in that great tall building on the riverfront that looked like a medieval tower. He tried to pick out her window; he imagined himself scaling the wall to her apartment. Then inspiration struck. If you want something, you have to go get it. Sitting around daydreaming and singing the blues wouldn't do it. Showing off wasn't where it was at. He had made one mistake after another with Kay. Slunk away this morning when he should have been bold. Only the brave, only the brave, only the brave deserve the fair.

Jerry called Kay and asked if he could come over and talk. Almost to his surprise, she said yes.

Jerry's spirits rose as he watched the floor numbers in the elevator of Kay's building light up: 10, then 15, then 20. When the 25 lighted up, Jerry did too. He was flying.

Kay answered the door and invited him into a beautifully furnished room. She had changed from her business clothes into a caftan that showed blue and gold when she moved. She led Jerry to her terrace to look at the view.

"I came to see you, Kay, not the view," Jerry said. "I love you. You know that."

Kay turned from the sliding doors. She looked as though she'd been struck. When Jerry reached out to embrace her, she put her hand on his lips.

"Don't say any more."

"What is it?"

Noise from the bridges and expressways rose from the river. Kay went back into the living room, and Jerry followed.

"I feel bad," Kay said. "I didn't realize what would happen when I got into this and asked you and Charlie to help me."

"I thought the other night you loved me. We–"

"That was the river – a spell – I can't afford to be in love."

"You can't afford not to."

"I should never have come back to this blasted river."

Kay walked over to her desk and sat down.

"I should sell the business. Charlie's getting hit was the last straw. I feel responsible."

"That's what the shooter wants."

"I suppose. But I can't let you and Charlie or anybody else take any more chances. Maybe if I quit, the shootings will stop."

"I think we're close to an answer."

"Maybe."

"Kay, quit if you have to. But don't go back to Iowa. Marry me."

"I can't do that, Jerry."

"Why not?"

Kay fiddled with a paper weight.

"It won't be like your marriage to Martin."

"Martin never had a chance. You and Charlie were my models, my whole world. Two wild boys."

"Then what? It's Charlie, isn't it? I'm fine in a pinch, but he's the one you really want!"

Kay said nothing and Jerry found himself blurting out stuff he didn't even know he felt.

"It's Charlie and I'm just here to be used."

Kay stood up. "How dare you! This is just typical; you think I'm a piece of meat for you and Charlie Summers to squabble over!" Her eyes were like welding torches.

"I guess I couldn't give you all this." Jerry swept his arm around the apartment. "I bet Charlie's operation would suit you. He's got plenty of money."

"You don't hear good, do you? But while we're on the subject of Charlie, at least he respects what I'm trying to do with the business."

"It's your curves he's interested in, lady. Not your business sense."

"Get out."

"You sure know how to lead a man on."

"I tell you I didn't want this!"

"Then why did you vamp us poor fish into risking our lives for you?"

Kay's open palm connected with Jerry's face and the slap seemed to reverberate around the room.

"I didn't vamp you. You've got me mixed up with my mother the belly dancer! I'm not like her."

Jerry had never seen Kay so mad. He was actually stunned for a second. He felt the place on his cheek where her hand had smacked his flesh.

"I'm outa here," Jerry said. "I've been a God-damn fool. Again. Risked my neck to show you how I feel."

"And show Charlie who's the better man! Step right up and win the prize! Gee, I've been stupid. I actually thought this was about me, but it's just the same old story."

"You have to choose, Kay!" Jerry said. "You've been playing us poor fish against each other since second grade."

"What makes you think I want either of you?" Kay yelled. "You arrogant bastard. Now you know why I married Martin."

Jerry stamped out of the apartment and down the hall to the elevator. He pushed the *up* button by mistake, stood cursing the damned thing's slowness, saw his mistake, and punched the *down* button with his fist. Through the hall window he could see the rain starting. Even the weather was going to hell.

Chapter 34

Evil was coming his way, but he couldn't see it. He didn't know evil like he didn't know God. You have to know God to know evil. To see what's beyond.

Nettie looked through the picture window her husband had made in their trailer. The rain was dimpling the surface of the river. Like the day the semi hit her son's cycle and killed him and the day her husband died. God damn his soul. The window was the only good thing he ever did for her.

She looked at her swollen ankles. She used to love to dance, to dance and drink, too. But that was over. The other was over, too. So many things over. The job on the river she'd always wanted, watching the towboats go by and wondering what it was like to be on one. What the people were like.

It was nice, having her own room and bath, no one to boss her around – till that rich bitch took over the line. Sent her spies around. And started telling a person that'd cooked all her life how to do things.

The bitch was part and parcel of it, sure. The evil hanging over Jerry's head she could see as clearly as the heat shimmer at the end of a row of sun-baked cotton, or the nasty tomato worms she used to pick off her father's crops – bright green and as big around as your finger. Wrinkled as an old man's thing. The evil was like her father's face when he took his belt off, loop by loop, and started toward her to "strap some sense" into her.

Jerry's problem was that he'd never hated anyone. He didn't know how a person could look at someone else with envy and hate, and wish them dead. He'd never wished anyone dead or even wished them bad luck. He was still a boy in a lot of ways. Still nice.

He expected people to like him. But some people couldn't like him. It wasn't in them.

Should she call him? He'd laugh. He'd blame her "hants." But she had known there was trouble the night she saw the boy on the tow. She thought the bad thing was coming to Dave, but she was still right. It came for Charlie.

She could hear in the distance the sound of a boat in trouble, signaling "May Day."

A buoy clanged on the gray water; it sounded of mourning. Stay off the river. Stay off the river.

Chapter 35

Every puddle made him madder. Then Jerry remembered that he had left all the windows open in his apartment. And the one in the living room was right over his record collection.

"Damn!"

By the time he got home, the sills were dancing with rain drops inching their way toward his records. He pulled and tugged at the warped windows, finally got them closed. In the gloom, his apartment, that had always seemed cozy and inviting, looked small and narrow and ugly. What a joke, thinking Kay would come here. He felt like getting rid of every evidence of his stupidity: he went to the fridge, wrestled the cork out of the champagne he had bought for Kay, and pored it down the sink. The bottle made a satisfying clank as he pitched it in the trash can. He needed action and wanted to get out of the apartment as soon as possible.

The tiny red light on his phone machine was blinking, so the one concession he made to routine was to hit the "message" button, which told him he'd had three calls. Number one was a loud asinine voice announcing he'd won the right to compete for a free tip to Hawaii. He had to let it play out, impatiently drumming his fingers. The second call was a hang-up and the third was a small, almost inaudible voice saying, "Nettie." Jerry started to ignore it, annoyed that she hadn't left a number, then turned back, looked it up and called her.

"Stay off that boat," Nettie said.

"Where are you?"

"Nevermind that. I'm tellin' you now, you're goin' down under the water."

Nettie's voice was high and hysterical.

"Should I come over?" Jerry asked. "Is there anyone there with you? Where's Dave?"

"You don't believe me. That girl will pull you under."

"Well, Nettie–"

"I warned you. She'll take you right to your mother and daddy."

Nettie hung up. Jerry held the receiver a minute, shuddered, then turned out the lights and left the apartment.

Chapter 36

When Jerry returned to the harbor, there was only one kind of work suitable for his mood: welding. There was an old gas tank that needed repair, so he got his torch, helmet, and gloves and set to work. The sparks that ate through his tee-shirt actually felt good. As compared with his session with Kay.

In the white-hot glare of the torch, he saw Kay's face changing – from Rapunzel to Lorelei combing her weedy hair by the water and leading him on to the rocks. Nettie was wrong only about timing. Kay had already pulled him under.

Smitty approached on the work barge.

"Nice. day."

"Looks just like yesterday and the day before to me," Jerry said.

"Wow, what's eatin' you?"

"This stupid dump."

"I thought you was real proud to have your name on it."

Jerry bored into the steel and threw a shower of sparks onto the barge. "I shoulda gone to college."

"Why Jerry, you're a college edgecation just to be around," Smitty said. "You musta ate somethin' didn't agree with you."

"Yeah – shit."

"Gotta eat a certain amount of that before you die," Smitty said.

For just a second Jerry hated Smitty, him and his down-home laugh and his girlie magazines and his total contentment with his small, out-of-the-way life.

"Couldn't be nothin' but a woman put a feller in such a bad mood," Smitty said. "I'll leave you to your sorrow. I just come down to tell you Daryl called in. He's got a lead on a new car up in Brandenburg and took the day off to go check it out. I said OK if he'd send a guy to deck for you."

"Good." Jerry barely heard Smitty's words. He resumed his welding. I'm carryin' a torch, he thought, a real one. Ha ha.

"Jerry, did you hear me?" Smitty asked. "Daryl says he's gonna check out this Bolton guy for you while he's over that way. Bobby Bolton, the guy told Daryl's friend about the boy from Gar's Hole."

"Fine," said Jerry. "Fine, fine, fine."

When Smitty had gone, and Jerry finished his welding, he went up to the office and washed. He glanced at the *River Queen*; she was just about finished, ready to float. What a dumb waste of time, he thought. Other men were out getting rich while he was living in the past, playing with a toy. And wasting his time on a woman. He could just feel his father's scorn. To old Homer Burnside, women were right down there with cows and roustabouts.

It was over with Kay, face it, Jerry told himself. Kill the dream. Dive into Sheryl's soft places and take the revenge of the flesh. He called the alterations shop. Sheryl was there as usual.

"Gosh, I thought you were mad," she said. "You were in such a hurry the last time I called."

"I'm sorry. Something on my mind. What are you doing later?"

"Nothing. How about you?"

"Not a god-damned thing. Can I come over?"

"What about her?"

"Who?"

"That Kay."

"What about her?"

"How's it going?"

"Forget it. Strictly business between us. Has been all along...."

"Oh. Well sure, come over. I'll look for you."

"Can I have a beer and a big double-deck sandwich?"

"Sure. I'll get the kind of fixings you like."

"And put on that negligee I gave you, the one that makes your breasts stand out."

"Oh Jerry."

"Don't forget now."

"I won't."

"And put on that Tony Bennett record...."

"I will."

"See you later, babe."

Jerry felt a little better than he had before. This evening would be fun. And maybe he could forget.

The deckhand Daryl sent was not impressive. He arrived in expensive pumped-up gym shoes and Ralph Lauren jeans. What on earth was happening to the river, Jerry wondered. There was a woman mate on the *Delta Queen*, and now this. Where had this yuppyfied youth ever run into Daryl? Had his faithful second banana taken to frequenting fern bars?

Jerry put him to work painting on the harbor boat. He and Jerry spent most of the day with their brushes and ladders, and sweating under the hot sun. About four o'clock, Smitty came down.

"*Plattner*," he said. "Roscoe called. Needs a barge put in tow. Down at McAlpine."

"Ho – I'm supposed to care...."

Smitty shrugged. "Should I say you ain't here?"

"Yeah, tell 'em Nettie predicted my death by drowning, and I'm hidin' under the desk."

Smitty started toward the office.

"Kidding," Jerry said. He pitched his paint brush into a paint can, and motioned for his deckie to follow suit. "Tell Roscoe we're on it."

"Roscoe sounded a little pissed," Smitty said.

"Thought he reformed."

"Could be. Last time I seen him, though, his breath coulda knocked a buzzard off a shit wagon."

"On duty?"

"No, I'll give him that. But I don't all the way trust him, Cap."

Jerry and the new man, clad in borrowed work shoes and gloves, untied the *Harvey*, picked up the barge from the fleeting area, and headed toward Louisville full speed. By the time he got that far downriver, Jerry's mood had improved. The river breeze always helped.

"Thar she blows," Jerry said, sighting the *Plattner*.

"Say what?" asked the deckie. He went to the first deck, shaking his head.

Jerry sized up the job to be done. The tow was a full one, lacking only the barge facing them, mostly empties riding high in the water, which could be even trickier than loaded barges. Jerry prepared to make a downstream landing, with the new man ready to detach the barge pushed by the *Harvey* and lash it to the tow. There were some strange currents at McAlpine, and Jerry could feel the boat working hard not to get caught in them.

"*Harvey C.* to motor vessel *Plattner*," Jerry radioed. Roscoe answered the call. Smitty said his voice sounded a little funny earlier. Did it now? Maybe. Pretty sad, Jerry thought, a man gets a reputation as a drunk, and even if he's dead sober, people suspect him. Maybe Roscoe had a cold or another alimony fight with his ex.

"We're about to approach," Jerry said. "Current's going every which way.

Might have to make a second try at 'er."

"Roger, cap," Roscoe said. Jerry could swear his words were slurred.

"Everything OK, Roscoe?" Jerry asked.

"A.O.K."

"Good." Jerry switched off the radio and concentrated on lining up the *Harvey*. In spite of the currents, he made a perfect downstream landing. He was directly facing the *Plattner*, with a thousand feet of barges in between. The deckhand made the lines of the delivered barge fast to the ones in the tow, and removed the face wires still holding it to the *Harvey*.

"Pick you up on the side of the tow and we'll head back for the harbor," Jerry called to him.

He backed the tug away, turned broadside to the head of the tow and proceeded to get out of the way. But just as the tug was broadside, the big boat came forward full ahead on both engines. The bows of the lead barges hit the tug on the port side, pinned the pilothouse door shut and rolled the *Harvey* over on her side; the port propeller was nearly out of the water. Jerry found himself on the starboard wall; he braced his hand on the ceiling, which had now become the wall. He slid down the wall which was now floor and reached for the engine controls and radio. He jammed both throttles as far forward as they would go, a pointless exercise in the case of the port propeller, which was only fanning air. He yelled into the radio, "All stop, Cap, God damnit, all stop!" By now the boat was slanting over, heading for upside down, and Jerry started to slide back up the wall toward the ceiling.

PART III

Chapter 37

Sirens sounded on the *Plattner,* and the big boat backed down. The crew on deck ran from one side of the barges to the other searching for some sign of Jerry.

Meanwhile a helicopter hovered over the turbulent water where the *Harvey* went down, and a small open Coast Guard boat holding two men appeared. They dropped a buoy overboard to mark the spot, headed for the Kentucky bank and slowly searched it, then went to the other shore and did the same there.

When night came, the moon showed the traffic piled up all along the banks, towboats tied off while the search for Jerry continued. The Coast Guard boat with its tiny red and green lights still zig-zagged along the shores like a bug. The moon was pale and thin, and the boat captains cut through the dark with their searchlights. The buoy clanked in the current, treading water like a tired swimmer.

Next day, the Corps of Engineers boat, a small cruiser with the U.S. Army insignia, moved around the area of the wreck. Inside their cabin, the corpsmen checked the depth-finder, which showed the bottom of the river in an up-down pattern like those on an E.K.G. machine. The line was jagged, but regular, then suddenly took a sharp dip where the *Harvey* cut into the river bottom.

A dredger tied off over the site of the wreck. Charlie was on her, overseeing the operation. He got three barges and a tug wired together, to make a square of water in which to dredge, and put a small outboard in the center of the square. A diver in a blue wet suit, and an assistant, sat in the outboard, awaiting orders.

Kay paced from one end to the other of the barge while the men worked. When Charlie had a moment to talk, she went to him, and Richard and Daryl joined them.

"Could he still be alive?" Richard asked.

"If he's not in the pilothouse," Charlie said.

"You see that Coast Guard boat?" Daryl added. "They don't look for bodies, they look for survivors. And he could still be alive if the glass ain't broke in the pilothouse. If there's enough air."

"Possible," Charlie said. "Pretty long shot. Don't get your hopes up."

Charlie raised his hand and signaled the crane operator; a bucket claw reared into the air like a prehistoric monster and dipped into the water. It dropped a giant spud sixty feet long into the middle of the hole. The sun was boiling hot, the men sweating, wiping their faces. The diver, at a signal from Charlie, slipped into the water, took hold of a cable on the spud and descended below the surface.

The observers could hear water rushing past the diver's mask from his sound equipment, then bubbles. They heard his voice. "Current's too rough. It's pullin' me away from the spud. I gotta come up."

The diver broke the surface and everyone looked disappointed. The diver grasped the side of the outboard and gasped for air. He rested, then gestured to his assistant, and was once again lowered below the surface.

"If he's in there, do you want to take him out or do you want the coroner?" the Corps of Engineer's officer asked Kay.

"Don't bother her," Charlie said. "I'll get him."

"Coroner has body bags," said the officer.

Charlie ignored him.

The diver broke the surface once again and shook his head.

"Can't see a thing. Water's solid brown down that deep."

The diver got into the boat and took his head gear off. Charlie conferred with the crane operator.

With the towboats tied off and no pleasure boats moving, the river was quiet, so quiet that when the Coast Guard's motor was no longer heard, people noticed the silence, and felt a collective let-down. The search for a survivor had been given up.

Charlie signaled the diver to try once again.

This time he reported from below, "I've made contact with her. I can't see, but I think I'm on the lower deck. She's in about three feet of sand."

In a minute his voice was heard again, as though from another world.

"I'm turning a corner. Current's gettin' me. Gotta come up."

"Get cables on her," Charlie ordered. "Move that riverward barge out."

The diver and his assistant stood in the outboard with a winch, sending the cable down. A helicopter flew above, with a TV logo on the side.

The cables were being pulled up. The water was slightly turbulent, and an object appeared just below the surface. It was yellow, metallic.

"What is it?" Kay said.

"Looks like the sunshade on the pilothouse," Charlie said. "Pull 'er up."

They were all thinking the same thing: what if he's in there?

The men pulled. The yellow object sank slowly out of sight.

"Wait, we lost her," the diver said. "Darned thing broke off."

"Get a cable on the stanchion, should be right handy there," Charlie ordered.

The cables were lowered, the winches spun, pulling the cable taut. The men reversed them, and soon the tip of the *Harvey* pilothouse broke the surface.

"Don't look," Richard said to Kay.

"Maybe–" she said.

More of the pilothouse emerged at a slant. There was part of a window showing. The diver slipped into the water while his assistant stood by with a grappling hook.

The diver pushed off and reached the pilothouse, and swam below the surface. He re-emerged and shook his head.

"He's not in there," he said. "Glass is all broken in a million pieces."

"Could he really still be alive then?" Kay asked.

"Not too many people have survived being sucked under a tow of barges, Kay," Charlie said.

Daryl turned and left the group, and headed for the johnboat he had come over to the barges on.

"I'm gonna go find him."

"We should never have trusted a drunk," Richard said.

"My fault. I should have stopped the boat." Kay stared downriver.

"Roscoe was OK when he got on," Charlie said. "He must have had a bottle hidden."

"Drunks are cunning." Richard hovered over Kay. He was making Charlie nervous.

"I of all people should know better," Kay said.

Kay touched the bandage on Charlie's temple. He was sweaty and sunburned, and looked tired.

"You get some rest."

"I gotta get this stuff knocked down." Charlie indicated the barges and equipment. He yelled some orders to his men.

"Well, the shooter's won. This barge line is for sale," Kay said to Richard.

"This was an accident, Kay."

"Was it?"

"You're not thinking poor old Roscoe–"

"Well where is he?"

"Nobody knows."

"Somebody has a real vendetta against me."

"It was Charlie and Jerry who got shot at. No one has touched you."

"They know how to get rid of me."

"Kay, please. This has been terrible for you. Take a few days off. Then if you still want to get out, of course, I'll do everything I can to help."

Kay saw Daryl's skiff moving downriver on a search for Jerry. She couldn't bear the thought of him in the heartless, mindless river.

"Jerry said whoever's behind this mayhem is trying to scare off every last person who remembers the *River Queen*. There was only us three, Jerry, Charlie, me – and one crazy old man."

"Now you're being melodramatic, Kay. Nobody cares about that old boat,"

"They have gotten rid of us all now, except for old Mac Lodder."

"This is nonsense," Richard said. "You're tired, dear."

Charlie intervened. "Go home, Richard." He put his arm around Kay. "I'm still here, and I'm not scared off."

But Kay could feel him shaking beneath his soaked shirt.

Chapter 38

Kay made herself go to the office the day after the dredging, but she couldn't concentrate. Richard insisted that she go home.

"You need time," he said. "Don't be hard on yourself. It wasn't your fault."

"But I have to make a report on what happened. I have to see about getting Jerry's boat back up. And find Roscoe...."

"We'll find him. Leave it all to me. That's what I'm here for, Kay."

She still hesitated, and Richard said, "Don't you trust me, Kay?"

"Of course." She had to give in. She felt a black veil coming down over her when she walked, and the words on the papers in front of her made no sense.

She felt like a trapeze artist who had just missed the hands held out for her. She was still flying through the air, wondering how far she'd go, and when she would land. What it would be like when she hit.

Back in her apartment, she still couldn't rest. She paced around the living room. Had she done anything right? This wouldn't have happened if she hadn't gotten Jerry involved in her problems. But still, wasn't the shooter bound to involve him sooner or later? It was the problem of the whole river. No one knew who would be shot at next, maybe killed.

Where was Roscoe? He must have been drunk. It was his fault Jerry went down. But it was her fault Roscoe was still working, though everyone had urged her to give him another chance.

She stared at the water with hatred, trying to become Jerry struggling to get out of the pilothouse, being pushed to the bottom of the river by the giant barges. Where was he now? She tried to picture what was down below on the very bottom of the river: big, moving, mysterious forms, half real, half dead – old boats, houses swept away in floods, the decaying flesh of animals and humans, the monstrous fish and creatures of story....

Toward evening, Richard called with news; the body of a young man, wearing expensive gym shoes and Ralph Lauren jeans, had been found by a party of bass fishermen near Evansville, Indiana. He had been identified by Smitty as the deckhand on the *Harvey's* last trip.

Kay went into the shower, still in her clothes. She turned on the water and screamed and screamed.

Chapter 39

Jerry is crawling on glass walls. His feet crash through the glass. He is sucked into the water. He is going down, down, through black and green into a soundless chamber.

In this cold emerald place, he sees a world of shimmering forms. He swims into a sunken wreck and finds a treasure chest, while schools of smiling fish swim by. He is here at last: Davy Jones' Locker. He wants to laugh; he has found the river of myth. And just as Nettie said, he sees his mother and father. Their clothes trail slimy lime-green threads, like underwater line. Mom. Daddy. His mouth fills with water. His lungs are about to burst. He cannot unlock the treasure chest. He squeezes through the sides of the ancient wreck and can see no more. A monstrous black form rams into him: one of the giant catfish they say live deep under the water.

Chapter 40

"Oh," Jerry yelled. His eyes opened, sticky and slow as stubborn clam shells. The light hit his eyes like a laser beam. He could hear his own voice. Birds. He could see shadows on wooden boards. There was something around his legs. He must be alive. Then he was back in the dark under the great steel behemoth beating him down.

He waited for a new surge of strength, to open his eyes again. He was in a bed. But he could not move.

"Oh God, don't let me be paralyzed." The words bounced off the walls of the strange room.

He dozed again, and woke again, reliving again the smash of the thousand feet of steel against the *Harvey*, the crash of glass as he went through the windows. Nothing after that.

He looked around the room; the walls were wooden. There was one window that looked handmade, a chair across the room, a table made of an old wooden cable spool next to the bed. There was no clock, no calendar, nothing to tell him where he was.

"Hello?" Jerry called. The only answer was from insects outside the window scraping and humming. A dog barked in the distance.

Jerry drifted back into unconsciousness, back into the dark green chamber. Next time he awoke, the wooden walls and spool table seemed familiar. He resolved to try to get out of the bed. It was built-in, made of the same wood as the walls. The mattress was a thick downy quilt simply laid on a wooden surface.

Jerry pushed himself up with his hands and leaned on his elbows. Every bone and muscle ached as though covered with concrete. He eased one leg over the side of the bed. It hurt all over his body. He paused to let the nerve endings rest, then rolled over and arranged his feet to meet the floor. He moved like the Tin Woodsman. Maybe he'd been transformed. The place he found himself in suggested some weird metamorphosis. No one answered his call, yet someone, he noted, looking down at his faltering body, had dressed him in clean long johns and put socks on his feet.

Jerry staggered to the door of the room and pushed it open. Before him was a light, airy room constructed of the same hand-hewn wood as the bedroom. The windows let in light on a table, that also looked handmade. There was a huge fireplace of rough stone. A potted geranium and a quilt added to the charm of the room that he was sure had been swept clean by Snow White and the Seven Dwarfs.

Jerry walked, occasionally reaching out for support from a chair or wall, to the window, and looked out. Trees and sunlight. He was in a thick forest, the birds chirping and chattering – they must be what he'd heard as he drifted in and out of consciousness. Jerry steadied himself on one of the chairs at the table, which was set for two: two plates, two bowls, two spoons, and a small pot of golden nasturtiums. He found himself checking the crockery. It was a normal size, not made for giants or dwarfs or for Mama, Papa and Baby Bear.

"I'm awake," Jerry said aloud. "This is not a dream." He ran his hand over the wood of the chair back. It was solid and real. On the other hand, he'd had dreams where he gave himself this very kind of test and said, "This is not a dream," only to wake up and find out it was.

Jerry hobbled over to the door and stepped out onto the patio. Like the fireplace, it was made of huge rough stones. Jerry could see the river down below through openings in the trees. He sat on one of the low patio walls, automatically patting himself where his breast pocket normally was, searching for a cigarette. He heard a goat bleating. Jerry felt a sudden and intense euphoria, thrilled to be alive and in such an enchanted place. He had no idea how he got here, or how he had survived the pummeling of the barges. Or why it had happened. His landing and start-up were perfect. Roscoe may have been drunk, but that didn't explain it for Jerry. The *Plattner* had mowed him down as though on purpose. It wasn't just sloppy boat handling, and combined with the shootings made Jerry sure it was no accident. But why Roscoe? He had to be involved with others. Jerry wondered if those others could have anything to do with the place he was in. The scene around him seemed less enchanting now, the woods beyond the patio dark, impenetrable, and frightening.

Jerry looked at his wrist, trying to check the time. All he saw was a bad tear in his flesh where his watch should be. He looked at his other hand: scratches and cuts all over it. He pulled the long john sleeve up, and peered into the neck opening; he was bruised all over as a rotten plum. The bruises were black, the nastiest looking things he'd ever seen. He let the cloth fall. These wounds would be with him for a while, and so would the stiffness and dizziness that were overtaking him as he sat here. Laboriously, Jerry got to his feet, and stared at the sky, trying to ascertain the time. It looked to be near noon. This was confirmed by a voice from inside the house.

"Louisa, put on another plate for lunch. Our guest is awake and I'll bet he's good and hungry."

Chapter 41

Jerry turned to see a man push open the screen door and step onto the patio. He was small, thin, and taut as a barge cable. He wore no shoes, just a pair of old dungarees and a cotton shirt. His feet and hands were large for his size. He had a fine head of snow-white hair and a friendly smile.

"I'm Matthew Johnson." He extended his hand.

"Jerry Burnside."

"Come in, come in. Come meet Louisa."

Jerry followed Matthew into the house and was introduced to the loveliest and most serene-looking woman he had ever met. He judged Matthew and Louisa to be in their late seventies, but their unforced smiles and relaxed manner made age irrelevant.

"I don't know what to say," Jerry stuttered. "I seem to be dressed in your clothes and living in your house but I haven't the faintest idea where I am or how I got here."

"I found you on the river bank," Matthew said. "I went down to check my trot lines two evenings back, and there you were lying on the bank, all scratched up. Looked half dead."

Jerry shook his head.

"I was delivering a barge to a towboat near Louisville, and my tug was pushed over. I operate a harbor." The thought of the *Harvey* at the bottom of the river, stuck in sand and mud, made him feel even heavier. He tried to think back to what had happened after the *Harvey* went down, but nothing came. "Somehow I survived," he said.

"Well, you're in River Hollow now," Matthew said. "Our home."

"And welcome." Louisa's voice was as lovely as her face.

Jerry felt a wave of hunger and nausea as the odor of the stew Louisa was cooking began to waft his way.

"Do you mind if I sit down?"

"Oh of course." Both Johnsons rushed to his aid, Matthew pulling out a chair for him, Louisa offering tea.

"You haven't had anything to eat for two days," Matthew said. "We couldn't get anything into you. And you wanted nothing to do with liquids."

"I swallowed about a hundred gallons of the Ohio," Jerry said. "Did you notice the water level going down?"

"I'm relieved you can make a joke," Matthew said, "that's a good sign.

When you didn't come round again this morning, Louisa and I were beginning to worry we'd done the wrong thing in not trying to get you to a doctor. But the nearest one is miles away and we have no car. You were breathing – your cuts and scratches are nasty but nothing seemed to be broken and we judged you'd be better off resting and letting nature heal you."

Louisa was ladling stew into the three bowls on the table. Everything she did, Jerry noticed, was done with grace and precision, as though each task were part of a sacred obligation.

On the table, sun and shade made a pleasant leafy pattern. There was a clean cloth napkin at each place, a basket heaped with thick textured bread in the center of the table. Jerry waited to let the Johnsons say grace – they seemed like the type who might – but when Louisa had filled the bowls, Matthew simply nodded and started in.

Jerry went slow, beginning with a piece of bread which he chewed deliberately and swallowed cautiously, to make sure it would meet with a decent reception from his deprived and no doubt outraged stomach. When it seemed to go down with no problem, he turned his attention to the other good-smelling things on the table.

The tea was the worst stuff Jerry had ever tasted: hot water with a few herbs giving it a little pale color. Home grown, Jerry judged. The salad, too, seemed to come from the premises; it was a combination of wild greens, dandelion being the only one Jerry recognized. He took a large bite of the stew. It tasted wonderful: rich chunks of meat surrounded by tomatoes, onions, herbs, potatoes, and cabbage. Jerry's eyes narrowed with pleasure. His whole being relaxed and expanded with a revived will to live.

"Mmm," he said. "This is great. What is it made of?"

"Groundhog," Louisa answered.

Jerry's stomach did a quick flip and he rushed to the terrace, leaned over the side, and vomited violently. When nothing more came, he sat gasping on the wall, embarrassed at his refusal of the food Louisa had provided.

Matthew and Louisa let him alone for awhile, then Matthew joined him on the terrace.

"Guess your stomach'll need a little time to adjust back."

Jerry nodded. Matthew handed him a sprig of mint.

"Whereabouts are we?" Jerry asked.

"A good little way below Cincinnati – Kentucky shore."

"Where's the nearest city?"

Matthew named an Indiana town, one Jerry had recently heard mentioned.

"I can row across the river after while and get a ride into town and call your folks for you."

Jerry looked around. There were no electric wires, no phone lines, no power of any sort.

"You're in no shape to move for a day or so," Matthew said. "You need to take it easy."

Jerry's aching muscles agreed.

"We take mail up to the road every other day or so. I can take letters for you."

"Thanks. You and Louisa are so kind."

"I'm sure you'd do the same for us."

What a beautiful spirit, Jerry thought. He'd gotten so used to people trying to outdo each other just to win, he'd almost forgotten there were people like the Johnsons. And since the shootings, he sometimes felt downright despair about his fellow man. Then, being plowed under by 24 thousand tons of barges hadn't done anything to help.

"How long have I been gone?" Jerry asked.

"I don't know. You've been here two days. Two and a half now." Matthew gave Jerry the date.

"Then the accident was three days ago," Jerry calculated. "You didn't hear anything about it?"

"We don't take the papers. When we chose to live our own way, we decided not to keep up with the outside world."

Louisa came out on the terrace with a fresh cup of tea for Jerry.

"Better?" She settled herself in a rocker made of branches and rough wood, and began shucking peas into a pan.

"I haven't seen anyone do that since my mother," Jerry said.

"We grow all our own vegetables. Matthew has a large garden on a terrace down closer to the river."

"We buy our clothes across the river," Matthew added. "Otherwise, we figure the earth will provide what we need."

"And it does."

Sitting with the Johnsons on their sun-dappled terrace, Jerry slowly gave in to the feeling of peace that was around him. He observed the shaded ferns under the big ash tree about to unfold, now tightly coiled like green question marks. He listened to the birds, the susuru of the trees, the tinkle of goats' bells from somewhere nearby. He watched the river flowing past the growing green hill of peas in Louisa's pan. How he loved the natural world, river, water and willows, human hands and feet. He wanted to kiss Matthew's large, tanned toes, bury his face in Louisa's sun-filled apron.

During that first afternoon, Matthew and Louisa went about their routine while Jerry just sat, staring into space, trying to reacquaint himself with his arms and legs, his own toes. Matthew weeded his garden, picked fresh vegetables, milked his goats, baited his trot lines, cleaned fish. Louisa swept and dusted the cottage, washed the towels and bedding and hung them in the sun to dry. She pumped water flowing downhill through troughs Matthew had built.

When darkness fell, the Johnsons lit candles and kerosene lamps, and the two of them talked about their life. They seemed at peace with themselves and each other.

"I wish I could live like you do," Jerry said.

"You could," Matthew said. "It just takes a decision to do so."

"And lots of hard work," Jerry added.

"The work is a joy to us. We appreciate our food because we have to plant it and care for it, or kill and slaughter the animals we eat. It makes us independent of cities – of the turmoil and – ugliness."

"I have a friend I'd like to bring down to visit you."

Jerry pictured himself and Kay living like the Johnsons.

Chapter 42

"Charlie, come in," Kay said. "Have you heard from Roscoe?"
"Roscoe?" Charlie sounded as if he had forgotten who Roscoe was.
"He's just disappeared?" Kay said.
"He must be in Alaska by now, or some place like that."
"The whole thing is so strange. I can't understand it. This terrible thing coming on top of the shootings."
"Kay please...."
"Oh, I'm so sorry." She suddenly realized Charlie was probably as upset as she was. He was the only person who cared as much about Jerry as she. He still wore a bandage on his head where he had been shot. He was sunburned from his long hours trying to pull up Jerry's tug.
"Come in and sit down."
Charlie came into Kay's living room and sat on the couch farthest from the terrace doors. The two of them sat facing one another awkwardly. The moon and Kay's lamp made twin bright spots in the glass.
"I tried to find Jerry's ex and notify his kids; I didn't get very far," Kay said. "Kept thinking about going with Daryl and searching downriver."
"It's hopeless."
"I just can't believe...."
"I know."
"Charlie, would you like a drink?"
"Yes, Kay."
Kay went to the bar and took a tray of ice cubes out of the small refrigerator.
"Scotch alright?"
"Good."
Funny how you drink appropriately in bad times, Kay thought, just as you dress in black: nothing fancy, scotch.
Kay handed Charlie his drink and sat next to him on the couch. Charlie downed his quickly. Kay looked into his eyes: his pupils were black, bottomless. Her own grief seemed magnified there. He had dark circles under his eyes and his bandage was soiled.
"You did all you could," Kay said.
"What do you mean?"
"Trying to find him. You were great."

"Oh."

Kay finished her scotch and poured two more. She felt only half there, as though a part of herself was missing. She knew Charlie felt the same. She felt a terrible urge to throw herself on his lap and cry.

"Our *River Queen* days meant so much to Jerry," Kay said.

Charlie looked away.

"Did you ever see the model he made of her?"

"No, no I didn't."

"It's great."

Charlie finished his second scotch.

"Oh, Kay, I...." He groaned as he reached out and roughly pulled Kay to him. Kay was surprised, but she let him hold her. She put her arms around him. In a minute, she pulled back and looked into Charlie's eyes. They were flat as a low river when there was no wind. She stroked Charlie's hair. After a moment, Charlie let go of Kay and sat with his head in his hands, his face hidden. Minutes went by and still Charlie did not move. Kay began to worry, to feel out of contact, as though he were somewhere else – like Jerry.

"Charlie?"

Charlie did not rouse himself, but stayed bent over, despairing. Kay touched the back of his neck. It was burning from the long hours of dredging for Jerry's boat. Her own skin burned as well. She felt hollow, dead. She wanted to comfort Charlie, and herself, but there was nothing to say.

Charlie looked up at her; his face was the saddest she'd ever seen. His hunger for her so naked it made her stomach drop. Charlie held out his arms again and she let him pull her close.

"Kay, I feel so...."

He kissed her neck, her shoulders, her ears. When he reached her mouth, she opened it wide, surprising herself. Her sides ached with desire. She could feel Charlie's heat through her blouse.

"Oh God."

Charlie had her on her feet now, and picked her up. He was so strong. She could feel the decks of the *River Queen* shudder, and felt the breeze on the top deck where they'd kissed like this before as kids – knowing she shouldn't be doing what she was doing.

Charlie's chest was a mass of black hair and his arms were covered with it. Kay seized it in her fingers and twisted as they stretched out on her bed. He buried his head in her neck, burrowed under her arms. Wanted to eat her alive. She couldn't get enough of him, holding on to his lips when they kissed hers, holding his hand in place wherever he touched. Kay was almost frightened, had to remind herself she knew this man trying to devour her. He was strong as a bull, needy as a baby.

The sun went down on their moans and Charlie's saying "I love you, Kay," and Kay crying, "Oh God. Oh Jesus."

Afterward, in the darkened room, Kay kept seeing Jerry's face, down under the water, down among the oldest fish who gorged on the dead and all that the river had taken.

"You're my golden girl," Charlie murmured into her ear.

I'm worthless, Kay thought. How could she be doing this, with Jerry out there in the water?

She stared at Charlie's face. With the small night light from the hall casting shadows around his eyes and jaws, his hair, he appeared strange, an animal, some mythic demon from the riverbed. Mud man.

"You better go, Charlie."

"Marry me, Kay."

"I can't."

"You have to. It would make everything right."

"I don't think so."

Charlie got up from the bed and put on his clothes. He left the apartment hurriedly, neglecting to close the door.

Kay got up and locked it, then sat on the terrace and stared at the river.

She wished she were down under the water, with Jerry and the *River Queen*. Washed clean as the empty clam shells she pulled from the water as a kid.

Chapter 43

Jerry sweat and shuddered like an overworked engine. Awakened from a nightmare, he heard Nettie's voice as though through a telephone. She had predicted this one. Was the woman truly psychic or did she know something? The mowing down of the *Harvey* had not been an accident. Though harbor tugs were top-heavy, what happened was rare. Who? Why? He recalled Roscoe's slurred voice, and thought now he'd heard another voice behind him in the pilothouse. Why did no one stop Roscoe from piloting? Why had Nettie and Dave run off after Charlie was shot? He thought about Richard's suspicions of Cliff Cooper. Roscoe, Richard, Donny, Slag, Cliff, Nettie. What was the thread holding them all together?

Jerry was thankful when daylight came, and he was greeted by the smell of coffee and bacon.

He spent most of the morning on the Johnsons' patio in the sun. Every move still hurt.

For lunch Louisa filled him with herb tea, porridge, corn muffins, cold goat's milk, and red ripe tomatoes still warm from the sun.

Filled with good food, he felt less weak, and walked down to the river bank. He stooped on the pock-marked bank, and stared into the water, trying to find a pattern in the attacks. Maybe Richard <u>was</u> at the center. Charlie said the river was all about money. The money was in Kay's business. Maybe Roscoe was part of a whole scheme to terrorize Kay and anyone who worked for her. Richard had access to that clever electronic board telling him the exact location of every Kenny boat, and he kept in touch with the pilothouses. He could do a lot from the nice safe Midwest America office far from the river and the shootings. With Charlie and himself out of the way, Richard could terrify Kay into selling the barge line or letting him take over. But then....

Jerry's head hurt so bad he couldn't go any further.

In the afternoon Matthew showed Jerry his studio, a space he had built across from the main house. He had painted many of the steamboats, and later the tows, that passed his property, as well as his family and animals.

"I recognize your hound in that one," Jerry said. "Oh, and there's Louisa's favorite goat."

"And there's the old *Americana*. She was the *River Queen's* one rival." Jerry told Matthew about his background on the *Queen* and about the model he was working on.

Without a word, Matthew went to the closet and pulled out another painting. There she was in all her glory. Jerry could see the name *River Queen* on the side of the boat, and he recognized his father and mother as the small figures standing on the top deck on the pilothouse steps.

"I did that in 1930, long before we came here. It's yours."

The painting was dark, but Jerry could see the vague shapes of cattle on the first deck. The man standing by the stage was Mac Lodder, the purser; as always, he had his notebook and bills of lading in his hand.

The *River Queen* again. She seemed to be trying to tell him something, the way her image kept returning to him, through his model, his reunion with Kay and Charlie, the Fitzgerald twins, now Matthew.

A new pattern began to form in his mind. Kay was definitely at the center of everything. But maybe it wasn't money her unknown enemy was after; maybe it was something else. Fifteen people had been killed on the *Queen*. Some demented relation of one of them, who believed Kay's father responsible, might have decided to keep her off the river. No, it had been too long ago. Though as Tom said of Chief Cornstalk, hate like that doesn't die. The shootings definitely started when the three *River Queen* survivors were about to come together, and they had all been targeted in one way or another. Maybe it was somebody who had heard about Jerry's model and his intention to look up Mac and get the truth at last. There was something Mac knew that would blow this person out of the water.... No, this new account didn't explain all the pieces. But then neither did any of Jerry's other ideas....

He recognized the name of the town across the river that Matthew had mentioned, and he would be going there....

Louisa called Matthew and Jerry then, and insisted they sit on the terrace and rest. She brought out bowls of blackberries.

"Tomorrow I should take the skiff over to town," Matthew said, "and make calls for you. Your people must be worried."

It suddenly struck Jerry that no one in the world knew where he was or that he was alive. Everyone thought he was dead; why not stay that way a little longer and try to find Mac?

"I couldn't put you to all that trouble."

"But your wife," Louisa said.

"I have no wife. Unfortunately, there's no one who will be really frantic. I'm pretty much a loner."

Kay was the only person Jerry would feel really bad about deceiving.

"I'll write a letter today to my dispatcher," he said.

"The mailbox is a good three miles uphill. You'll have to heal up quite a bit before you hike that far. I'll take it," Matthew said.

Jerry was thrown off guard for a moment. What could he say to Matthew's kind offer? But his "death," if it were to do any good, had to be absolute. Phone calls could be listened in on, and letters intercepted. He quickly thought up a fake name and address to put on an envelope.

Fear that Kay might be in danger shook him, but he would have to wait and hope that she was all right and gamble on her being all right a little longer.

Jerry stayed one more day with the Johnsons. He helped Matthew in the garden and sat on the terrace cracking walnuts and cleaning vegetables for Louisa.

He spent the evening curled up in a chair in the living room while the Johnsons read. Every once in awhile one of them shared a passage from a book. Outside the screen, the insects and tree toads kept up their steady song. An owl hooted, and a towboat whistle sounded. Theirs was such a big world. Jerry wanted to stay here forever, protected by good people; it was like being a child, safe and loved by your parents in the days before you realized they had faults and unhappiness in their lives.

He had not told the Johnsons about the shootings; he wanted to protect them as they were protecting him. He still had not told them of his scheme to stay officially dead either, but as he had planned, had given Matthew a letter to a fictitious person to mail. Thinking of Daniel Zecariah, he asked God – if there was one – to forgive his lies, and especially to forgive his letting good Matthew hike three miles uphill to mail a phony letter.

Chapter 44

Mist rose from the river as Matthew and Jerry pushed off in the rowboat. The sun was far upriver, slowly throwing its light westward like a flashlight beam down a long corridor. The air was as humid as the day before, and the crows had suddenly joined the cicadas and tree toads in the constant chorus of noise from the shore. Thinning walnut trees suggested that autumn was coming, though the sun would be blazing hot by noon.

Matthew insisted on rowing. Jerry sat in the stern, watching the older man's arms and legs as he strained against the water, amazed at his strength. Jerry felt no fear of the water, though it had come close to killing him. It was his element. His home. Its green depths threw back only shadowy reminders of its grip on him. He must have fought hard to stay alive, been bashed and knocked out by the barges, but somehow popped up and escaped their pull. Then what? How had he washed up on Matthew's bank? It was like trying to recall an elusive, especially complicated dream.

A towboat with a load of coal coming toward them got larger as Jerry and Matthew approached the Indiana shore. Even this behemoth did not frighten Jerry. It was moving slowly. There was plenty of time to clear its path.

Matthew tied the rowboat off to a willow tree. Next to it was a path through the heavy foliage.

"Let's hike up through there," Matthew said. "There's a little settlement and you can get a ride into town."

They headed in the direction Matthew pointed to, Jerry beginning to wonder just how long finding a ride into town might take. The path was almost grown over with willows, scrubby locust trees, evil-looking red sumac, and devil's broomstick. He and Matthew walked a long, hot half-hour with no sign of habitation.

Jerry had to admit to himself, though he fought it off, that the heat was making him slightly dizzy. His muscles ached as he trudged along behind Matthew. He was glad when they saw some rooftops among the trees. But the little settlement they approached turned out to be a block of boarded-up stores and one or two run-down, probably abandoned, houses.

"Hmm," Matthew said. "Looks like the folks I usually see in that house are gone." He pointed to a dirty gray frame that probably hadn't been painted for twenty years – though its proportions and front porch had the elegance of a lot of the old houses along the Ohio.

"Let's sit in the shade and see what comes along." Matthew squatted under the full branches of a box elder. Jerry joined him, patting his breast pocket for a cigarette. Matthew looked perfectly content. Jerry didn't have hope of anyone coming along in this remote spot. He felt depressed – on another wild goose chase.

Jerry looked around; there was no sign of life anywhere.

"Oh," Matthew said. "I almost forgot...."

He reached in his pocket and brought out a handful of one dollar bills and some change.

"You'll need this for the phone in town, and maybe have to stay a night someplace."

Jerry started to decline Matthew's offered cash, but he knew Matthew was right; he would need money. He accepted it, planning how to pay it back, as he tucked it in his shirt pocket.

"Wait," Matthew said. "I hear a truck coming."

Jerry heard it too, and momentarily a rattly pick-up slowly approached down the road. Matthew flagged it down, apparently not even noticing that it was filled with men carrying bows and arrows.

"Whoa," Jerry said. The bunch looked pretty scary to him. Not one of the men smiled as the truck came to a stop.

"Deer hunters," Matthew said. But they could have been an escaped chain gang or the criminally insane for all Matthew seemed to care. He must be protected by his own goodness, Jerry decided, for the hunters listened respectfully as Matthew told them what he wanted, and with only time for a quick handshake and thank-you for Matthew, Jerry was wedged in between the riders standing in the truck bed.

Jerry's interest in hunting was nil, but he did know it was a little early for shooting deer. He couldn't think of a thing to say. He had his secrets and the men had theirs. And in view of the situation he was in, it behooved him to keep quiet about both.

Jerry was left off just outside the small town where Mac lived. He hiked to the town center, where a block of mostly vacant stores and some houses were grouped around an old red brick courthouse with fat white Colonial pillars. He found a drug store with a soda fountain. The smell of it was a zephyr from childhood. He ordered a soda, and asked the young man behind the counter about hotels and whether he knew Mac Lodder.

"Ain't but one hotel," the boy said. "The Palmer House. That's it right across the square there – red brick building. Mac Lodder? You mean crazy

Mac? Real old man...."

"He's in his sixties." Where I'll be in a dozen years, Jerry thought.

"Like I said, real old fucker...."

"What do people do around here?" Jerry asked.

"Not much. Most everybody's on welfare."

Jerry paid his check, bought a packet of cigarettes, and headed for the Palmer House.

It was just the kind of small-town hotel that river crews and old-timers were likely to frequent: plastic chairs, ashtrays on stands in the tiny lobby. No elevator. Rows of flat key holders Jerry remembered from the *River Queen*, from his childhood. They tasted slightly salty. The clerk was a friendly-looking woman with leathery tanned skin and a fresh perm and finish.

Jerry had shaved and was wearing a clean shirt of Matthew's. He must not have looked too threatening, for with only a glance of mild curiosity at his request to see Mac, the woman said, "102."

"Can I call him from here?" Jerry didn't want to give out his name, but he had to be sure Mac knew who was asking for him.

"Sure. Wait a while though. He's watchin' his soap opera now. Watches it every day exactly this time."

Jerry took a seat and lit a cigarette. Was he crazy, sitting in a small-town hotel, waiting for an old man he knew thirty years ago, while someone was shooting at his friends and the woman he loved?

Suppose Kay were in trouble, hurt, or dead? He had to know if she was all right. For the first time since nearly drowning, he recalled the fight they had last time they met. Was she sorry now? Did she mourn for him? Maybe she was regretting the way she had treated him. He resisted enjoying the thought. He loved her and that was that, and he had to find out if she was OK. He went into the old-fashioned wooden phone booth and dialed the barge line.

Chapter 45

"Ms. Kenny, please," Jerry said to Kay's receptionist. He tried to disguise his voice.

"Mrs. Kenny is at a meeting this afternoon. May I ask who's calling?"

Jerry hung up. She was OK. That was all he needed to know.

When he took his seat again, the hotel clerk said, "You can call Mr. Lodder's room now if you want. Though in five more minutes he'll be taking his walk. He always comes down right after his program, says 'hello Loraine,' goes over to the drug store, buys a package of cough drops, walks down to the river, turns around and walks back. Always says 'Good afternoon, Loraine' – you could set your watch by him."

"Maybe I'll just wait for him." Jerry decided that he might do better presenting himself to Mac in person. He might not remember Jerry or want him to come to his room; it had been thirty years.

It became very important to Jerry that Mac remember him. Never mind what Mac might be able to tell him. This was personal. It was as if Mac must identify and recognize Jerry as the boy who had lived on the *River Queen* – who had seen it blow up. When Jerry heard slow, old-man footsteps on the stairs, he felt like an actor with stage fright: sweaty palms, the fear he would forget his lines.

Then he saw Mac. It was he. The old familiar figure of Jerry's childhood: a tall, heavy-set man, dressed in a formal black suit and carefully polished black shoes, his gold watch chain reaching from pocket to pocket across his impressive front. Mac was the symbol of order, of security; the man who got the passengers to the right staterooms, checked the cargo off and on at each stop, paid the grocery bills, kept the books, and let the captain and the owners know how much went in and out of the till.

Mac was walking with a cane now, his weight and age and a lameness – probably his injury from the *River Queen* explosion – working together to slow him down. He was so intent on the careful navigation of the stairs that he did not notice Jerry, until Jerry stood and placed himself in the way.

"Mac, remember me? Jerry Burnside."

Mac seemed perplexed as he looked Jerry over.

"I'm sorry to drop in on you so suddenly, but I happened to be in town and I knew you lived here so I looked you up."

"What did you say your name was?"

Jerry repeated his name. He had probably changed more than Mac had; he'd been a boy when the purser last saw him – a skinny adolescent with a lot more hair.

"Oh yes, Captain Homer Burnside's boy." Mac looked taken aback, unsure as to what to say to Jerry further, now that he'd identified him.

"May I walk with you? I understand you're about to take your regular walk."

Mac pulled out his pocket watch.

"I'm a little late. I always take a stroll about now. Go to the drug store, then down to the river and back."

Mac started off, out the finger-smudged door of the Palmer House and into the sunlight, leaving Jerry to follow or not. With difficulty, Jerry paced himself to Mac's slow gait. He tried making conversation, but Mac seemed barely aware of him. Jerry could swear the old man was counting his steps. He was. When they reached the drug store, Mac said, "200 left foot, 201 right foot." He pulled a small notebook out of his pocket and jotted down the figures.

"Pardon me, I must obtain some lozenges for my catarrh." Mac went into the drug store, leaving Jerry staring into the container of blue liquid and the faded poster for sun-tan oil in the window. Jerry's heart sank further than ever. Would he get anything out of this pathetic old man?

Mac returned in minutes, his cough drops nowhere in sight, presumably stuffed into a pocket. He looked surprised to see Jerry.

"Mac, I'm Jerry Burnside," Jerry reminded him. "I'm walking with you? We met back at the hotel?"

"Captain Burnside's boy. How have you been?" Mac proceeded toward the river. When they reached the bank, he pulled out his watch. "The train to Indianapolis leaves at eleven-forty. Connects for Mr. and Mrs. Marshal in Cabin A."

Jerry wanted to cry. Mac was obviously living completely in the past.

"Would you like a cough drop?" Mac asked. He had taken the box out of his breast pocket and put a lozenge in his mouth.

"Eucalyptus."

Jerry took a cough drop and wondered what in the world to do next.

"Mac, I wanted to talk to you about the *River Queen*."

"Captain Dan Gray's boat."

"Remember, you used to give me and Kay Slack and Charlie Summers pennies, and we were always hanging around, borrowing paper and being general pests, remember?"

Mac was staring at the river, apparently not even listening to what Jerry was saying. It was hopeless, Jerry thought. He felt desolate. For Mac, for himself. It was as though he saw a life raft and it floated right past him.

Mac offered Jerry another cough drop, took another himself and replaced the box carefully in his pocket. Then he raised his cane above his head, his eyes full of maniacal fury. He took Jerry completely off balance. Jerry stepped back, raising his hand instinctively to protect his head. But Mac bypassed Jerry. He whacked his cane with all his might against a tree. He whacked it again and again, then he attacked a wooden bench, and a waste can, striking with absolute fury.

After his initial alarm, Jerry just stood aside and watched. He didn't try to stop Mac. As he watched the precision and deliberateness with which the old purser dealt a vicious beating to his surroundings, he figured Mac did this every day at this time and counted the blows.

After his seizure was over, Mac tucked his cane under his arm like a proper boulevardier, and turned toward the Palmer House.

Watching the old man, Jerry felt convinced, still, that somewhere in Mac's addled brain was knowledge that he must retrieve. But how to get to it? He needed time.

He was glad Kay was safe. He stowed his jealousy. For once he was glad Charlie was around. He would watch out for her until Jerry returned.

Chapter 46

Kay stroked the black silky hair on Charlie's arms and chest. It was soft as a spider. She had sworn not to see him, but taking in his tormented, restless body was the only way she could black out images of Jerry: Jerry under the water, Jerry swelling, floating, decaying in the water.

They had not found his body, and Kay could hear him in the night, wandering around like a ghost, crying for burial. She could not rest until she saw him, though seeing him would be awful. Seeing the river's ultimate cruelty, and the ugliness of his death.

She should never have come back to this river, these men. How I can pick 'em, she thought: a feckless dreamer, a charming, tender drunk, and now a riverbank Caliban. Richard was the future she'd planned on – expected to happen. The hell with him, she thought. The hell with the business. Let it go. Let him go.

"C'mere," she said.

Charlie's eyes were open and he was staring miserably at the ceiling with a loneliness she only knew one way to fix.

Charlie twisted Kay's arms behind her back and bit her on the shoulder hard. His lovemaking was getting increasingly rough as his demands that she marry him got more insistent. He was taking over her life.

They were lovers in flames. He was her punishment.

Maybe she would marry him.

Mud man. Mud man. Mud man.

Chapter 47

Jerry and Mac did not say a word on the way back to the Palmer House. Jerry debated with himself about whether there was anything he should do or could do about Mac's condition. The man was obviously confused, maybe sick. He would talk to Loraine. But what could she do? If she knew about Mac's violent streak, she might even throw him out of the hotel.

When he arrived at the door of the Palmer House, Mac turned to Jerry.

"Would you like to come in?" He seemed more rational than he'd been all afternoon.

"Sure." Jerry followed Mac into the hotel lobby.

"Good afternoon, Loraine," Mac said.

The clerk turned from the mail boxes she was stuffing bills into, and looked up at the big clock over the desk.

"You're a little late, Mr. Lodder."

"My old friend Mr. Burnside was with me and I'm not used to company."

Jerry was shocked at the old purser's sudden lucidity. Maybe the strange tree-whacking had done him some good.

Mac sat down in one of the plastic chairs and Jerry joined him. Jerry decided to try and get to him with some *River Queen* memories.

"Remember George the cook?" Jerry said, "You used to get so mad at him 'cause he'd always put liver on his grocery list and then not serve it."

Mac smiled for the first time. "That was George's 'don't get no' list. 'Don't get no margarine, don't get no sardines, don't get no liver'."

Mac's old self was definitely returning. Maybe, Jerry thought, the fact that he had observed Mac's outburst and not said anything had made Mac feel more at ease, more trusting.

"Would you like to visit my room?" Mac asked.

"Sure." Jerry followed Mac up the steps. The old man paused at each landing to get his breath.

"I'm slow but sure."

Mac's room was a small dark cubbyhole on the third floor. The bed and dresser took up most of the room. Clothes bulged out of the closet and onto the backs of the doors; magazines and newspapers covered the one chair and end table. The small window faced a brick wall. The smell in the room was funky, of half-washed socks, cigars, and shoe polish.

Among the litter and junk were a Seth Thomas pendulum clock in a wooden case on the wall above Mac's bed, and a battered but genuine leather suitcase serving as a night stand – a few small treasures that might be from *River Queen* days. A rack of nicely carved canes sat by the door. He'd need those, Jerry thought.

Mac moved a pile of newspapers from the chair, and invited Jerry to sit. Mac sat on the bed, resting his hands on his cane.

"Well."

"Well," Jerry repeated.

Were he and Mac going to know each other now and have a perfectly rational conversation?

But they were still on shaky ground.

"Where do you eat dinner?" Mac asked.

"I don't live in town. I'm just visiting. I wanted to talk to you about the *River Queen*."

"Do you smoke?" Mac took a cigar from a pocket and lit up. The smell was overpowering in the small room. Even a smoker like Jerry found it difficult to breathe.

"You remember me, don't you?" Jerry asked.

"Of course," Mac said. "My young friend Jerry. You were always running around the boat with that little Slack girl and Wendall Summers' boy."

"Remember the time you and George brought a ferret on board and it bred those monster rats?"

"That was well before your time…."

If Mac was hazy about everyday events, there was nothing wrong with his recall of the distant past.

"You came on the boat with your father, after Captain Patterson retired."

"True, true." After a pause, Jerry asked, "What do you remember about the day the *River Queen* blew up?"

"July 4, 1958, 1:30 p.m., Central Time." Mac took out his watch as though to confirm his statement. "We were preparing for a big excursion; three hundred passengers had booked."

"But exactly what happened? I mean – you lived through it – what was it like?"

"Hell."

Jerry could almost see the flames in Mac's eyes, the burning river he jumped or was blown into. He hoped he hadn't pushed too far.

"But what caused it? There's this story about Kay Slack's father–"

"Not true."

"I thought not, but Kay...."

"I could have saved Joe's reputation but no one wanted the truth from me. My name had been blackened by rumors."

"I do, Mac. What was the truth?"

"Wendall Summers, Chief Engineer, blew up that boat."

Jerry could only remember once before being this breathless: when socked in the stomach by a fast medicine ball in a gym class.

"Charlie's father? But why? He was on the boat when she blew."

"So was I." Mac extended the bad leg that made him require a cane. He pointed to his head. "But he knew when it would go and he jumped. I didn't know. He killed fifteen people just to get rid of Joe Slack."

"You think he blew up the boat that was his livelihood and killed fifteen people to get rid of Joe Slack?"

"To get Linda."

"But Joe wasn't on the boat when it blew...."

"Maybe Wendall didn't know that." Mac looked less sure of his story, and as though he might slip away into dementia again. He obviously didn't like his story challenged. Jerry thought it over; it was no crazier than the rumors about Kay's father. That triangle between her and Joe and Wendall must have been some hot stuff. As kids they knew about it vaguely, but had not realized how strong the passions were. You didn't, Jerry thought, until you felt them yourself.

"But how did it happen?" Jerry asked. "What makes you think Wendall Summers caused the fire?"

"I don't think," Mac said. "I <u>know</u>. I myself saw Jimboy Dix – he was the oiler – welding near some paint that was highly inflammable. I told him to stop, but he said his boss, Wendall, had told him to finish up what he was doing, so I went up to the pilothouse to tell Captain Burnside. Wendall and Captain Burnside were in the pilothouse, and Captain Burnside told Wendall to go tell Jimboy to hold off on his welding. There was a strong wind and it was especially dangerous that day. Wendall left. About fifteen minutes later, I, too, left the pilothouse and went down on the texas deck where Jimboy was welding. I asked him if Wendall had told him to stop; he said no, in fact, he had told him to get a move on. Again I told Jimboy to stop, but he was afraid of Wendall. I ran back to the pilothouse to tell Captain Burnside, but before I got there, the ship blew!"

Jerry felt like he was breathing paint. The idea that the fire was on purpose changed his whole life. As suddenly as the explosion had changed his life. If it were true. But why would Mac make up such a story?

"Why didn't' you tell this at the time? Wasn't there a hearing or something?"

"The hearing was over way before I remembered. The persons I told later didn't believe me. They said I was crazy from being hit on the head."

They weren't far wrong there, Jerry thought.

"How long after the blow-up was your memory?" Jerry asked.

Mac looked as though he were going to retreat into his nutty old man mode again. It seemed to come over him whenever he felt threatened.

"I don't recall."

Jerry was beginning to feel dizzy and confused himself. He had to think about this story of Mac's. It made little sense. Surely Mac himself was not involved in the triangle of Linda and Joe and Wendall. But, if there was anything he'd learned it was to avoid conclusions about people's passions. In spite of Mac's fondness for boys, maybe Mac had some reason for dreaming up a lie. As for his mind, he was senile and forgetful, but did perfectly well with anything having to do with the *River Queen*.

"Now that you know what happened, I hope you'll see to it that Wendall Summers is brought to justice," Mac said.

"He's dead. Died a few months ago."

Mac's eyes burned with the maniacal light that Jerry saw in them just before lashing out at the tree with his cane.

"I hope he burns in Hell." Mac was fingering his cane nervously. Jerry hoped he wasn't about to use it again. "He blew up the best boat I ever served on, and I never got another."

Mac's voice was the bitterest sound Jerry had ever heard.

"There was nothing wrong with my head when I got out of the hospital. I could run a boat better than any man on the river. Why, I knew every town and city on the Ohio and their train schedules by heart: Pittsburgh, Rochester, Steubenville, Huntington, Marietta, Parkersburg, Portsmouth, Point Pleasant, Manchester, Aberdeen, Maysville.... I knew every little farmer's house and every tree good to tie off on, and every small stop: Smith's Landing, Piney Rock, Red Fox Crossing. I never even had to look at my book to tell Joe the load to be put on and taken off, or what belonged to who on the wharf boat. But those new people that bought the line from Captain Gray didn't want me back. They said, 'You haven't got anything we want. Your knowledge is no good anymore.' If Captain Dan Gray had still owned his own boats I'd have had a job, you can be sure."

"What do you mean?"

"He sold the line to that big syndicate right around when the *River Queen* blew. Didn't you know that?"

"No," Jerry admitted. At that time he'd been dealing with his own head injuries, caused by bar fights.

"They just turned me out," Mac said. "Just turned me out. Captain Dan would never have done that."

A faint memory of his father talking about the *River Queen's* money problems came back to Jerry. And didn't the Fitzgerald twins say something about her changing owners in her last days? Jerry had let that slide right by.

"Did Captain Dan own the *River Queen* when she blew up?" Jerry asked.

"I don't know."

"How come you...."

"I kept books for the boat, not the boat line. I do know the *Queen* was losing money."

Jerry was beginning to get an idea; Mac's story could be true. With Mac's memory for all things past, weak as his grasp on the present might be, Jerry believed him. It was his version of Summers' motive that did not make sense. Of course, Charlie's father would not be crazy enough to blow up the *River Queen* to kill a man who was not on board. Something was missing. Wendall had to have a reason to destroy his own livelihood. Maybe, the thought occurred, it was not his livelihood, or would be more profitable for him out of commission. Suppose Wendall had been part of the group that bought the *Queen*? The insurance would be worth more than a money-burning, superannuated old steamer. But how to find that out? Would Charlie know? How to ask him without admitting why he wanted the information after all these years? He had to get to Charlie. Jerry felt bad about what this story, if it were necessary to tell Charlie, might do to his old friend. He would try to find out about Wendall's investment in the *Queen* from him without letting Charlie know about Mac's accusation. But the truth had to come out eventually, for Kay above all, for Mac. For himself.

Jerry left Mac with a promise to prove his story.

"I believe you," Jerry said.

Mac looked surprised that there could be any doubt of his word.

"I'm going down Paducah way. I'll be back soon, Mac."

Jerry took Loraine to dinner and borrowed her car. He still hadn't called Kay.

He drove south as though in a dream. Maybe going in the wrong direction.

He felt like one of those two-headed snakes people claimed to have seen on the river: one of his heads was pointed to the present, one to the past. He was taking a big chance; whoever was behind the shootings had to be getting more desperate, more dangerous.

Chapter 48

Jerry rehearsed what he would say to Charlie when he got to his house: you see, Charlie, right in the middle of these shootings, I return from the dead, telling no one, and just decided to drop in on you to talk over old times. And where have I been? Got washed up this far downriver, near Paducah, where you just happen to live. Oh by the way, I heard your father might have been one of the owners of the *River Queen*. I wanted to know if that was true – part of the general research I've been doing, along with the *River Queen* model.

Terrific. He couldn't sell it to a half-wit, much less to an intelligent guy like Charlie.

He'd have to go slow: tell Charlie he'd been hiding out, been in a coma. Needed a pal to help him figure out how to come back from the dead without scaring everybody silly. Don't want to upset Kay by appearing so suddenly. Say, by the way....

Jerry followed the map to a little town just outside Paducah where Charlie's home and business were located. Once a steamboat stop, now it was living on welfare. There were one or two nice-looking houses, some brick ruins among the weeds along the river, which were probably once a furniture factory or grain store, and spoke of some former moment of prosperity. Now rusted cars disfigured the waterfront. A dark bar from the open door of which came jukebox music, clouds of smoke, and small-town guffaws, was the only lively place on the main street. Jerry could see Charlie's operation a bit downriver, its impressive cranes looking like gigantic praying mantises.

Jerry's stomach was rumbling like the *Harvey's* engines, and the smell of food coming from a little dive called the Blue Bird pulled him in. He had to have food; besides, he was postponing his visit to Charlie. No matter what he found out, it was bound to be painful. If Wendall had not owned part of the boat, his errand would be pointless; if he had, it would open a great big vat of Ohio River gars, the nastiest creatures in the river.

Jerry was the only customer in the eatery. It was Sunday, but still, the place was abnormally empty.

"Where is everybody?" he asked.

"Up at the mall," the waitress said. She had a world-class beehive, and the longest, reddest nails Jerry had ever seen.

Jerry picked up a menu and studied it; he ordered something called Manhattan Beef, which turned out to be an old-fashioned roast beef and gravy sandwich with mashed potatoes. The waitress, whose name, Ruth, was embroidered on her uniform, seemed to be doing the cooking as well as the serving. When she had plunked down Jerry's lunch, she studied her nails.

"Some fingernails you got there," Jerry said. He dived into the roast beef.

"You shoulda seen 'em before. These are short."

"You don't look like a Chinese Mandarin."

"I'm not," she said seriously. She held out an egregiously clawed hand for study. "These are all mine, not those phony ones. But I broke one, and had to file the rest to match." Jerry finished his roast beef and mopped up the gravy. Ruth poured him a fresh cup of coffee.

"Do you know where Charlie Summers lives, which house?"

Jerry figured if Charlie was ever at home, it would be on a Sunday afternoon. He would try there, and if he couldn't find Charlie, move on to the harbor.

"Sure. Everybody knows the Summerses. That's their house at the top of the street there, with the fancy trim and the white porch." Jerry had noticed the house as he looked around town for a place to light. It was red brick with a kind of steamboat gothic porch, an oldie, probably built soon after the Civil War. It was a fine house, the kind he'd like to have himself if he had the money. He even liked the unkempt bushes around the front, lilac and rose-a-sharon. There were hollyhocks by the garage, an outbuilding which could have been an old kitchen, remodeled.

"Charlie Summers' son comes in here a lot," Ruth said. She looked around at the empty kitchen. "Makes you feel kinda creepy."

"Why's that?"

"After him killing the old man."

Whoa, Jerry thought. He was taken completely off balance.

"Doing what?"

"I thought you must know about it if you're a friend of theirs." Ruth studied her nails.

"I don't." Jerry had barely known Charlie had a son.

"Charlie Summers' kid, Denver, the one that hardly ever leaves the house but just to come in here? He set old Mr. Wendall's mattress on fire. His grandfather was bed rid and couldn't get out of the house. Sometimes it makes me feel real funny being here alone with just him."

Jerry was meeting a new Charlie, one he had never known. And Wendall – died by fire.... So the *River Queen* finally had her revenge.

"Course it didn't kill old Mr. Summers," Ruth said. "But the firemen that eats here said the smoke was so bad, it brought on the heart attack. He went only a week after the fire that boy set."

"Why weren't charges brought against the boy?"

"He didn't kill the old man right out." Ruth shrugged. "Nobody could prove that. But he gives me the creeps. He's crazy is what he is."

Jerry couldn't believe Charlie and the townspeople let a pathetic psycho kid, maybe a dangerous one, run around loose, with nothing done about him.

"Shouldn't the boy be getting some kind of help? Some treatment?"

"Like what?"

Jerry thought for a moment. Don't take on the town, he told himself.

"Everybody knows he set the fire." Ruth scribbled out a lunch check.

Jerry took a last drink of water and wiped the ring on the counter away with his napkin. He had thought Charlie was still the kid he knew on the *River Queen*. But really, Charlie was a stranger, someone he knew little about after the *River Queen* explosion. Charlie had been married and had a child. His wife was dead. That's all he knew. The facts.

Jerry paid his bill, and left Ruth as much tip as he could. The money the Johnsons had lent him was dwindling fast.

"How's the mother? Charlie's mother?" Jerry asked Ruth. "I think I may stop up and visit her and Charlie."

"Oh, she's OK – been sick all her life. Ever since I can remember."

"What's their number?" Jerry thought he had better call first so as not to shock Charlie at his sudden appearance. Ruth pointed to a phone booth outside the diner, and Jerry left her studying her fingernails.

The glass booth was smeary and dirty, and half the twenty or so pages of the small phone book were torn out. The vandals hadn't gotten to the S's, and Jerry found what he was looking for. As he dialed, he looked around: ruins, weeds, a Pepsi machine – the ubiquitous symbols of the failing river town. There was no answer at Charlie's, but Jerry decided to walk up to the house anyway, just to take a closer look.

Chapter 49

As Jerry walked up the street toward Charlie's house, he noticed that its classic lines were marred by peeling paint. The gutters were rusty and about to give way in places where last fall's leaves were still packed. What had happened here? What had gone wrong with Charlie's son?

Jerry stood on the slightly sloping porch and rang the doorbell. From where he stood he could see the river at the foot of the street, indifferently leaving every kind of debris from rotten telephone poles and dead pigs, to plastic bottles, to whole towns along its banks. He heard movement inside the house, but no one came to the door. He rang again, and peered in through the long window. As he bent over, the front door opened and a young man about twenty-six or seven stood in the doorway.

"We don't want any," he said. The sound was harsh, with the erratic volume of people hard of hearing. "We've got all the carpet sweepers and Tupperware and makeup we need. My grandmother doesn't even wear makeup. She's in a wheelchair and never goes any place."

This must be Denver, Jerry thought.

The young man was tall and thin with a prominent Adam's apple. He was dressed in an oddly formal outfit for someone his age: a black suit, white shirt, and a string tie with a heavy silver tie-clip. He looked like an old-fashioned preacher.

Jerry introduced himself.

"I thought you were dead." Denver might have been saying, 'I thought you were in Pittsburgh.'

Jerry replied in kind.

"I managed to live. Here, pinch me, I'm alive."

Denver shrank away from Jerry's outstretched arm.

"Is your father around?"

"He's in Cincinnati. He won't be back until at least Wednesday."

Jerry hesitated, then decided that he could perhaps learn something about Wendall from Charlie's mother.

"I'd like to pay my respects to your grandmother. I'm an old acquaintance of hers...."

Denver yelled into the house, "Grandma, it's Mr. Burnside. That friend of Daddy's. Do you want him to come in?"

"Burnside? Didn't your father say he drowned?" The worn, tired voice was one that Jerry recognized even after all these years. "Tell him to wait. I'll be out in a minute."

Denver pointed to the living room, an old-fashioned parlor with lace curtains, stiff horsehair furniture, and lots of miscellaneous items that Jerry's mother called "gee-gaws." Denver pointed to a chair for Jerry, and plopped down in the rocker opposite him.

"She's putting her teeth in and getting her wig on. She's held together with glue and bobby pins like a corpse."

Jerry wasn't sure which was making him the most uncomfortable, the prickly horsehair stuffing in his chair, or Denver. Charlie's son had crazy eyes, and they returned Jerry's stare without blinking.

"I take care of her," Denver said. "I'm worthless at the harbor. Three generations of river men and then me. My father and grandfather probably wanted me to learn the family business, but I was hopeless."

Jerry automatically started to protest; no one was worthless and hopeless. But Denver and his family seemed to have worked out this scenario and it wasn't going to be changed by Jerry's tendency to play Mary Worth.

Mrs. Summers appeared at the threshold, propelling herself in a wheelchair. Of all the mothers on the *River Queen*, Jerry recalled, Charlie's was the least liked by the kids. Kay's mother was fun – demonstrating the latest dances for them and teaching them songs. Jerry's mother shared her reading and her thoughts with them. Charlie's mother complained or made them do errands for her.

She looked just like she always had, Jerry thought. It was amazing how she, the sick one, had remained so intact, while all the other parents were gone. With her wheelchair she was even more the invalid than when she was on the boat, but her bulk had protected her from wrinkles and her wig concealed changes in her hair.

"Mrs. Summers," Jerry said. "It's good to see you."

"I'm surprised to see you. Last I heard you were drowned in the river. Charlie said he looked and looked and couldn't find your body. What happened to you?"

"I don't know for sure. I was knocked out. I've been with some friends down this way. I wanted to see Charlie in person to let him know I'm OK."

"He's up in Cincinnati, I guess Denver told you."

"Right. I'll head up there later today." A sudden thought hit Jerry, that Charlie's mother might get to Charlie before he did. "I'd like to tell Charlie myself I'm OK – I'd appreciate it if you'd not – well, it'll be a shock."

"Don't worry. I don't even know where he stays up there. Do you? Does he go with that Slack girl?"

"I don't think so."

It felt strange to Jerry that this old lady rather than Kay or Charlie should be the first to be told he was alive. At the same time, it was somewhat easier to reveal his survival to someone who basically did not care and made no fuss. Being "dead" as long as he had had taken on a kind of reality of its own. He sometimes actually felt dead. Felt he'd have to do something supernatural to return to his former life. He was a different person now, too, a man someone had tried to kill, with a revised life story.

Looking from Denver's jittery face to his grandmother's oddly preserved features, Jerry had difficulty believing Charlie's son, weird as the young man seemed, could have tried to kill his grandfather, and that Mrs. Summers continued to live with him in the house where it had happened. In spite of his experiences with the people on the *River Queen*, in the army and in towboating, Jerry had remained somewhat of a Candide, believing that if he got himself straight, the world would fall into place. Silly me, he thought.

"I'm sorry about your husband," Jerry said. "I remember him so well. A good engineer. My father thought very well of him."

"Hmm." Mrs. Summers did not seem to be taken in by Jerry's flattery.

Jerry tried again. As he spoke, he concentrated on a single dish in the bowed-front oak cabinet that was full of glasses, platters and china. It was a cut-glass bone dish of the type used on the *River Queen*.

"I've been building a model of the old girl," Jerry continued. "Been looking up old river buffs for information. I actually saw Mac Lodder recently. Remember him, the purser? He raised the question I never thought of before: who owned the *River Queen* when she went down? Mrs. Summers, you're now, believe it or not, one of the only survivors of that boat."

The woman still did not seem moved. She called Denver, who had been skulking about as she and Jerry talked.

"Denver, get my purse."

Denver brought his grandmother a large flat black leather bag. Mrs. Summers took a change purse out of it and handed Denver two dollars from it.

"Go down to the Blue Bird and get a root beer float," she said. Denver took the money and left Mrs. Summers and Jerry alone. Jerry shifted his gaze to a framed picture, a black and white reproduction of a stag surrounded by baying hunting dogs.

When the front door was shut, and Denver's footsteps could be heard going down the wooden porch stairs, Mrs. Summers said, "Charlie wants to put him in an asylum."

I think I would too, Jerry thought. He tried to keep his face composed for Mrs. Summers. He let her talk.

"He was never nice to Denver, neither was Wendall. Now he wants to put his own son away in some hospital."

"Perhaps he feels Denver needs help...."

"What for?"

Because he tried to kill your husband. Jerry couldn't say it aloud, or even hint at it; the story was only something he'd heard at a cafe – though having met Denver he was inclined to believe it.

"Charlie is mad because of Wendall's will," Mrs. Summers said.

"What will?"

"I shouldn't be talking about it. My lawyer said so."

"Maybe I could help in some way."

"Well, since my husband died, Charlie found a copy of a will Wendall supposedly made when he got sick, just before the fire. It leaves everything to Charlie, nothing to me or Denver."

"But surely, Charlie would share...."

"It's no good to him. All Charlie has is one of those xerox things. The lawyers won't accept it. Charlie wants me to sign everything over to him, says it was his father's intention, but I won't do it. The real will leaves it all to me. You see, I own Charlie's business, this house, the money, everything. Charlie don't own a thing."

So the successful, always-in-charge Charlie was in deep shit! Jerry felt disloyal listening to all this, although to his most spiteful self it was music.

"He thinks if he threatens to take Denver away from me I'll sign everything over to him. Denver's my legs. What would happen to me without him?"

Jerry debated how he might ask what was in the will concerning the *River Queen*.

"Maybe you can talk to Charlie," Mrs. Summers said. "Remind him Denver is his own son."

"I doubt he'd take that from me."

"You've always been his best friend."

Sure, Jerry thought, I just never knew him. He tried to imagine what it would be like to have all the stuff you worked for dangled in front of your eyes, then snatched away, and to be under the thumb of this querulous old woman.

Mrs. Summers stirred in her chair. Jerry thought of the old witch in Hansel and Gretel. He glanced toward the dark passageway to the kitchen. Did he really expect to see a blazing oven back there?

"I guess Mr. Summers owned a good chunk of the *River Queen*," Jerry said.

"Why do you want to know that?"

"Oh – like I said – I'm interested in anything having to do with the old girl."

"What did Mac Lodder have to say?"

Jerry thought for a split second, felt like a diver about to try a swan dive, and said, "He told me some crazy story about your husband being responsible for the *River Queen* fire."

Mrs. Summers didn't throw Jerry out, or even react to his words. She seemed to be trying the story on for size.

Finally, she said, "It's not crazy. It's true. He did it for the insurance. He was an evil person. He made me sick."

Had he thought this conversation couldn't get weirder? Jerry hit the water flat.

"How do you know that? I mean, is there proof?" Jerry thought what this would mean to Kay. He could cut Kay loose from the *River Queen*.

"Papers, checks. My word. He told me so."

"Did Charlie know?"

Jerry figured this would kill Charlie. Old Wendall was a hard man, even harder than Captain Burnside and Joe Slack in some ways – secretive and aloof. But he was the only person Charlie had....

"He does now. I showed him the papers when he was fussing about the will."

My God, Jerry thought. Now Charlie has lost <u>his</u> father to the *River Queen*, too. It just took him a long time to die.

"Charlie will put Denver away if I don't stop him. He thinks Denver stole that so-called will."

He probably did, Jerry thought.

"You tell him what I told you," Charlie's mother said. "He don't believe I would tell anybody. He said nobody would believe me. But you believe me, don't you? And I told you, didn't I?"

As Jerry left the Summers' house, he saw that Denver had returned from the Blue Bird. He was in the weeds by the garage, carefully fitting a brown paper bag over the head of a small dog.

"Denver!" Jerry called.

Charlie's son dropped the bag, and gave Jerry a weak smile and a wave. The dog ran away yelping.

Chapter 50

That bastard Wendall Summers! Jerry's fury made the car shake so hard he could feel it. Too bad Denver hadn't burned Wendall to a cinder so he could have a real taste of fire.

He was furious with Charlie, too. Letting Kay go on thinking her father had something to do with the *Queen's* demise. He was supposed to be in love with her.

Jerry's friendship with Charlie was over. Another piece of the past blown away.

And Charlie's mother – what a manipulating old bitch. Jerry could almost feel sorry for Charlie. It would be hard to face Wendall's crimes, much less tell anyone about them, but knowing the truth and not telling Kay was unforgivable.

Jerry was desperate to get to Kay now, but he had to think how to do it. He didn't want to scare her or upset her any more than necessary. He decided to drive directly to the harbor, have Daryl return Loraine's car and take a note to Mac telling him what he had found. No, Mac would have to wait until things settled down, then Jerry would go in person. First, Smitty should call Kay and prepare her for the shock of seeing him alive.

Luckily, when Jerry called the harbor, Smitty answered the phone. Jerry paused a second at his dispatcher's unsuspecting, "Burnside Harbor, Smitty here." So the world had gone on without him, Jerry thought. He paused. Dropping in on Smitty this way was like hitting a child.

"Smitty, it's Jerry."

"Who is this?" Smitty's voice was hostile.

"It's Jerry."

"I ain't listenin' to no more crank calls. Go play your shitty jokes on somebody else...."

"Wait," Jerry said. "Honest to God, Smitty. It's me. I'm on my way to the harbor. You'll see me in a few minutes. I didn't want to scare you."

Silence.

"Ask me something only I know...."

Jerry could almost hear Smitty thinking.

"What's your favorite country and western?"

"I don't have one. I hate the stuff and you know it."

"Sounds like him – you–"

"Know how to keep goats outa your yard?"

"Jerry! I can't believe it! I can't believe it. After all this time? What happened? How come you ain't drowned? Where've you been?"

"Tell you everything when I see you, buddy. Right now, I gotta get to Kay. You call her, Smitty. She's gonna be awfully upset. I should have called her before, but I've been doin' some stuff needed doin'. Take it slow and explain I'll be over as soon as I stop at the harbor and get rid of this car I'm driving."

When Jerry saw the harbor, he felt all the way alive for the first time since the *Harvey* went down. Home! There was the float, the work barge, the office perched up high. He ran down the hill and over the gangplank, loving its reassuring clank. He took the metal stairs two at a time. Smitty was at the office door and shifted from foot to foot with pleasure.

"Well, I'll be!" Smitty said. "I'm seein' a miracle! A God damn miracle! Since you called I thought maybe I was startin' to hear things that wasn't there. I sure am glad to see you!"

Jerry filled Smitty in on his rescue by the Johnsons and promised to tell the rest when he came back from Kay's. Daryl was gone off on a job, using a tug Kay had lent the harbor.

Now for the hard part, Jerry thought: seeing Kay. He would be glad when these emotional scenes were over. He couldn't stand them. As he drove toward Kay's building, he recalled their fight. Surely she wasn't still mad; after all that had happened, they would both see things differently. He had realized how pointless his jealousy was, and she couldn't hate a guy who came so close to being killed. Could she?

As he rode up toward her apartment in the elevator, he tried to rehearse what he would say. He got off at her floor and walked down the hall. His head was pounding, as though he were still under those barges. Kay's apartment was open, and he tapped on the door frame. Hearing nothing, he stepped inside. No arms reached out for him – no Kay flying into his arms. She was sitting at the desk, staring out at the river.

"Kay, I–"

Jerry walked over to her. Her eyes were like stones. He tried to touch her, to pull her to her feet.

"You bastard!" Kay pulled away from him and pounded him on the neck and shoulder. One of her blows hit his Adam's apple and cut off his air. "How could you do this? How could you?"

"Kay, I had to–"

"You've been gone a week. We thought you were dead." Kay hit him again with all her might, but he turned and took the force of the punch with his arm. "Daryl went up and down the river for days looking for you, and Smitty said you were with some people all along!" Kay stopped her attack and stood glaring at him. "Why didn't you call? Why didn't you write or send a note or a telegram? I've been frantic. I thought you were <u>dead</u>."

Kay sobbed, tears spurting onto Jerry's shirt. She sat down at her desk again and the tears spilled onto the papers on her desk. Jerry watched the paper curl slightly, with a kind of mindless concentration. He patted Kay on the back and she didn't draw away, but she didn't look up either. He was hoping the storm was over, though he was touched at her reaction.

"We gotta talk, Kay. Let me put my arm around you. Let me hold you."

Kay pulled away.

"I thought it was best to let people think I was dead."

"I'm not people."

"I should have called, but I wanted to check something out, and I guess I was afraid someone might listen in on a phone call or intercept a letter...."

"By someone you mean Richard."

"Anyone."

Kay clenched her fists.

"You and your goddamned jealousy."

Jerry let that one pass.

"You've got to admit I have reason to be a little on guard. I was mowed down by the *Plattner*...."

"Oh my God, that was so awful. I'm so sorry. That must have been terrible. Tell me how you came through. We thought sure you had drowned. We watched and watched while Charlie dredged and then when the pilothouse came up and you weren't there, it was like – I kept hoping you were alive. Then I gave up."

"I don't know how I survived," Jerry said. "Somebody must have picked me up and dumped me at the Johnsons', this wonderful old man and his wife. They took care of me for a few days till I could get on my feet."

"But why didn't you call? I still don't understand."

"Because it was on purpose."

"On purpose? Roscoe was piloting. He was drunk."

"Have you talked to him? Did the Coast Guard look into it?"

"Not yet. He was too drunk, and then he disappeared. We're trying to find him."

"That boat came forward when it shouldn't have. It was not pilot error."

"It's these shootings. Everything is bound to seem on purpose."

"Have there been any more?"

"Not since you've been gone."

"Tell me how things have been going here. Then there's something else I have to talk to you about."

"I of all people should never have trusted a drunk," Kay said.

"You of all people would want to give him a second chance, and if I remember correctly, Charlie and I urged you to keep him on."

"I could kick myself."

"I wish we could find Roscoe," Jerry said. "He might have been drinking, but I swear there was more to it."

Kay smiled for the first time. "I'm just so glad you're alive. I can't believe you got out from that pilothouse and from under those barges. Do you know the odds on doing that?"

"Somebody up there wants me back for more fun and games," Jerry said. Then all of a sudden, he felt weak, weak as a rubber band that's lost its snap.

"Say, you wouldn't have a drink would you?"

Kay looked concerned. She went to the bar, and held up a bottle of bourbon.

"This OK? Or brandy maybe?"

"Brandy's fine."

"Are you OK?"

"I feel like I've got the bends."

"Delayed reaction."

"Too much, too often."

Jerry longed to crawl onto Kay's couch, curl up like a baby and go to sleep. Kay handed him his brandy.

"I'm glad you're back. I'm glad you're OK," she said. "I'm sorry I hit you, but I was so—"

"That's the second time you hit me."

"I'm sorry about the other time, too."

Kay poured herself a brandy. Jerry felt the alcohol relax his body.

"How's the barge line going?" he asked.

"Lousy. Everybody thinks the *Plattner* is cursed. And that I'm a hex or incompetent or both. Maybe they're right."

"But no more shooting...."

"If I'm right, and someone's trying to put me out of business, they don't need to shoot anymore. They've got what they want. Morale is shot. I can't get anyone to work for me."

Jerry held out his glass for another drink. His hand, for the first time in his life, was shaking.

"I can't hold onto the boat line. Pretty soon I won't be able to give it away. Richard has a buyer lined up."

Jerry did not tell her of the image he had had at the Johnsons' of Richard watching the electronic board and manipulating everything that had happened. He still couldn't put it all together, put Richard in touch with Slag or Donny or whoever else might do the actual shooting. Roscoe yes, Nettie and Dave maybe. Jerry filled Kay in about the Johnsons and how he had gone to see Mac. He told her about what Mac said about Wendall Summers blowing up the *River Queen*, and how Mrs. Summers, Charlie's mother, backed up Mac's story and showed Jerry the proof.

Kay looked as though she had been hit in the stomach. She was quiet for a long time, long enough for Jerry to become uneasy.

"Kay?"

"That bastard. Wendall killed your father and mother. And thirteen other people."

Kay went silent again, then spoke as though from a tomb.

"I thought all those years.... People said...."

"I know."

"I should have trusted him."

"And I should have gone into all this sooner. Not wait half a lifetime."

"I couldn't stand to hear her name. The *Queen*."

Jerry put his arms around Kay and she clung to him. Then she pulled away. Her face was dead white.

"I can't believe Charlie...."

"It's hard."

Kay blushed. "How long has he known about Wendall?"

"Weeks. Months. Long enough to tell you the truth."

Kay got up and paced about the room.

"It would be hard to tell you," Jerry said.

Kay opened the sliding door, went out on her terrace and looked down at the river.

"I'm going to tell Charlie what I found out," Jerry said. "Not that it can change what he's done to you."

"No," Kay said, "nothing can change what he's done to me."

Chapter 51

The story of how Wendall Summers blew up the *River Queen* had to be told. Joe Slack deserved to have his name cleared, and Mac's credibility should be restored. But how? Maybe Jerry could lay it all out to Captain Jesse and Captain Harold. They knew all the river people. If Jerry went that route, he knew, Charlie would become a pariah on the river. Of course the sins of the fathers should not be visited upon the children. But they always were, Jerry thought, they always were.

Kay had told Jerry that Charlie was at a nearby terminal doing some repairs on the *Plattner*, and he resolved to go down there and confront his old friend. First, he decided to check in with his own harbor. The *Harvey* was due to be brought in this afternoon.

Jerry dreaded his reunion with the boat almost as much as those with Kay and Charlie. What would she look like? Would she be worth saving? When he pulled his car into the space up on the hill, he reminded himself to be careful. The news of Jerry's not being dead would be getting around. In his preoccupation with the *River Queen* and the past, he had almost forgotten about the fact that the shooter who had been terrorizing the river was still out there.

In the office, Jerry went through a week's worth of mail, and checked Smitty's records of what the harbor had been doing in his absence. He went into his inner-office and looked over the *River Queen* model. A lifeboat had slipped – glue must of dried and cracked – and Jerry adjusted it with his finger, meaning to squeeze out a little fresh Elmer's and tack the johnboat back in place as soon as he got time. All his vessels were in disrepair, he thought. He was pulled away from his ruminations by some commotion in the office, and the sound of someone calling his name. Charlie. Damn. He couldn't put off seeing him any longer.

"Anybody home?" Charlie knocked a familiar "beer and a whiskey, six bits" on the door frame. He came into the room, and grabbed Jerry by the shoulders in a bear hug. It was all Jerry could do not to push him away.

"I can't believe what I'm seein'. You must be made outa cork, man! What in hell are you doin' alive? We thought we got rid of you for good!"

Charlie sat on the edge of the desk, while Jerry remained standing.

"Only know one other man survived what you did. When they brought him up, he said to the guy who ran him down, 'Well, Cap, I done scraped and sanded your barges for you. But if you want 'em painted you'll have to do it yourself.'"

Charlie guffawed. At Jerry's feeble response, he added, "Guess you're still hurtin'. What you been off doin' all this time?"

"Nothin' much."

"Got any coffee?"

"Oh sure." Jerry searched his mind for something to say, anything to talk about besides what he had to. He was so mad at Charlie, he choked up. He was sorry, too, that they could no longer be friends. "We're expectin' the *Harvey* pretty soon."

"We had a devil of a time gettin' her up off the bottom."

"Kay says you're workin' on the *Plattner?*"

"Yeah, something ails that boat. God, that was the worst thing I ever hope to see."

"Somebody on that boat tried to kill me."

"Now wait," Charlie said. "You been hit on the head one too many times."

"Seriously. Roscoe knew exactly where I was. We were on the radio."

"Roscoe was drunk. It wasn't on purpose."

"If he didn't do it on purpose, where is he?"

"There you got me. But Roscoe just wouldn't do anything like that, I know."

"Then why did he disappear?"

Charlie shrugged. "We're lookin' for him. He's got family in Canada. Could be anywhere. But tell me, what happened? How'd you beat those barges? Where you been?"

Jerry told Charlie what he knew of his experiences after the *Harvey* went under.

"I can't remember anything till I woke up at the Johnsons'."

"Your number just wasn't up. Like that guy I know got caught in one of those drums at Meldahl Dam."

"I was lucky," Jerry said. "Real lucky."

"But why didn't you let us know right away when you were conscious? We were pretty upset."

Jerry could not avoid any longer telling Charlie what he had learned about his father.

"Charlie, I have some bad news to talk about – I saw Mac Lodder."

Charlie's face changed like the surface of the river when a cloud drifts between sun and water. He obviously knew what Jerry was going to say.

Jerry spelled out what Mac had said about Charlie's father being responsible for the burning of the *River Queen*, and the fact that Charlie's mother had confirmed Mac's story.

"How come you to go to my house?" Charlie demanded.

"I was lookin' for you."

"You didn't have to talk to the old lady. Sounds like you were pumping her behind my back!"

"Now wait a minute, pard," Jerry said. "It seems like I'm the one ought to be mad. We're talkin' murder here. My parents–"

"Something that happened over thirty years ago. And you got no proof."

"There is proof, Charlie. Your mother has it."

"She's crazy. You could see that."

"I don't think so. Why didn't you tell us what Wendall did, when you found out? Kay was upset and worried all these years over the rumors about Joe."

"No one believed that–"

"The stories never stopped–"

Charlie lifted his cap and ran his hands through his hair. Jerry noted that he had not once really looked at the model of the *River Queen*.

"If I could catch the damned maniac that started this shooting – stirred this whole thing up...."

"I was planning to see Mac soon anyhow. Ever since I started my model. This was bound to come out."

"Jesus H. God." Charlie looked so miserable Jerry almost felt sorry for him.

"Why can't you let sleeping dogs lie, Jerry?"

"Because they never do. Your father blew us all out of the water. We were never the same. It's been buggin' me ever since that day, but I ran away, couldn't face it. Maybe–"

"So what are you going to do with this so-called news of yours?" Charlie asked.

"Mac deserves to be told. Somehow you should set the record straight for Kay's sake."

"Mac is so over the hill, from what I hear, he don't know his hindquarters from a hole in the ground."

"He's pretty down on his luck. He could probably use some financial help. But mostly to restore his pride. He was right when he said everybody thought he was nuts."

"Dirty old fag."

Charlie didn't ask if his mother had told Jerry about the fight they were in over Wendall's will.

"Even if my father did what you said, it wasn't my fault. I didn't do anything. I didn't even hear about it till a few months ago."

"So are you going to just start another whole set of lies?"

Charlie stonewalled.

"You should have told me and Kay," Jerry said.

"Kay will understand."

"I doubt it."

When Charlie left, Jerry watched him through the windows. His usually vigorous step was slow. At the top of the hill, he turned and looked up at the office. Jerry sensed that his old friend had come to him, not so much to see if he was all right, but to find out what Jerry had discovered at his mother's house. He tried to recall what Charlie had said when Kay mentioned the *River Queen* model, when Jerry said he would be looking up Mac Lodder. Jerry was sure all this was connected to his close shave on the *Harvey* and the shots taken at him and the other pilots. But how? How was Wendall's crime connected to Cliff and Slag and the man called Donny who had an eye like a bloody egg?

Chapter 52

The *Harvey C.* would be sticking her nose around the big bend to the west any minute. Jerry was very keyed up as he waited for his first glimpse of his beloved tug. Daryl and Smitty stood alongside him on the float, equally excited. The bend downriver was extremely sharp, and the boats would be pretty close before anyone would be able to spot the *Harvey*.

Daryl was the first. "I think I see her." The others caught sight of a boat coming their way. As it got closer, they could make out that it was indeed the *Harvey*, being pushed by the *Millie B*.

Jerry's heart sank. The *Millie B.* was her usual sparkling white, with the Kenny colors sharply painted on her stacks. She looked vigorous and strong. But instead of her usual bright mounds of black coal, she pushed the most dismaying wreck Jerry had ever seen on the river. The *Harvey* was mud brown. Her decks were slanting this way and that. The pilothouse roof was gone and the windows were broken out. The doors to the galley and engine room were torn off.

As she came closer to the dock, Jerry could see that the furnishings of the pilothouse and galley were piled up in a pathetic heap of wood, plastic, and twisted metal. A tv antenna poked through the rubble. The life rings hanging on the rails were mush and the johnboat in splinters. And these were only external injuries.

"She was stuck in ten feet o' mud," Smitty said. "You shoulda seen her before we cleaned her out some."

Smitty's encouraging words did nothing to lift Jerry's spirits. He felt as though he were stuck in ten feet of mud. His tug was ruined, his debts were growing, he had lost another friend and possibly his harbor to this blasted river.

Jerry watched as the *Millie's* deckhands readied the lines. One lad Jerry hadn't seen before stood on the bow of the *Harvey* and another newcomer was on the stern of the *Millie*. Dude was running here and there giving orders, his hair actually flying around his face, and Whitey, in his usual bikini, waved from the second deck. Jerry and Daryl stood by to catch the lines and help tie off the two boats.

"Hey Jerry!" Whitey yelled. "Hear you had another close call."

"Story o' my life!"

"We never thought we'd be havin' this conversation with you!" Dude said.

"You the guy that went down with this tug?" asked the deckhand pitching a line to Jerry.

"'Fraid so."

Jerry left Daryl and the new boys to finish the task of tying off, and jumped onto the lower deck of the *Millie*.

Whitey and Dude joined him, smiling happily at his being alive.

The three walked the deck to where the *Harvey* was attached, and looked her over.

"She may look a mite under the weather," Dude said. "But it won't take so much to put her back into commission."

Jerry raised an eyebrow and plunked his finger at a water-soaked life preserver.

"We'll help," Whitey said. "Me and Dude are about due for days off."

"Thanks," Jerry said. "'Preciate your offer." He was touched, but he wanted to be alone with his boat.

He climbed onto the *Harvey*, while Dude and Whitey tactfully stayed behind on the *Millie*. Walking along the mud-caked deck was like being caught in a terrible dream. A repeated dream of dashed hopes, endless work. The boat would have to be almost totally rebuilt. His right foot went through a rusted-out place on the metal deck.

Jerry peered into the engine room. The machinery was there, but would have to be pumped out and refitted and rebuilt. Nothing was left in the galley but the sink and a water pipe sticking out of the wall at a crazy angle. The stairway to the pilothouse was perilous, with missing steps and bent handrails. Jerry was breathless as he entered the small room of gouged-out windows rimmed by jagged glass. Here he had crashed through the glass, struggled to breathe, been thrown so close to death he could feel the old man's cold fingers. Jerry shuddered, returning to his waiting friends.

"See?" Whitey said when Jerry stepped onto the *Millie*. "It ain't as bad as it could be, is it, Jerry?"

"I guess nothing ever is," Jerry said, "by definition." He just couldn't feel the hope Whitey expressed.

"A little sanding, paint. A new roof. Fix up the engines," Dude added.

That sounded like a whole new boat to Jerry; even the hull was full of holes, but he tried to drum up a little gratitude for his survival, and arranged a smile for Whitey and Dude. Their offer to help was generous and it shouldn't be rewarded with a glum face and a lot of complaining. Good companions were worth a lot, and maybe his insurance, meager as it was, would help pay for some of the damage.

"Hey, we want you to come say hello to somebody," Dude said. "Come on in the galley." Jerry followed his old crewmates to the open door from which he could smell the odor of fresh baking. A dumpy woman in a muu-muu was bending over the oven, taking out a pan of some of the prettiest biscuits Jerry ever saw.

"Nettie," Jerry said. "What are you doin' here?"

"It's you?" Nettie put her pan on the stovetop and wiped her hands on her apron.

"Now do you believe he's alive?" Dude asked.

Nettie looked doubtful. She stepped back a bit, as though unconvinced of Jerry's reality.

"It's me," Jerry said. "Honest."

Nettie pushed a pan of biscuits onto a dish, and extended it as though making an offering to a ghost or greedy spirit. When Jerry took it, she said, "Well, you owe the Lord one, you sure do. Now sit down and eat some of these biscuits."

Jerry still wasn't sure if this was a test of his reality or a gift, but he sat down and let Nettie pour him some coffee while he slathered butter and jam on a biscuit.

Whitey and Dude joined Jerry at the table, and the two deckhands, having secured the *Harvey* to Jerry's float, tromped in looking for some reward for their brief labors. Jerry looked them over: a couple of farmboys from Kentucky. In a minute, Daryl came into the galley and joined the group.

Nettie continued pulling fresh biscuits out of the oven and piling them on platters. Her face was red with the effort.

"Nettie, come on and sit down," Jerry said. "How come you're on this boat anyhow? I thought you and Dave took off."

"We come back when we heard you was saved. After you went down, one night Dave and me heard the *Harvey* whistle signalin' arrival: two longs and a short. An' we knew you'd been saved. But we thought you was in Heaven sendin' us a signal...."

"Me in Heaven?" Jerry asked. "Now you know I'm not headin' that way, Nettie."

"God sees things in people they don't see. You got as good a chance as the next person even if you don't believe."

"I believe in you," Jerry said. "You called it right the day you said I'd be seein' my mama and daddy."

"I heard a Mayday signal, Jerry. Clear as could be."

One of the new deckhands, who identified himself as Byron, spoke up. "Some strange things happenin' on this river."

"Sure is," Whitey said. "We was missin' a deckhand one time, oh years ago. Figured he fell in and just got carried away so far downriver we never could find him. Then one day me and Dude was lookin' out across the water down around Golconda and we saw this something sticking up in the river way across the channel, couldn't figure what it was. Didn't look like no buoy nor was it driftwood, remember Dude?"

"I remember."

"Well, we got in the johnboat and rowed over to where we saw this thing, and there was a drowned man standin' straight up in about forty feet of water. We figured there wasn't no way a body could drown standin' up. Well we pulled him out of the water and found a cement block 'tached to his leg with a length of number-nine baling wire. That held him to the bottom, and his head was so swelled up with water it was out to here–" Whitey gestured with his arms, making a circle about three feet in circumference, "– and that kept the body floating straight up."

"Weirdest thing I ever seen," Dude said.

"It was the boy we lost."

"You have any idea who trussed him up like that?" Jerry asked.

"No sir," said Whitey, "and we don't to this day."

"I hope nothin' like that happened to the guy that disappeared from down at Summers' place," Byron said.

"What are you talkin' about?" Jerry asked. A bell rang in his mind, loud as the old school bells from childhood.

"One of the boys we used to work with, did odd jobs, not real bright, just up and disappeared."

"You work for Charlie Summers?" Jerry asked.

"Did some time back," Byron said. "This was some time ago that boy disappeared."

"I reckon Slag musta fell in like Captain Burnside did," said his buddy. "But he ain't likely to be comin' back after all this time, is he?"

"Slag?" Jerry asked. "That was your friend's name? He worked for Charlie?"

"Sure did." Both boys nodded.

"Big kid, real big head?"

"That's him. You could always tell which was his hat in the equipment room. It came down around my ears."

"Jesus God," Jerry said.

Everything fell into place. Charlie.

Jerry couldn't believe what he had heard.

"Whoa," Daryl said.

Jerry saw the truth reflected in Daryl's eyes.

Chapter 53

"Let's go get him," Daryl said.

Jerry shook his head.

"I have no proof, just suspicions."

"Good enough for me."

"This is all speculation. Slag is dead. We have no idea who the boys are that shot at me from Blennerhasset. Roscoe is missing. My story probably sounds like a jealous suitor trying to get rid of his rival. Charlie's told a lot of lies. But lies don't prove a man guilty of attempted murder."

"Yeah, but we know he is."

"I'm goin' over to see Mrs. Kenny," Jerry said. Kay would be a good judge. She'd tell him if he was being overly suspicious for his own reasons. First he wanted Richard to be guilty, now he was sure it was Charlie.

"That can't be," Kay said.

She looked sick when Jerry told her what he believed.

"I just can't see it. Charlie's lied and I hate him for it. But to deliberately try to kill his best friend...."

"I agree, he's not a killer. Face to face, he couldn't take a gun and shoot me. But I could see him letting an accident happen. With all he's done, all the shit he's in, I do believe he's capable of it."

"But why? Why would he do all this?"

"You said it was somebody wanting the barge line – trying to make you feel incompetent."

"How could he get the barge line?"

"He wanted you too."

Kay's face sagged. She sat down wearily.

"So what are you going to do now?"

"Go see him. See what he says when I tell him I know he had Slag on his payroll."

"If he really tried to kill you – should you take a chance like that?"

"I have to."

Jerry borrowed Kay's phone and called Charlie's number. No answer.

"I'm goin' back to the harbor. I'll keep trying to find him."

"I just can't believe all this."

"I know. This whole thing is tearing me up, Kay. Bad."

Jerry went back to Burnside Harbor, and immediately tried Charlie's number again.

"Why don't you just turn him in?" Daryl said.

"We hold a man innocent till he's proven guilty."

"I don't."

After several more tries, Jerry put Smitty in charge of phoning Charlie.

Daryl looked disappointed. There would be no showdown at the OK Harbor.

"I'm outa here," he said.

Jerry looked at his watch. The day was over for his deckie and co-pilot. Jerry walked Daryl down to the lower deck, and waved him off. Then he picked up a bucket, and lovingly began washing the *Harvey*'s face. He cleaned off enough mud from her bulkhead so that the name could be seen.

What Jerry really needed to do was to examine the boat and make a list of where to begin repairs and to estimate the costs, but his mind was on the telephone and Charlie.

He put down his bucket and climbed back up to the office. He was very depressed.

"No answer," Smitty said.

Maybe Charlie was down on the boat. "Ring up the terminal for me, will you?" he asked Smitty. "See if you can get in touch with the *Plattner*."

Jerry tried Charlie's harbor downriver. No answer.

He was dead tired. He called Kay.

"If he contacts you, call me right away. Don't be alone with him anywhere."

"Jerry, really."

"I know it seems weird. But wounded things are dangerous."

Chapter 54

Charlie could hear the phone ringing up in the pilothouse, but he ignored it. He felt his head where the bullet hit. The wound still sometimes throbbed, especially when he tried to sleep. That night on the boat, Nettie had told him and Dave something was about to happen. How did she know?

The spooky feeling got worse after the divers went home. He could swear he could see Jerry's face in the water over the *Harvey*. But there was no way on earth he could be there, he thought; Jerry's body would be miles downriver, bloating up on its own waste. It would probably never be found. What if it were, though, and he had to identify it? Look into the empty eye sockets that the river sucked clean?

Raising Jerry's boat took forever. The *Harvey* was so bogged down with mud, it was hard to get her to the surface. Charlie didn't want the job, it spooked him bad, but Kay had insisted; she wouldn't let anyone else touch the boat. Every time some part of the *Harvey* had popped to the surface, Charlie jumped.

And then Jerry turns up. Like a miracle.

Could he have actually wanted it any different? Could he have wished his old friend dead?

The river was sparkling with the last few rays of sun. This same river where he and Jerry played as kids. They had some really good times. The day they discovered a hidden beach and spent the whole afternoon pretending to be castaways. The time they found a tree full of ripe pears on the bank and climbed into the branches and ate the sweet pears until they couldn't hold any more. The afternoon they ate the top crust of George's mulberry pie. Camping on the shore in a pup tent and fishing at dawn.

Jerry was his best friend, probably his only friend. When you grow up you don't make friends like that. It's all competition: kill, kill, kill. Get them before they get you.

Nettie had tried to warn them. God the woman was scary, talking about seeing that boy on the tow. Charlie had never believed in spirits, but he sometimes wondered – could some murdered person in some way come back? There were so many stories. Probably the "ghosts" were seen by people with vivid imaginations because so much talk about them kept them real.

"Hi."

Charlie jumped and turned at the sound of a voice right behind him. It came from the *Plattner*'s captain. Roscoe's puffy cheeks and babyish mouth were right in Charlie's face. He could smell Roscoe's Sen-Sen.

"Jesus, you scared me," Charlie said. "Where the hell have you been? Everybody's been lookin' for you."

"I needed to think."

Roscoe tugged at his shirt collar and tried to light a cigarette, but his hands were shaking so badly, he finally pitched the match and cigarette into the river.

"I musta blacked out," he said. "What'll the Coast Guard do?"

"I don't know."

"I just can't figure it. I can't remember a damn thing."

"You were pretty wasted."

"I'll lose my license. And they could charge me with manslaughter I guess."

"Or murder. People are sayin' it wasn't an accident. That Richard guy is on your case."

"Why would I want to hurt Jerry Burnside?"

"You tell me."

Roscoe's features drew together in an ugly frown.

"That's nuts. Nobody could pin anything like that on me."

The shadow of the barge crane had darkened and fell across Roscoe's face. Charlie's heart pumped madly. He stepped around Roscoe and pretended to check a line.

"Gotta get these wires tightened up," he said. "Crew's all up the hill."

"Listen–"

"You better turn yourself in, Roscoe."

"You were with me that night. You'll have a lot of explaining to do."

"I don't think so."

Chapter 55

Kay was getting out of the shower when she heard Charlie's knock at her door.

She knew it was he. She recognized the peremptory rap, and this was about the time of night he usually visited her. She pulled on a jogging suit, and went into the living room and stood in the middle of the room, pondering what to do. The moon peered in at the window like a voyeur.

"Kay, I know you're there," Charlie called, "the super said you were. Let me in."

She could hear him breathing.

"Come on."

"Have you seen Jerry?" Kay asked.

"No, why?"

Should she believe him? Kay looked at her watch.

"Kay–" He sounded like himself, not someone who's been accused of murder. But he would know by now that Jerry had told her about Wendall. And that she knew he, Charlie, had kept the truth from her.

She wondered how he would act, now that she knew he'd betrayed her.

"Kay, I need you."

He wanted to go to bed, of course.

She wondered what it would it be like to make love with a man so angry, a man who might kill for her.

The lies Charlie had told could never be forgiven. Never. But she had known Charlie since she was three. He was not the terrible boy that the *River Queen* crew made him out to be. They were all too hard on him. She needed to see his face.

Kay went to the door and opened it, holding the chain in place. Charlie's face was enormous in the opening, like the moon.

"Let me in," Charlie said. "What's wrong?"

"Nothing."

Kay didn't want to make Charlie any more suspicious than he already was.

"Please, Kay."

"Wait."

Kay played with the door chain. Hate and desire made her blood sing.

She slid the chain off the hook. She would soon know if Charlie was a killer.

Chapter 56

Nightmares of sinking boats and women's hair covered in mud gave Jerry little rest. He awoke tired and groggy, wanting to run away, as he had after the *River Queen* went down. He had to do something. But what? He couldn't go to the cops with his not-very-foolproof story. He had to get hold of Charlie, force the truth out of him. He tried to reach him at the *Plattner* again. No luck. He thought a minute. Picked up the phone again. When the connection was made, he said, "Denver, let me speak to your grandmother."

The wait seemed interminable while Denver went to get Mrs. Summers to the phone. Jerry could hear his uncontrolled, scratchy voice saying, "Grandmaw, it's that Mr. Burnside, my father's old friend. Well come <u>on</u>. You don't need your glasses and shoes just to answer the telephone."

"You told Charlie what I told you, didn't you?" Mrs. Summers said almost as soon as Jerry identified himself.

"Yes, I did," Jerry admitted, "and I'm worried about him. He just up and disappeared. I need to talk to him."

"Try the harbor."

"I did. I got no answer. He's not there."

"Oh, he's there all right," Mrs. Summers said. "Been there most of the night. Harbor's all shut down. Nothin' goin' on. He's hidin' down there."

"Hiding?"

"That's what I said."

When Jerry hung up, he turned to Smitty and Daryl.

"I'm goin' down Paducah way, to Charlie's. He's down there."

"Great!" Daryl rummaged in his jacket, and pulled out a shiny, well-oiled Saturday Night Special. "Take my little buddy here along."

Jerry hated the sight of guns. He pushed it away.

"Be careful with that damned thing."

"Ain't loaded."

"My father always said there were more people killed with unloaded guns than loaded ones."

Daryl went to the door and pointed the pistol toward the river. "See?"

He pulled the trigger and an explosion echoed across the water.

"For Jesus' sake," Smitty said. He held his ears.

"I rest my case," Jerry said.

Daryl squeezed the trigger again. Click.

"It was virtually unloaded," he said. "That was the last one." He opened his locker and took out a box of bullets, and dropped six of them into the gun's chamber.

"You keep your little buddy. I'm just going down to talk to Charlie."

"Gosh, Jerry," Daryl said. "You remind me of that guy in the movies. Mel Gibson played him."

"Road Runner?"

"That guy had to kill his uncle and he couldn't seem to make up his mind and go for it."

"You mean Hamlet?"

"That's it. I only sat through about half of it."

"He didn't have no balls," Smitty said.

Jerry sighed. There was a time when he would actually have agreed with these two.

"This is not a matter of balls," Jerry said. "If you want balls, go to the State Fair and look at the sheep. They got balls the size of Indiana melons and they're the world's dumbest creatures."

Daryl looked stricken and Smitty seemed to be trying to think.

"Just do what I tell you," Jerry said. "Smitty, keep the phone clear. Daryl, you start scrubbing the decks on the *Harvey*."

"You better take me with you, Jerry. You're gonna need somebody with a hair-trigger temper. This guy tried to kill you and he might find this the golden opportunity to do it again." When he saw Jerry wasn't going to change his mind, Daryl said, "At least take this." He offered the gun again.

"Charlie won't commit cold-blooded murder face to face." He'll let the controls slip and hope he can't avoid plowing me under, but...."

Daryl looked disappointedly at the gun and returned it to his jacket pocket.

"Don't you want to take the bullets out?" Jerry asked.

"I will," Daryl said. "I'm gonna shoot a few tin cans before I start moppin' up that mess we're still callin' a boat."

He trudged out of the office and toward the *Harvey* recalcitrantly, muttering, "I never made no truck with fish that feeds on the bottom."

Chapter 57

Charlie looked out over his harbor, a big sprawling operation with several tugs, work barges and dredging machinery. A tall, spider-legged gantry reared up into the sky. His harbor tug, the *Jenny,* was named after his wife – years ago when he still pretended he loved her. Be funny if she had pulled him under, trying to get Jerry's tug off the river bottom. He almost wished she had.

Business was down. The equipment was just sitting idle, as though waiting – like he was, for something to happen. He saw a pickup truck pull up to the office on the bank. He took his time in approaching it. He knew who it was.

Two men sat in the cab. The older one, about forty, was deeply tanned, with white gullies along his one or two etched-in lines. The other man had an eye like a fertilized egg.

"What do you want?"

"We're runnin' low on cash," Donny said.

"Learn how to save."

The older man, whom Charlie knew as Kennis, said, "You never paid us for our trip to McAlpine lock."

"You almost killed me. Can't you shoot straight?"

"How was we to know you was at the controls? You said that other guy would be there."

"You almost got Jerry Burnside, too, at Blennerhasset. I didn't hire you to be hit men. "

"You said come close."

"My shack had to be tore down and I had to shoot the dogs," Donny whined.

"Wait here." Charlie went into the office and took two hundred dollars out of the safe and put it in an envelope. He took it back to the truck and handed it to Kennis.

"Don't ever come around here again," Charlie said. "This is the last I want to see you."

Kennis rifled through the envelope.

"Two hundred bucks? That won't cover my boat."

"You tryin' to hold me up?"

"Good bitin' dogs cost money," Donny said.

"We could tell the cops what you're up to."

"Sure – they'll love hearing from guys that took the shots at those towboat pilots."

Donny looked puzzled. Kennis put the money in his shirt pocket.

"Can we fill up our tank?"

Charlie nodded at the gas pump. He slapped the door of the truck.

"Take it easy. And don't let me see you again. Ever."

Charlie talked tough, but he knew he had not seen the last of these two creeps. The thought made him feel tired.

Donny held the gas pump a long while, letting the gas flow over the truck's fender.

God, they must have been running on pure air, Charlie thought. Don't they ever think ahead?

Kennis clapped the lid on his tank and grinned and he and Donny started off. They waved good-bye.

"Have a good one," Donny called.

Chapter 58

Daryl felt more and more frustrated after Jerry left for Charlie's place. He went down to the river near his home with his little buddy, and shot a few rounds. He was rusty. Aimed at a dead log and missed. He set up a few tin cans and popped a couple. He couldn't concentrate. Kept worrying about Jerry. Then he noticed a willow branch bending to the water, snagged on something.

Something good-sized in the water. Daryl waded over to the bent branch, and looked down. Oh my God, Roscoe's face was staring back at him – what was left of it. Daryl pulled the branch that held Roscoe's body away from his shirt. The skull was bashed up pretty good. Couldn't be accidental: too deep. So Roscoe had not run away to Alaska or any place else. He had not killed himself. This was murder. The head wounds proved it.

Daryl tried to tug the body to the bank, but there was a strong eddy and the branches of the trees got in the way. Damn! He lost his footing in the soft mud, the river out-tugged him, and Roscoe's body went out into the channel and down under the surface. Daryl struggled to a grassy place on the bank.

Jerry said Charlie wouldn't kill in cold blood. But what was this? He had done a real number on Roscoe's skull. And now – soon – Jerry would be facing Charlie with nothing to protect himself. Daryl rushed to a phone to call Smitty, and then he called Kay.

"Oh God," she said. "Oh God."

Chapter 59

Charlie pointed a small handgun out the window of the *Jenny's* pilothouse, practicing his aim. He tilted back in his chair. There were two bullets in the gun, one for Jerry and one for himself.

Why couldn't Jerry leave things alone? After the *River Queen* blew, everybody wanted to forget all about it. That was that. He and his father started their business and got big and successful. Kay was to crown it: his beautiful golden girl. Then she turned him down. He felt like nothing. Years of a hateful marriage. His son a disappointment. A disgraceful sissy or moron or whatever. He worked like a dog – dragging up old rusty wrecks and factory waste, with only his father as an anchor. The old man was tough, not a big talker, not one to take you fishing or baby you along. Demanded a full day's work from everybody, including, especially, his own son. But that was OK. He was the same way himself. Then his father's death, the fire, which he knew Denver set, and the old witch and the boy plotting to destroy him. He could not let them win.

Once again, Kay comes along. More gorgeous than ever and as independent as ever. He could not ask her again – get turned down. He would make her come to him. He'd show her she was not cut out to run a boat line. But he <u>was</u>, and once he got her good and scared, she'd be right in position to take. But every calculation went wrong. He had no luck. No luck at all. No one was supposed to be really hurt, until Jerry got in the way. Forced him to run him down. And that led to Roscoe. He would never have killed Roscoe, but he had to, and now he had killed someone. And Jerry knew. Jerry was getting bigger and bigger, while he was getting small. His father had said to stay away from them; Jerry was trouble and Kay was a slut and a whore like her mother. What could he do?

Charlie laid the gun on the console and poured himself a cup of coffee. He looked at his watch. Jerry would be along soon, and he would be able to see him coming a mile away through the big pilothouse window.

Chapter 60

Jerry marveled at Charlie Summers' Harbor; it would hold five of his operations. There was a well-built one floor office building, strictly functional and modern, and a truck ramp going down to the waterfront where several work barges and assorted craft were anchored. A large empty barge reared up out of the water, riding with its hull high above those loaded down with dredging cranes, winches and all the rusty, oily, machinery and junk of a river business. On the riverward side of all this were a hangar for welding and boat repair, and two harbor tugs. Jerry looked in the window of the office building. The fluorescent lights were on, but no one was stirring. He tried the door; it was locked.

He's not gonna come running out to meet me, Jerry thought.

He noticed a Volkswagen that didn't look like Charlie, and a truck parked just beyond it.

Jerry shielded his eyes and looked over the acreage of boats and buildings, of rust and blinding metal and water reflecting the wavy patterns of sun on tin. He walked down the ramp and onto a work barge, poked his head into the hangar.

"Charlie?" His voice echoed among the empty barrels, the stored canvas, line and paint, an old boat hull turned upside down for repair. A welder's torch, cruel and capable of ruining eyes and hands, lay on the boat hull, the vest and helmet beside it like medieval armor. This was one of those "meet me at the old warehouse at midnight" situations so popular in movies – which Jerry had always scoffed at. Still he entered the large dark chamber.

Click.

Jerry stood still. He was halfway through the hangar. He listened carefully. The sound was that of a gun being cocked, he was sure of it. He had been so sure Charlie would not hurt him. He looked right and left, behind him and to where he had been; he saw nothing. He continued on quickly. When he reached the outdoors and the sunlight, he breathed a little more freely.

The sound must have been the creaking and cracking of old wood, of water and sun-stressed metal.

Jerry looked over at the big tug, the *Jenny*.

Someone appeared to be in the pilothouse, but the backlighting was so extreme, it was hard to tell.

Jerry called Charlie's name, but the pilothouse was high above the float, and the engine of a downbound tow was making so much noise, it drowned him out.

Jerry climbed the ladder to the second deck. There he looked up, saw something and called Charlie's name again. He crept warily up the steps to the bridge and over to the pilothouse. It was abnormally quiet, as though someone were waiting for him. He slid over to the window. Charlie was in the pilot's chair. Jerry jumped.

"Charlie!"

His old friend didn't answer or even look at him. He was focusing straight ahead, looking downriver as though piloting through a dangerous stretch of water. Jerry pulled open the door.

"Charlie?"

Jerry ran to him. Charlie had a bullet hole in the side of his forehead.

Jerry seized Charlie's wrist and felt his neck. He was still warm, but there was no pulse. Gone. Jerry looked around. Charlie's wound was matched by a hole in the window on the landward side of the pilothouse. Was Charlie not behind the shootings after all? Someone was still out there. Jerry choked on his horrible mistake.

He ran toward the inside steps. He was a sitting duck for whoever shot Charlie. He needed to get off this boat.

Jerry crept toward a window in the galley and cautiously peered out. Crack! A gunshot rang out and he dodged, but it was not coming in his direction. He heard a ricochet sound on the water and the anguished yell of a familiar voice.

"Jerry!" It was Daryl. Jerry ran out on deck, forgetting about his own safety. He could see his deckhand on the work barge, limping out of the hangar.

He was holding one leg with his hand and gesticulating madly toward the crane barge. A man was running toward the gantry.

"He shot me!" Daryl yelled. "Got me in the thigh. Over there!"

Jerry sped onto the barge and chased the man to the gantry, a four-story set of stilts with a long boom delicately balanced at the top.

"I slowed him down a little," Daryl called.

Jerry caught up with the shooter, who was desperately trying to get the cab started to scale the thing high above the water.

He was almost in the door when the cab began to move. He was expecting the shooter to be Donny or the other half of the Blennerhasset two. But on a closer look he recognized the unkempt black hair and deeply-lined face. Mr.

Huff pushed at Jerry with his foot, and the cab started up the steep gantry with Jerry hanging from its door. Jerry hated heights.

"Get away!" Harlan Huff said. He tried to close the door on Jerry, but Jerry crawled into the cab and tried to tackle him. The little man raised his gun threateningly. He pushed Jerry toward the opening and Jerry caught a dizzying glimpse of the metal stilts going by. He reached for one, but didn't connect. He was back on the floor of the cab, wrapping himself around Huff's legs.

"Listen to me. Stop this thing!"

"I ain't goin' to no jail," Huff yelled. He was obviously planning to shoot it out with the police from the high ground. The cab kept going up and up, with Jerry pleading and Huff getting more desperate. They were at the top of the gantry now, a structure that could easily tip over – the whole thing held together in an uneasy balance. Only the best and most intrepid operators were allowed up here. It was worse than a harbor tug.

"Gimme the gun, Mr. Huff," Jerry said. "Stop fighting, you're gonna tip this thing over. Whoa-a-a."

The cab swayed sickeningly. The boom out over the water dipped like a giant toy duck.

Jerry lunged for Huff's gun, but Huff pulled away. Jerry scrambled for the controls. Again, as Huff tried to prevent him, the whole structure threatened to go over. Jerry edged toward the door, to start climbing down, hoping Huff wouldn't shoot him in the back of the head. Huff reached out to grab Jerry back, and the gun in his hand slid out through the door. The two men watched it fall, hitting the struts of the gantry's legs as it careened barrel over stock into the river. Huff was transfixed long enough for Jerry to climb onto the top strut. Huff reached for him and slipped. For a moment, the little man was falling freely.

Jerry reached out and grabbed Huff, who clung to Jerry's legs until he could get his own grip on the steel girders. The two men swung on the swaying stilts for the longest moment of Jerry's life. Jerry reached repeatedly for the cab cable that was jumping up and down from the stress they'd put on it. Finally, he made contact and caught hold of the rubbery cable. Together the two men slid, Tarzan-style, down its slippery length. They hit the barge with a crash and lay on the deck in a heap, stunned, entwined for a moment like lovers.

But there was no time to even think about how close they had come to dying in each other's arms. Harlan Huff was up and on his feet faster than

Jerry, and he darted among the equipment like a rabbit.

Daryl let out a yell, grabbed a line. He waved it above his head and it went flying slowly, like slow motion, above their heads. Jerry, watching in hope and despair, thought it would never land. A nice stationary timberhead was one thing, a moving target was another. Huff was still running toward the hangar, like a man doing an obstacle course. Until he fell – Daryl's line pulling him tight to the deck of the barge.

Jerry was there now, holding him down until he stopped struggling.

Daryl came limping over. He had his gun pointed at Huff.

"Pretty throw, Daryl," Jerry said. "But who invited you on this outing? How'd you get here?"

"Flew. Pal o' mine has a Cessna – 172. Who is this guy?"

"Mr. Huff, the man I told you about, saved me and Smitty from that nut with the dogs down in Gar's Hole."

Jerry nodded at Daryl's gun. "Put that stupid thing away, and help me tie this guy up." Jerry could see that Daryl's wound was not fatal, and that he was able to walk. "I'm gonna go and call the police."

He looked down at Harlan Huff. Daryl was pulling the man's hands behind him, and working with the rope.

"How'd you know about Charlie?" Jerry asked.

"Bobby Bolton told me," Mr. Huff said.

"Oops, I guess I passed the news to old Bobby the night we found out Slag worked for Charlie," Daryl said.

"Wow." Jerry sat down and lit a cigarette. He offered a puff to the tied-up man.

"Why'd you do this?"

Huff turned away from the offered smoke.

"Tell me," Jerry said. "I was fixin' to kill Summers myself. He tried to kill me."

Huff spoke then, through clenched teeth, still seething with anger.

"He got my boy into trouble and got him dead."

Jerry felt deeply sorry for the man, in spite of the fact that he had almost gotten the two of them killed. Not to mention killing Charlie and wounding Daryl. Still, the feelings of a father for his son sometimes swayed juries.

"You might get off light," Jerry said. "Jury might understand."

"I didn't do this thinkin' o' light or not light." Huff's deep-set eyes snapped, his Abe Lincoln craggy chin stuck out defiantly. "Anyway, I took care of the two other guys he hired, too. They got Slag into this."

Three of them. Huff was right, that didn't add up to light.

"Why didn't you just come and tell the cops, or get in touch with me?" Jerry asked.

"I told you if I found out who got my boy into this I'd take care of 'em, and I did. He hadn't ought to of coaxed no half-witted kid into shooting people."

Jerry threw his cigarette into the water, and looked up at the pilothouse where Charlie sat silently staring at the river he had spent his life on.

Huff asked Jerry for a cigarette now, and looked concerned about Daryl's wound.

"You ain't hurt bad," he said. "I was just aimin' to slow you down some. If I'd a meant to kill you, you'd be makin' explanations up yonder."

"God," Jerry said. "I'm going up to the pilothouse. I'll call the police and Charlie's mother and Smitty. Daryl, you watch Mr. Huff."

Back in the pilothouse, Jerry made his calls. He gazed at Charlie's body in the pilot's chair. They were together again: Jerry and Charlie, waiting for the police to arrive.

"Remember when we got in trouble with George for eating all the lattice work off his mulberry pie?" Jerry said. "He said he'd call the cops on us."

Charlie had slumped a little, but still wore his captain's hat. His grip on the pistol was hardening.

"George said we'd end up in prison, all three of us."

We had so much fun, Jerry thought. But maybe there was always one who's not having any fun.

Jerry touched his old friend's face. It was cold as dough. The coffee cup he had been drinking from lay in his lap, and the spilled coffee was staining his jeans. Jerry took the cup and placed it on the console.

Soon he heard the police cars on the hill, and then after a while footsteps on the stairs. They were running.

"I thought the excitement was over," Jerry said.

A young policewoman and her partner came into the pilothouse.

"Shooter got away," the woman said. "Wow." She had caught sight of Charlie. She joined her partner, looking the dead man over.

"That deckhand on the barge says you were up here when the sniper shot him in the leg. He couldn't identify him. Did you see the man? Could you describe him?"

"He –" Jerry stopped himself. "Not from this distance." He couldn't call Daryl a liar. And he owed Mr. Huff – for Slag's death, which he would never forget – and for Mr. Huff saving him from Donny.

While the police and coroner did their work, Jerry walked out on the deck. The sun was sliding down toward the water, coloring it rose.

Daryl came up behind him.

"Did I do right?"

Jerry sighed. He didn't believe in vigilante justice. And he would probably have a guilty conscience the rest of his life.

"Charlie killed Roscoe," Daryl said. "I found his body with a hole in his head big as a soup plate."

What was done was done, Jerry thought. He had become part of the river's most ancient code.

"You never could tie a decent knot, Daryl." Jerry did not turn around to look when the coroner took Charlie's body down the pilothouse steps. He and his deckhand stayed at the rail and watched the sun dissolve. This was the moment the hero and the girl kiss and look into the sunset and dream of a new day. But the girl was not here. Just Daryl. And Jerry felt little relief at the end of the summer's terror and the long mysteries of past and present. Only a deep deep sadness.

Chapter 61

Jerry held the hose steady on the *Harvey*'s deck. The force of the water biting into the mud on the hollow metal made a familiar sound. A binding sound, linking the years of his life. But he refused its comfort.

When Jerry and Daryl had cleaned up most of the mud, Jerry got out a hammer, pliers, rivets, and a large sheet of steel which the two men fashioned into a new roof for the *Harvey*'s pilothouse.

Whitey and Dude joined them to help with the work. The whole crew lifted the roof into place and secured it. Then they began straightening the rails and replacing the broken window glass.

The trees across the river and up on the hill were all colors. A few were beginning to shed, and yellow leaves had blown onto Smitty's geranium. It had gotten spindly, and Smitty stopped watering it.

"The days are gettin' short," he reminded Jerry.

"Tell me about it."

Jerry felt his thinning hair.

Work on the *Harvey* went on. The buckling paint came off like sunburned skin. At first easily in sheets, and then stuck tight. The men could almost feel pain as they scraped and burned it off the metal. When the bulkheads and decks were in shape, the group began to paint.

The clean white paint looked and smelled like hope. But Jerry ignored it as he did the glowing reds and oranges of the trees on the hills across the water – signs of fall he usually enjoyed. This year the blazing beauty of the horizon was just an unwelcome portent of winter, with obvious symbolism for a near-fifty year old man.

Neither the sounds nor the sights of the river, none of the things he was usually so alive to, could help him forget Charlie sitting there dead in his pilothouse, Charlie trying to kill him. With Charlie's death everything had fallen apart.

The police officers on the scene had questioned Jerry and Daryl. Did Charlie have any enemies? No. What were they doing there that day? Charlie was Jerry's best friend. Could they think of anyone who would kill Mr. Summers? No, only the mysterious shooter who had been terrorizing pilots all summer. Were they sure they did not recognize the man who shot at Daryl? Positive.

A terrible silence had developed between Jerry and the people he cared about most. He could not say anymore than what he and Daryl had already said. He and Daryl even avoided talking to Smitty, who felt betrayed and left out.

Daryl and Jerry had kept their mouths shut even with each other, as though Burnside Harbor were bugged. The only words they exchanged were these:

"What did you do with your little buddy, Daryl?"

"River."

And again, at another time, Daryl said, "Jerry, I told you you shoulda had a gun."

And Jerry replied, "No, he shouldn't have."

Jerry could not tell Kay the truth; the police had harassed her enough with questions, and he did not want to put her in the position of having to lie for him and Daryl or get them in trouble.

"It had to be one of the men Charlie hired to shoot at the boats," Jerry told her. "He'll be so far back in the hills by now he'll never be found."

Kay clearly did not believe him.

Jerry had the eery feeling she might suspect him. She knew his hatred of guns, but he'd been known to use one on a dying dog or a deer with its guts on the highway. And in defending himself, as with Beany Fuller, she had seen he could be relentless. But she did not press him further, just walked him firmly to the door of her apartment.

"I hate this river," Kay said. "It's so full of lies, you can hear it in the water, on the radio and on the boats, everywhere there are lying voices."

Was she talking about his lies or the stories about her and Charlie that were making the rounds, stories that kept him awake at night? Was what he kept hearing true? The gossip was made more lurid with every telling – that Charlie bragged about sleeping with Kay, making Kay a subject of jokes like her mother. The beautiful woman who stood for the most enchanted years of his life. Gossip had a way of being true. Was she sleeping with Charlie all along or while he was under the water struggling for breath, or risking his life in Gar's Hole?

After their talk, Kay barricaded herself in her apartment and refused to see anyone.

Charlie was buried in the unkempt cemetery in the small town where he'd lived. The ragged dogwoods were turning red and the river flowed just beyond the tombstones. The names on many of the stones were smudged from time and floods. Tall grasses grew around the grave of Charlie's father, and a length of wrought-iron fencing lurched near the newly-dug earth that would receive his son.

A few river people, Charlie's secretary and second pilot, Nettie and Dave, Dude and Whitey, Smitty, and Daryl, whose scar was pulsing red, stood awkwardly beside the open grave. Tom and Cliff stood together under a weather-beaten tree; Tom raised his two-fingered hand and Cliff nodded.

Kay arrived with Richard in her Jaguar. Denver brought his grandmother in her wheelchair. He grinned compulsively throughout the service. Jerry repressed his tears as the clergyman read the twenty-third psalm from a blue Bible covered in plastic.

Jerry watched Kay as the coffin was consecrated with a handful of dirt. Her face was a mask. His fists in his pockets clenched. His teeth ached from gritting. Still, he could not let her slip away again.

When the service ended, Jerry approached Kay where she stood on the other side of the open plot. She sent Richard on to the car, and the others walked away. He took her by the arm.

"Don't," she said.

"Talk to me, Kay."

Her eyes were like the winter river.

"Did you shoot Charlie?" she demanded.

"Did you sleep with him?"

Kay turned on her heel, and stalked away.

Jerry struggled to breathe, to absorb the blow of what he and Kay had just done to each other.

Kay continued to her car without looking back, leaving Jerry standing in the long grass by Charlie's grave. He watched as she was helped into it by Richard.

Her car pulled away.

The gravediggers began shoveling dirt on the casket. Jerry turned to the river. It was the color of ashes.

Charlie had won at last.

Chapter 62

The next weeks were hollow and empty, like the hull of the old work boat being beaten by the autumn water and giving off a mournful "thunk." Jerry tried to keep busy. When the *Harvey* was on her way back to health he drove down to the Johnsons' to help Matthew cut wood for winter. The roof of the log house was covered with brown and red leaves, and smoke curled out of the chimney.

Matthew and Louisa welcomed Jerry and made him comfortable by the fire.

"We thought maybe you'd bring your friend," Louisa said. She offered him, as usual, a cup of herb tea, this time with a stick of cinnamon in it.

"Oh, yeah. The lady went back to Council Bluffs." Jerry had heard Kay had taken over the other Kenny interests, while Richard was now running the barge line. Jerry knew he'd been made a partner, but whether the partnership was personal as well, he hadn't heard. Jerry told them about Charlie being shot in his own pilothouse. By an unknown assailant. The Johnsons didn't believe him either.

Before Jerry left River Hollow, Matthew offered him the painting of the *River Queen* he had promised him. But Jerry asked Matthew to hang on to it a little longer.

He had given up working on his model of the *River Queen*. It was proof that he was the "day-dreamin'est" guy on the river – just like Joe Slack had said.

When Jerry and Matthew had piled up a good stash of wood, Jerry left the Johnsons' and went across the river to see Mac. In telling of Charlie's death, Jerry stayed with his story of being in the pilothouse while Daryl made a futile attempt to catch the shooter. He told Mac about Mrs. Summers having proof of Wendall's guilt in the *River Queen* fire. Mac looked annoyed. Of course, there was proof. Of course he was right. He had never been wrong on a single call in his life, except maybe the time he got the ferret on board the *River Queen* to clean out the rats. "I was going on good authority in employing that animal," he claimed. "It was recommended by the purser on the *Liberty Belle*, a man of vast experience and unique knowledge of his profession."

Jerry explained about Wendall's part ownership of the *River Queen* and how the insurance money was his motive for blowing up the boat.

"Well, don't underestimate the power of passion," Mac said. "True, Joe wasn't on the boat. But the fires that boiled up in Wendall Summers weren't rational. Linda Slack was a mighty attractive woman. Mighty attractive. She could get men dreaming about her at night."

Runs in the family, Jerry thought. And after all, what was the cause of Wendlall's greed? The small ember that started the whole conflagration? Could be Linda, or the Summers' love of gold or some other tiny spark long thought to be burned out.

Life was one complicated dude.

At the prescribed time, Mac took out his watch. Time for his walk. He and Jerry said good-bye to Loraine, and started out for the daily stroll to the drug store and the river. Jerry hoped Mac wouldn't go whacking away at the trees; they were going to put him away if he acted crazy. To his relief, Mac just stared at the water, and read off the name of a passing tow.

"Omar N.," he said. "United Freight Line. The old Omar operated a Pittsburgh-Cincinnati packet route, 1901-1951."

At dinner, Jerry proposed taking Mac up to Marietta and finding him a room there, where he could spend time with the other river veterans. Mac's minute knowledge of the packet days would be valued by the steamboat buffs. But Mac refused.

"They turned me out," he said. "Just turned me out."

Jerry, Mr. Fixit, Mr. Mary Worth, had to admit that some things just can't be fixed. Anymore than an old steamboat could be put together again.

Everything was moving on. Even the towboats. The *Plattner* had been sold. Jerry was surprised one day when he saw her going downriver lashed to a Midwest America tow. He took Daryl and the *Harvey* over to her and jumped onto the boat. A lone deckhand was in charge.

"She junked or something?" Jerry asked.

"Naw," the kid replied. "She's goin' to China. Be towin' on the Yangste River."

He took Jerry into the galley. In place of the ovens where Nettie baked biscuits were two giant woks.

Jerry often dreamed of being pulled under the *Plattner* and popping back up to the surface of the water like a fish jumping into the air. He would awaken sweating and trembling, still wondering what had happened to the days he lost and couldn't recover. Someone had pulled him out of the river and deposited him at the Johnsons' landing – but why had they left without a word? He figured it was one of the mussel gatherers who didn't want to be noticed by the wildlife rangers. Or it could have been a fisherman wary of the Coast Guard.

Jerry could not get Charlie out of his mind. How could he have gone so wrong, done such desperate things? Dreamed up such a crazy scheme? Then one day the mail brought a manila envelope. Inside was a newspaper clipping about a rash of mysterious shootings that took place on the Missouri River some time before any of Kay's people were targeted. Nothing had been discovered as to who was responsible or why. The date, in Charlie's handwriting, was scribbled in the margin. Perhaps this unsolved crime spree gave Charlie the idea to go after Kay and try to make the shootings look random. Such things could happen. Bullets from nowhere. Look at Daryl shooting that crazy pistol out into the water, not having the slightest idea that there was a bullet in it, nor who or what might be in its path.

A second item in the envelope was a worksheet from Charlie's business, with Slag's name listed as an employee. The envelope had no return address, but was post-marked Paducah – no doubt Denver's idea of an anonymous letter.

On the river Charlie's story was passing into legend. Daryl knew part. Jerry, Mac, Kay, Denver, Smitty, they would each eventually tell enough to someone that it would become part of the river's lore: the year the mysterious shooter killed Charlie Summers. Was it a serial killer? Or was it his crazy son, a kind of male Lizzy Borden? Or was it someone who had a money-grudge against Charlie?

Charlie's size and importance would grow like the giant catfish that no one could prove real or unreal – or like Jerry's love for Kay that seemed, no matter how hard he tried to forget it, to grow larger.

Jerry tried not to think about Kay. They'd blown it again. They'd always blow it.

One sunny November day, he decided to take off in a small boat and keep going until he got tired of the scenery and his own company. He stopped at the Devonian fossil beds just down river from Louisville, walking out on the layers of stone embedded with plants and creatures 400 million years old. A sign warned visitors not to go out on the beds, but no one paid any attention to it. If water from the river, which was let out of the dam occasionally and covered the beds, was about to flood them, a siren would warn sightseers. Jerry wondered how much time a person would get. Studying the ancient rock, he tried to put his own feelings into perspective; these fossils were 400 million years old. This should mean something. But Jerry only thought, so what? Next year they'd be 400 million and one.

The river at night between Kentucky and Indiana is the blackest place in the world. When Jerry tied off the boat, the hills on both sides of the water were like ebony velvet.

He remembered the river when Kay and he sat waiting for dinner at the little restaurant in Petersburg. Poor Kay, he thought, she will never be rich, no matter how much money she has. The girl the kids called a river rat, who hated the river. He had a brief urge to follow her to Council Bluffs – maybe he could win out over Richard. But he could never compete on land. The river would always be his home. This oily, polluted stream. His round table was just a rusty grimy harbor. His knights were Daryl and Smitty. The mythical gold was back under the water, waiting for the next fool to try and find it.

When Jerry got back to the harbor, he found Whitey and Dude hanging out with Smitty.

"Hi guys."

"Hi Jerry."

"Guess what?" Whitey said, "remember that painter we saw out on Blennerhasset Island?"

"Sure."

"It excaped from that roadside zoo. You know the one out on the old Dixie Highway, where they got that moth-eaten old gorilla that smokes cigarettes?"

"Figures."

Sure, Jerry thought, it was bound not to be the legendary cat glimpsed over the years. That was just poor drab mankind's way of working a little romance and excitement into the river. Charlie was right; the big fish eat the little fish. The river was nothing more than a low-rent restaurant on the food chain. A ditch about nine feet deep.

When the men left for home, Jerry went straight up to the office and took the model of the *River Queen* off its table, and carried it down to the river. He laid her in the water, and set a match to her.

The flame on the *Queen* warmed Jerry's face.

"You're history," he said.

The days of steamboats were gone. In fact, they had never been....

Chapter 63

"I told you so," Jerry said.

"You said it, not me."

Jerry picked up a pin that was standing upright in Sheryl's carpet. "I could hear you thinking it."

"So how do you feel?"

"OK, now. OK."

"That's good." Sheryl ripped a garment apart with a loud tearing sound.

"Good God," Jerry said, "you're so violent."

She pitched the two ragged pieces into a basket. "Mine," she said. "And it can't be patched again."

"Is that a symbol?" Jerry asked.

"What do you mean?"

"We've been patched a lot...."

"Oh yeah. No, it's just a worn out blouse, Jerry."

Jerry looked around her little place. She had a cozy room. No books, but a nice gas fireplace and rather tasteful furniture. A new bird pushed bird seed onto the papers around its cage. If he ever moved in he would shoot it, he decided. He made a gesture toward leaving, but didn't make it out of his chair.

"Are you doing anything Thanksgiving?" he said.

"Going down to my sister's in Bowling Green. You?"

"Not much."

"Gonna be alone?"

"I'll be OK."

"Jerry, all you have to do is ask. I'll cook you a turkey and all the trimmings."

"Sounds pretty tempting."

"Be here at noon."

"Deal."

Jerry kissed Sheryl lightly on the nose. She raised her face for more, and he kissed her again on the mouth. She had lips like ripe peaches and tasted good. He decided he'd ask her to marry him. At Christmas.

West Memphis, 1987

Jerry read the newspaper stories about the drought and the old steamboats that had been found as the Mississippi shrank. One was right on the West Memphis bank where the *River Queen* went down. Though he had vowed no more looking back, he couldn't stop thinking about it. By late August there was still no rain, and the whole inland waterway system was all but closed down.

"I wouldn't mind goin' to Memphis a spell," he told Smitty.

"See that old boat? There wouldn't be much left of her, would there?"

"Probably not."

Still, Jerry kept wondering what the remains of his old home would look like, until finally Smitty could stand no more talk on the subject and threatened to quit if Jerry didn't go to Memphis.

Jerry packed a light suitcase and turned the harbor over to Smitty. He gassed up his pickup, and headed for Tennessee. He drove past Louisville, past Paducah, and old failing left-behind Cairo where the Ohio and Mississippi become one.

Jerry arrived in Memphis at dark, and realized he hadn't the faintest idea of how to find the *Queen*'s remains. He got a newspaper to see what stories there were on the drought. One mentioned the wrecks and a local archaeologist who was supervising a study of them. Jerry called his university and got hold of the man. After making sure Jerry had some legitimate purpose in visiting the site, he told him how to find it.

Next morning, Jerry crossed the bridge to West Memphis as he had been told, and drove through the maze-like cotton fields that lined the river banks. He was nervous as a lover going to meet his sweetheart. It took him awhile to find the right place, and his gas was getting low. The dried mud ruts of the road nearly tore the guts out of his pickup.

I gotta be crazy, he thought.

Finally, he arrived at a point that might be the "woods" that had been mentioned. He walked out onto the beach the drought had made, and contemplated the river.

The Great Brown God with prostate.

There wasn't a single towboat operating down here on the undammed miles between St. Louis and New Orleans. Old junk from every age, stuff that was routinely left beneath the water, appeared where the river had pulled away from its banks.

All around, driftwood in strange human shapes reared up out of the mud. A rusty barge, half-buried in sand, lurched beside a willow. The trees that had been at the water's edge were stranded farther up on the bank, tangled in dead grasses, and full of insects that sang in a high, merciless pitch.

Looking upriver toward the city, Jerry saw that he had overshot the archaeological site, and he began plodding upriver in the sand. Ahead he saw orange flags marking the boat, and he trudged on.

There wasn't much left of the *Queen* to look at: just a gray, weathered skeleton. It was hard to believe that this washed-out relic emerging from the sand had once been his home. That he had actually walked these rotting boards. That the calliope had played on the deck and music came from the salon.

Jerry crouched down and took a handful of sand and let it fall over the *Queen's* remains. What was she doing on the Mississippi anyway? She belonged on the Ohio.

He looked downriver. Though the sun was in his eyes, he was sure he saw someone among the trees. Then a person stepped onto the sand and came toward the boat. It was no idle stroller or sight-seer. Everyone connected to the *Queen* was either dead or scattered far and wide, and whoever it was walked purposefully in his direction, straight toward him and the orange flags. Now who but himself would care about this old wreck?

It was a woman, he could tell, when she got about half-way to him. When she caught sight of the wreck, and of him crouching among the boards, she paused. He thought he must be seeing things. He knew who it was by her beige and gold colors.

He went to her and said, "Hello Kay."

"Jerry."

"What're you doing here?"

"Same as you, I guess."

Kay looked good, maybe a few more tiny lines around her eyes. In spite of himself Jerry rubbed the top of his head where the sun felt warmer every year. He hoped the extra thinness of his hair didn't show, and he was glad he was still in good shape.

Jerry and Kay walked to the Queen's remains and circled the boards buried in the sand, each going in a different direction. They met at the bow.

Was she still mad Jerry wondered. Was he?

No. He was so damned glad to see her he wasn't capable of anger.

"I can't believe we once walked on these actual boards," he said.
Kay reached out her hand and touched the dry wood of the boat's ribs. She and Jerry looked in every direction except into each other's eyes.
"I'm surprised to see you here, Kay."
The two walked around the boards again, stood in the heart of the wreck.
"Don't you wish you could be there the day the *Queen* blew up," Jerry said, "and somehow be able to shout, 'don't go on the boat – stay on shore!'?"
"A lot of things would be different if we could see what's coming."
Jerry stooped down and smoothed an inch of wood. He tried to grasp the mystery of time and of what was destroyed and what was saved.
"So what have you been doing since I saw you last?" Kay asked.
"Same old thing. The *Harvey*'s good as new. She's workin' hard."
"That's good."
"How are Smitty and Daryl?"
"Takin' nourishment. How 'bout you?" Jerry said. "What have you been up to?"
"I got the business out of the red. Made the final payment on my last kid."
"So what now?"
Kay shrugged. She looked toward the trees where they had parked. Jerry did the same.
"There were some other wrecks upriver," Jerry said. "On one of the boats they found some hats."
"Hats?"
"Perfectly preserved."
Kay looked interested.
"Near St. Louis, and they found a log book and a steamer trunk."
"I heard that."
Was Kay more tied to the old *River Queen* days than she had said? Jerry resisted a feeling of hope. It wouldn't be fair to Sheryl.
"How's my pal Richard?" he asked.
"He moved up and out."
The insects among the trees were screeching louder than ever.
"Do you still hate the river?"
Kay pushed an inch of sand off one of the weathered boards of the *Queen*. She moistened a finger with a little spit and wrote *RQ* on the wood.
"She'll always be here, in some form or other," Jerry said.
"She will, won't she?" Kay smiled, lighting the dark river that had covered Jerry's heart for three years.

"I'll always love her," Jerry said. "Even though she was a killer,"

Jerry could swear he could hear the music of the *River Queen,* her steam building, the passengers walking the second deck, the animals shuffling restlessly in their stalls, the song of the roustabouts. She would never be dead to him.

Could the third time be a charm for him and Kay? Thank God Sheryl had turned him down.

"Why don't we go some place and talk?" Jerry said.

"You want to? I almost got you killed three times."

"At least you were never boring."

"Will you tell me the truth about Charlie?"

"Will you?" The words were on Jerry's lips, but he swallowed them. He had learned a tiny bit in his lifetime of acting on impulse and making smart comebacks. He would not let Charlie come between him and Kay one more time.

Kay turned toward the trees.

"Meet me at the Peabody bar where they have the ducks. You know the one," Jerry said.

"I know it."

Kay didn't say she would, but walked on toward her car. Jerry didn't say anything more. He had gone as far as he could.

If she showed up he would tell her everything. And who knows?

He took one last look back at the remains of the *Queen.* Then he headed for his pickup. It could happen, he thought. The river had been working its magic a long time. It was full of strange and wonderful things. Why, only last week, a diver saw a turtle the size of a Volkswagen.

Printed in the United States
25081LVS00004B/204